MW01073676

REVERSE PASS

MAGGIE RAWDON

Copyright © 2023 by Maggie Rawdon

Editing by Kat Wyeth – Editor (Kat's Literary Services)

Photographer: Michelle Lancaster - www.michellelancaster.com

All rights reserved.

No part of this book may be reproduced in any form or by any electronic or mechanical means, including information storage and retrieval systems, without written permission from the author, except for the use of brief quotations in a book review.

This is a work of fiction. Any names, characters, places or events are purely a work of imagination. Any resemblance to actual people, living or dead, actual events, or places is purely coincidental.

REVERSE PASS

Violet
He's the star wide receiver and the most wanted player on campus. He has it all—the body, the voice, the charm and the dimples. Plus he flirts constantly and cooks dinner shirtless in my kitchen.

There's just one problem—he's my best friend's younger brother.

She sent him to live with me so I can help him get his life back in order. Which makes him off limits in every way possible. But now we share a wall and secrets. Like the confession he makes after he accidentally walks in on me one night.

Ben
I'm usually so good with women that my teammates come to me for advice. But they don't know my secret. They don't know about *her*. The one woman I want—the one I can't stop thinking about—barely knows I exist.

Until everything goes wrong, and I land on her doorstep. The worst day of my life might just turn out to be my luckiest. Because she's fresh off a broken engagement—single for the first time in forever. And she can't keep her eyes off of me.

I just need to convince her I'm worth breaking the rules.

ONE

Ben

Somehow, the right place wrong time has become my own birthday party in my home. I know this for sure when I see one of the younger guys on the football team launch himself off the top step of a Jell-O slip and slide set up on the main stairs of the house. It's a problem in and of itself, but the fact the man who owns the home I live in is currently at the bottom of said stairs, and he and one of our biggest linebackers are about to experience a very important lesson in physics, all set to the background track of cop sirens? Yeah. Right place, wrong time: population me.

I grimace as I watch it happen from the overlook upstairs, white knuckling the banister as I see the explosion of Jell-O, flailing limbs, parts of the drywall, and what I am fairly certain is an expensive Italian leather loafer go flying. I immediately yell for one of the slightly more sober guys downstairs to help, and then take off down the hallway banging on the doors as I go. One of them has their window open, letting the smoke vent out, and I can hear the sirens getting closer in the distance.

"That us?" His pupils are wide, and I nod.

"Fuck!" He immediately starts gathering his shit up and nudges the half-naked girl on his bed. "Time to go, baby doll."

I vault down the back stairwell. One of the benefits of the old house is even when the main stairwell is a mess of Jell-O and linemen, the old servants' stairwell is still neat and tidy. When I get to the bottom of the steps I see Colton—our quarterback since Liam graduated and he transferred in— standing immobile, eyes wide with horror.

"Get Jake and any of the rest of the guys and get out. The cops are on their way, and Old Man Griffin just ate shit on the steps thanks to one of the junior guys. We're royally fucked."

"What about you?" He looks me up and down.

"No hope for me. It's my house and my birthday. Just get the guys out."

Colton frowns, but he takes off through the kitchen toward the main part of the house.

"Eric!" I yell across the room to one of the frat brothers who's currently still swigging keg beer like nothing interesting's happening.

He jerks his chin up to me like we're just saying hi, and I shake my head.

"Cops," I mouth the word, using my hands to imitate the lights on a squad car, and he puzzles for a minute until he understands and nods.

"Everybody get the fuck out!" He screams at the top of his lungs. "*Exit drills now*! Jones! Thomas! Brown! Get it cleared!"

The frat has their own little method of madness in preparation for raids and since it's never been a problem for us before, I'm gonna let them handle it. Especially since right now I am deeply regretting the fact we didn't just have this little get together at his place. This party has been way over capacity for hours and has been out of control for almost as long.

"Benny Boy?" A very drunk Chelsea stumbles into me.

"Sweetheart, you gotta go." I nod to the door.

"What? Why?" She looks at me like I'm making zero sense.

"Cops."

"What?" Apparently, everyone is going to act wide-eyed and confused when I say this tonight.

"Hurry up." I give her a little helpful shove out the door. "And trash the beer first or you're gonna get cited for public intoxication."

Jake slams into me as I turn the corner.

"Come on Ben, let's go."

"It'll look worse if I leave. Everyone's gonna say it was my party. Just save yourself, okay?"

He shakes his head giving me a forlorn look as he turns to head out the door, and you would think we were going down on a sinking ship. Like I'd just volunteered to stay behind on the Titanic and play everyone out.

And I guess I might be. The athletic department is going to be furious, especially if it makes the news and depending on the severity of Old Man Griffin's injuries, the university consequences are going to come down hard. He's big money for the university and the athletic department in particular. He owns this house and lets football team members stay rent free because he loves the team so much. But I have a feeling that love affair might be over, or at least on a long-term break after tonight.

I walk toward the staircase, listening as the sirens get louder and obvious that it's more than one car coming at this point. I'm dreading seeing what's become of Griffin and the sophomore linebacker. A linebacker who is no doubt underage, and I'm praying hasn't been drinking.

3

Taylor, another one of my roommates, is standing over them at the bottom of the stairs. Griffin is cursing up a storm at him and the sophomore. I try to remember his name. CJ? DJ? EJ? I honestly don't remember, but it's one of those, is on his feet, rubbing his ass.

Griffin's eyes land on me the second I'm in his field of vision, and if looks could kill, I would have been dead on the spot.

"Get this fucking kid out the back door before the cops get here. You all deserve major fucking consequences, but it should stay in house," Griffin grunts at me.

I jerk my head at the kid. "Let's go, man. Get the fuck out of here. That way"

"I think I bruised my ass," he mutters, rubbing circles on it still, like that somehow trumps him getting arrested.

"You're gonna have a lot more than that to worry about if you don't get out of here. The cops are gonna be here any second, and I doubt you're sober. So go!"

The mention of the cops finally has him up to jogging speed, and I watch as he and a few more stragglers from the living room exit through the back. I just hope none of the cops decides to be wise enough to block the back alley.

A moment later there's a knock at the door and the distinctive shout of "Police. Open Up."

———

THE NEXT DAY I'M IN COACH'S OFFICE, HIS HANDS steepled and his head down. The sound of the fan above us clicking as he makes a low frustrated noise at the back of his throat.

"You're gonna tell me you had a party, at the football house, with no other players there?"

"Other than my roommates, but again, they had to be there because they lived there."

I'm lying my ass off. Coach knows I'm lying my ass off. But we have to do this dance because he has to be able to say he interrogated me in good conscience.

He stares at me for a long minute.

"You know this is going to be a lengthy suspension. At least a month. And Griffin is agitating for more than that. Which frankly, you're lucky the man just has a slipped disc and not a broken spine."

"I know, sir."

"You can still call me coach. It's fuckin' serious but not so much we're going to act like a bunch of assholes about it." He leans back in his chair.

"Okay, coach." I nod.

"He's pulling the housing. Do you have somewhere to go?"

"For everyone, or just for me?"

"All of you. His wife is pissed about the 19th century wall-paper that got stained and says some of the wood on the stairs is irreplaceable."

"Shit."

"Yeah. So you have somewhere?"

"I'll find somewhere."

He gives me a doubtful look, like he's not sure I won't just sleep in my car and shakes his head.

"I'll put you up in a hotel tonight. Just keep it between us, and then you gotta find somewhere else. Get your boys to help and get your shit out today. There's a storage place on Santa Fe that's reasonable if you need it."

"I don't have that much. I think I can figure it out, but I appreciate it."

"Losing you for the suspension is gonna fuck us out there.

You're too vital to lose." He frowns down at the papers on his desk.

"I'm sorry, coach."

"Fuck." He curses and shakes his head. "You sure you don't want to spread this blame around a bit? I know it was your birthday, but if we have to lay this all at your feet..."

"Just me, coach."

Because if it's more than just me, that means more players benched. Colt. Jake. Half the guys on the team were there.

"You're a first-time offender, at least. How're your grades?"

I wince.

"Decent."

"Decent C or Decent D?"

"In between?"

"Get them up. Go to the academic center. Get whatever you need but get them up. When they reconsider your suspension, and I'll press to end it early, you need to look like a model fucking student, you hear me?"

"Got it."

"Fuck." He curses again, staring out the window.

I'm sure he's seeing his future wavering along with mine and the rest of the team, because we need the championship this year. Especially after we got all the way last year and came apart in the final stretch.

"All right. Get going. Keep your phone close. The other coaches and I will be in touch when we know more."

"Got it. Thanks, coach. And again, I'm sorry about all this. I'll apologize to Griffin and his wife as well."

"Get the kid who did it to apologize, will ya?"

I nod, and then I start to head out the door when he calls my name again. I look back.

"You're a good kid. I just hope you're not ruining your career to save the rest."

"It is what it is." I shake my head, not knowing what else to say.

He nods and waves me on my way.

———

WHEN I GET TO THE CAR, I CALL MY SISTER. BECAUSE right now I need family and I haven't figured out a way to tell my mom I might have blown my whole fucking future. Nora answers after the fourth ring, and she sounds like she's in a good mood. Maybe that'll help the blow of what I'm about to say, because she's unlikely to be much happier than my mom will be about it. Just slightly less devastated.

"What's up? This is an odd time for you to call."

"I fucked up." I decide to just rip the Band-Aid off.

"Shit." I hear her let out a little sigh. "What happened?"

I explain the whole situation, the party, the accident, the lack of housing and the fact I'm on the verge of taking a suspension for the team. There's a long pause after I finish talking, so long I'm almost worried she might have hung up.

"Nora?"

"Yes. I'm here. Sorry. I'm deciding whether to praise you for helping the team and your friends, or yell at you for taking the risks and then all the blame."

"It can be both."

"Right."

"I don't think I can tell mom. I just... I can't deal with disappointing her like that. Especially when I don't know all the details."

"I'll tell her, but you know she's going to call you anyway."

"Yeah. I know. But at least I don't have to hear her cry. I can't... if she does, you know? After everything."

"I get it. Don't worry. That's the least of your worries right now, and she would tell you the same thing. Is there anything I can do to help?"

"I don't know. My biggest problem is I have a hotel room tonight but then I'm going to be out on my ass. All the guys are already full at their places, and my roommates are couch surfing with their friends. But if I have to get my grades up couch surfing isn't going to work."

There's another long pause but this time I can hear her tapping on something in the background as she thinks.

"I have an idea, but I need to see about a few things first."

"Care to clue me in?"

"Not yet. But I will call you later either way, okay?"

"Okay."

"And it's gonna be okay, all right? We're gonna figure this out and get you back on track. I still don't know if you needed to fall on the sword quite so hard, but we will get it sorted."

"Thanks, Nora."

"Anytime. I'll call you later. Love you."

"Love you."

I hang up the phone and sit back in the car, taking a deep breath. I'm thankful because my older sister is a Type A—take the bull by the horns and sort shit out type—and knowing I've got her on my side makes me feel like I might actually have a chance at getting out of this mess.

TWO

Violet

I SIP THE DRINK JOSS HAD THE BARTENDER FILL FROM THE giant steampunk looking tank at the bar, wondering how it's possible for a drink to actually taste like a color, because this one tastes distinctly purple. She's chatting with several guys at our table, talking about local bands and some of the photography work she's doing. I'm normally her wing woman on nights like this as she needs me, but now I'm single, I guess technically we're each other's wing women.

One of the guys at the table has grown bored with her story and has made his way closer to me. His blue eyes rake me up and down before they stop at my lips, watching me as I drink. A lazy grin spreads across his face, and I can already imagine the lines that might be coming next, so I drink the rest of it quickly, stand abruptly, and hook my arm with Joss's.

"I need a refill, come with me?" I give her a pointed look and she nods.

"Let me guess, you don't like him either?" She raises a brow at me when we get to the bar.

"He barely talks. He just looks and grins and looks some more." I glance back over my shoulder at the offender.

"He's pretty. He's not used to having to talk." She shrugs like it's not a problem.

"I need more than one-word answers to keep a conversation going." The exasperation seeping into my tone.

"So, what was that thing Elvis said... a little less conversation and—" she counters with her own dose of sarcasm.

"Yes, I know. Elvis has the answer to everything. But what's the point when it's going nowhere fast?"

"To have a one-night stand, Violet, not find your next great love. There's an in between stage you know. Between the jerk who breaks your heart and the next guy you're willing to take a risk on. You're in the middle of it, and not using it to your advantage if we're being honest here." She shakes her head in disappointment, and I resist the urge to roll my eyes again.

My roommate is one of my favorite people on earth. We met in the first week of grad school when we took our Intro to Art Theory class together, and she moved in with my ex and me a week later when her relationship ended after an argument at a metal concert. She'd shown up at my door at 3 a.m., given me a giant hug, a box of fresh donuts, and we stayed up the rest of the night watching Pulp Fiction and discussing '90s Britart.

But she was always way more of a free spirit than I ever could be. I aspired to her levels of broken give-a-fuck-lessness but had yet to achieve them. She was still determined to make this the "best breakup of my life" though. Which, considering it was one of the only, meant it was a sink or swim situation at this point.

"I'm just not feeling it." I shrug.

"What about the bartender?" A little smirk starts to form on her lips as he approaches us.

He grins back at her as he reaches us and leans his elbows on the counter.

"I feel like you're plotting something, and I might need to be worried," he says loudly over the music, as he runs his eyes over her.

"Maybe." Her smirk gets wider, and she gives him a similarly lascivious review.

"What can I get for you?" He licks his lower lip and raises his brows.

I'm starting to feel like a third wheel in this scenario and start looking at the bottles of alcohol stacked against the wall as though they hold fascinating secrets.

"What do you think of my friend?" She nods to me, and I roll my eyes in response.

He looks me over for a moment, shrugging as though he doesn't hate what he sees before his eyes return to her.

"Why? You come as a package deal?"

She gives him a wicked little grin in response, and I groan.

"Two more of your purple drinks, please," I yell over the music and their eye fucking.

He glances at me and winks. "Coming up, doll."

Then he wanders off and Joss turns to me, the smile still on her face.

"That's all you, obviously," I say, clicking my tongue at the idea of hooking up with someone who clearly wants my friend.

"Only because I'm giving good vibes. You're giving sad poutiness. You've gotta fake it til you make it, and I guarantee a couple orgasms from him, and you would be making it."

"I appreciate your effort, but I think I'm good." I look down as my phone lights up with Nora's name, my best friend who still lives back in our hometown. I miss her lots but it's strange to see her name and an odd hour of the night for it. She rarely ever calls me, and we usually talk by text or the occasional video chat. So the ringing of my phone has my heart racing with worry, and I don't even think when I answer it in the middle of the club.

"Nora?" I ask.

"Violet! Oh wow. Where are you? It's loud."

"Is everything okay?"

"Yes. Well sort of. I mean I'm fine. Can you talk or are you in the middle of something?"

"Um. I'm in a club. I think I saw a patio though, just give me a second."

I look up and motion to Joss that I'm heading outside, and then make my way through the crowd, confirming I did in fact see an exit to a patio. I'm thankful the nights are still pretty warm, and I slip outside, where luckily, I find myself alone.

"Okay. I'm outside. What's up? You're scaring me with the call."

"Well, it's nothing horrible but it's time sensitive and I wanted to talk rather than text."

"Okay?" I say, frowning because she has me worried still.

"Do you still have space in your apartment, now that Cam's roaming Europe?"

The mention of my ex-fiancé has me scrunching my nose.

"Yeah, his old room that we used as an office is still open. We're looking for someone to rent it to. Why, are you thinking of running away here?" I laugh.

"No, but you remember Ben, right?"

"Your brother?"

"That would be the one. You know he plays ball for Highland, right?"

I frown. I guess I remember her saying that at one point or another, but I'd been too busy with grad school to pay much attention to the athletics department roster. I also can't imagine Ben being old enough to be at the university since the last time I remember seeing him, he was a scrawny teenager.

"I think I remember you saying that."

"Well, he got himself into some deep shit on his birthday."

"Ben? He was always a good kid."

"Yeah, he is. But he took the fall for some other guys, and they suspended him from the team. They're still deciding on how long for."

"Wow. I'm sorry to hear that," I say, still unsure how I figure into the scenario or why it's urgent for me to know.

"Yeah. He's going to have to bust ass to get back in their good graces. But the worst part is he also lost the place where he was living in the process."

"What? Can they do that?"

"Apparently, yes. They had a huge party, did some damage. The cops were called, and so it effectively broke the lease."

"And now he has nowhere to go I'm guessing?"

"Right."

"Yeah. He can come stay with me for a few days. I don't think my roommate would mind too much. And we already put the bed back in there out of storage."

"It might need to be more than a few days. Like a couple weeks? He's talking to the athletic department to see if they can find him housing for the rest of the semester, but they said it might take a while."

"That might be a harder sell. But I can talk to her and text you back. Definitely a few days to give him a place for now though."

"All right. I'll tell him. He's in a hotel until tomorrow. Is that too soon?"

"No. The room's ready. He'll just have to come by when

one of us is home. After I talk to Joss, I'll give you her number too. That way he can get a hold of one of us."

"Thank you, Violet. You're a lifesaver. He'll be so grateful. I love you!"

"Of course. You guys are family."

"All right. Text me and I'll let him know. We need to talk soon! Lots to catch you up on."

"Yes, let's do it. Love you, Nora. Bye."

"Love you! Bye!"

We hang up, and I stare at my phone for a second as I contemplate the potential consequences of what I've agreed to. I'm so swamped with school and exhibits and all the grading work from my teacher's assistantship. Taking on a new roommate, one who might need supervision if he was throwing parties that got raided by the cops, is more than I bargained for right now. I just hope Ben is the good kid I remember. I probably should have asked more questions before I agreed, but I also can't say no to Nora.

THREE

Violet

WHEN I GET HOME IN THE EVENING I CAN BARELY THINK straight. I'm starving, tired, and more than a little hangry. I got wrangled into a much longer than necessary meeting with one of my advisors when they decided to give me a rundown of the ins and outs of the politics of academia. All thanks to one of my undergrads complaining about my grading rubric which had landed me in their office in the first place.

"Thanks for that," I mutter to the student who likely doesn't even remember me in the first place.

So when I walk in the door and throw my bags down in the hallway to take my boots off, I don't immediately notice the intruder. It's not until the distinct sound of a male voice humming drifts out from the kitchen and into the hallway that all the hairs on the back of my neck go up. Cam was obviously long gone, and Joss's hookups never stuck around, and certainly never made their way into the kitchen. My mind reels, trying to make sense of it and decide whether or not to call for help.

If it was one of Joss's hookups, it was either way too late or way too early, however you looked at it, for them to be in the apartment. Plus, they usually had the common decency to slink out the door without making their presence known. Dallying about in the kitchen? Nope. Singing and humming? Not a thing they ever did.

I don't recall her saying we needed maintenance either, which really only left the possibility we were getting robbed. But robbers don't typically hum their way through an old punk song in your kitchen while they work to steal from you, do they?

I stop dead in my tracks when I reach the end of the hall and my jaw nearly hits the floor. He is definitely not a robber—or at least not a conventional one.

Because a tall, shirtless man is standing in our kitchen—cooking. Gorgeous dark brown hair, at least a half a foot taller than me if not more, he takes up the entirety of our small kitchen with his broad frame. His tattooed shoulders are sculpted with muscles, his shoulder blades and biceps working in time below them, chopping food to the beat of his humming. It all tapers down to a cut waist where his back tattoo disappears below his low-slung gray sweatpants. I squint, trying to make out the tattoos when he dips over to search through a lower cabinet. And for the record, his ass is just as phenomenal as the rest of his body.

We'd had someone accidentally walk into our apartment before, but I can't imagine getting undressed and starting to cook before you realize you're in the wrong place. So he must be Joss related. And Joss is insanely lucky. In fact, my mind might be changed about picking up random guys at bars if Joss could tell me where she found ones like this. I was going to be giving her a hard time about holding out on me.

I let myself enjoy the show for another few seconds before I remember how exhausted and hungry I am. And seeing as this guy is already hers and she is nowhere to be found, I had no time for a veritable stranger rooting around in our cabinets, making a mess, and creating dishes. If he was hungry, he could grab a burger on the way home.

Just then a timer goes off and he pulls his headphones down to his neck, creating the perfect opportunity for me to ruin his good time.

"As much as I appreciate the view, generally the rule is hookups don't get to use the kitchen." I cross my arms over my chest, feigning more irritation than I actually feel and daring him to argue with me.

He flinches ever so slightly, clearly surprised by my presence, and turns around slowly to face me. His warm brown eyes meet mine, and a slow smirk spreads across his face as his eyes search over me with interest. I'm distracted again, because his chest and abs are, well, a lot. All of him is *a lot*.

I've never really been envious before, and certainly not of Joss as we're polar opposites. She likes guys in rock bands. I like nerds in lab coats. I had been happy with Cam, and happy for Joss. But now, in this moment? The green-eyed monster might finally be rearing its little head.

"Violet," he says warmly, with a voice that sounds like what honey over gravel might if it had a sound.

My eyes snap back up to his face at the familiarity with which he says my name, like he knows it all too well. I almost ask him to repeat it. Maybe I misheard him.

His smirk reaches his dimples at my confusion, and then my brain catches up with all the clues I should have put together, making it obvious exactly who's standing in front of me. Who I'd just been lusting after like an absolute idiot.

Fuckity fuck.

"Ben!" My voice hits an irritatingly high-pitched note I didn't know I was capable of as I attempt to cover my tracks.

I rush over and throw my arms around him like I would have if he were still the little kid I remembered instead of the hot-as-hell man who is currently standing shirtless in my kitchen. Bonus points that the hug was giving me the opportunity to hide my face and the hot flush of embarrassment I'm sure is spreading up my neck and cheeks as we stand here.

His arms loosely and hesitantly wrap around me for a moment before bringing me in for a tighter hug. He smells and feels as amazing as he looks, and I immediately regret the rush to hug him. His warm skin against mine is setting off tiny sparks of interest, quickly chased off again by my embarrassment and the result is me just feeling like an entire pool of awkwardness. It's like my otherwise very sensible brain is short circuiting trying to make sense of this.

Best friend's little brother. Best friend's little brother. I'd just keep saying it as a mantra, and it would stick, right?

I glance up at him and then back down, realizing it was a bad idea as I seem to have zero control over my eyes or anything else in this moment. I feel like I can barely contain my reaction to him, and I'm just praying I seem awkward from tiredness and time and not your sister's-friend-is-perving-out-on-you awkward.

Focus.

"I'm so sorry. I forgot you were going to be here today. Class was a mess, I had to deal with a student problem and got locked in a meeting with a professor, and then I just assumed you were Joss's..." I trail off.

"Chef?" he offers, something dancing behind his eyes as he watches me.

"Something like that." I turn toward the counter, pretending it holds interest for me as I grasp for something else meaningful to say. Vegetables are sprawled out over the surface, rice is cooking, and there's some meat in a pan with sauce, and are... Are those herbs?

I blink. It's possible I'm dreaming. That I've fallen asleep in my little closet-sized office on campus and my mind is taking wild liberties with reality. That has to be what's happening.

"I'm sorry for the mess and using the kitchen without asking first. I just got done with a workout and shower, and I was starving. I thought maybe you and Joss would be hungry too, so I was going to cook. A thank you for giving me a place to crash. Mom's old recipe," he explains, looking a little sheepish.

"Oh god. You're fine. I mean it smells amazing. And here I am being all bitchy. I didn't know guys your age cooked, but I will take a Mama Beth recipe any day." I smile sharply.

I wish this was a dream, that I could escape this because the awkwardness is making my skin crawl.

"Mom taught me a few things. Said it would help me survive college, and maybe impress some women on the way." He shrugs, and his smile is gorgeous, but my eyes are drawn back to his shoulders.

This boy really needs a shirt, stat. I feel like I'd be doing so much better at this if he had a shirt on.

"She always was a great cook. How's she doing?" I bring my eyes up to meet his, pretending I was just momentarily distracted by something over his shoulder, and not him.

"She's good," he says slowly. But I can tell he's watching me carefully. Studying me.

He knew it. I knew it. He'd caught me flat out ogling him.

And I have a sinking feeling he's tucking that little nugget of information away for future amusement.

Where was Joss when I needed her? I glance at the door.

"She said she'd be back before dinner was ready. Had to run and pick something up." He reads my mind. Hopefully, not all of it.

But Joss had known he was here and said nothing. Not a call. Not a text. What a traitor! She was going to pay for that. Netflix was going to magically disappear from the TV one night right before one of her favorite shows premiers.

"Speak of the devil and she appears!" Joss's voice calls from the hallway as she closes the door behind her.

Devil is right. She and I will have so many words later.

"Sorry I didn't text you about your friend being here. It's been a day." Apparently, the mind reading is going around. She heads me off at the pass with a devious smile and unlaces her boots like she didn't just set me up for disaster.

"Same." I smile tightly at her, hoping my eyes are saying " you traitorous wench!" Or she can read my mind some more.

She smiles back, a little too tight, making it clear the message is received, and she thinks it's hilarious my best friend's little brother has turned into a tall, sexy, Roman sculpture come to life without me knowing it.

I try to glance furtively back at Ben, but it's obvious he's watching us with amusement. The alarm on his phone goes off and saves the day.

"Fifteen minutes and dinner will be ready," he says, breaking the tension in the room.

"Great!" Joss cheers. "I got some wine."

I am going to need it.

"In that case, I'm going to run to my room and get changed." I gesture down the hall and give a little wave as I head off. Which was just great. Fantastic. Very normal to wave goodbye in your house going from one room to another.

"Are we sure the dress code's not *no shirt and service?*" Joss teases behind me.

"Right." I hear him answer her. "Let me grab a shirt."

"Oh no! You should definitely stay like that. Violet needs the excitement in her life." She raises her voice to make extra sure I can hear her.

When I reach my doorway where I know Ben can't see me, I flip her off, and she laughs whole-heartedly at my misery.

Someday I'm going to get her back for this.

FOUR

Ben

THE UNIVERSE IS TESTING ME. IT HAS TO BE. Just when I absolutely need to get my shit together, it places the one temptation I've wanted since I was 13 years old right in front of me.

Violet Kennedy.

She's single for the first time since I can remember. And now I'm staying in her apartment, and she's standing in front of me looking sexy as hell.

And then, the part I'm going to put on rerun like it's a scene from my favorite movie, she ran her eyes over my body with very clear interest. *Very* clear. Fuck, she'd even admitted she'd enjoyed it.

At least, she did when she thought I was someone else.

Then she'd realized who I was, and we'd run slam back into the same routine we'd had as kids where she is the older, wiser one who scruffs my hair and tells me to run back home and be a good boy.

Probably the exact reason Nora put me here.

I throw on a shirt from out of my bag and put dinner on the table. I guess in addition to getting my shit together, I'm going to have to figure out how to live one thin wall away from my own personal kryptonite.

———

AFTER DINNER AND A FEW ROUNDS OF HOMEWORK, I emerge from the room they're letting me crash in and go to get a glass of water. Or at least that's my cover story. In reality, I'm looking to see if she's around. I fill my glass and then peer out from the kitchen in what I thought was a nonchalant way until half a second later.

"She's in her room working. You can knock." Jocelyn startles me from the couch where she's got her legs up on the coffee table editing photos on her laptop.

I nod, feeling a little sheepish that my intent had been so obvious.

I'm hesitant to interrupt Violet, but I'd barely gotten a moment alone with her today. I wanted to at least be sure she was okay with me being here, not just under pressure from Nora, and thank her for giving me a chance.

I also just want a chance to look at her again, see her smile and joke with me like she had earlier. Dinner had been mostly formalities, introductions and info about where things were in the house.

"And just so we're clear." Jocelyn's eyes remain on her laptop as she speaks softly. "You have my support. But you better not tell her that."

Had they already talked about me? This got more and more

interesting by the minute. I took a swig of the water but then abandoned the pretense, heading to Violet's door to knock.

"Come in," she responds.

I creak the door open, but just like Jocelyn, Violet's hyper-focused on her laptop. I wish I could have that kind of focus on something besides football. Especially now when I may need the backup plan.

"Am I interrupting?" I ask.

Her eyes snap up to me, and it's obvious I'm not who she's expecting. I could tell this "new roommate" thing was still in the early adjustment period for her.

"No, it's fine." She presses the lid down and sets the laptop aside.

She looks less intimidating now, her dark brown hair out of her bun pooling messily around her shoulders. The prim outfit she'd had on before replaced by shorts, a hoodie and knee-high socks. She looks more like one of the girls I'd find in the dorms than the intimidating force she normally is, and I think I might like it almost as much.

"I just wanted to check in and make sure it's all right that I'm staying here."

"Of course! Nora told me you're going through it right now." She frowns a little, and the furrow of her brow deepens.

Fuck. Not her too. I really couldn't deal with disappointing anyone else right now. And it's the last thing I want to talk about. Dinner here, laughing with them, thinking about old times is the distraction I need. Something to get my mind off freaking out about football.

"Yeah, something like that." I shrug.

"Do you want to talk about it?" She sits up a little, her voice a bit more serious than before. I can tell I'm about to get the big sister act, and I do not want it.

"About the way you were looking at me earlier? I thought

maybe we should... I mean, I know it could be awkward having a thing for your roommate." I give her a wide smile.

Dick move. I know, but I am desperate to change the subject and even more desperate to explore the depths of this whole—Violet actually noticing me—situation.

Her jaw drops. Literally drops. She hops up and sits on the edge of the ottoman and points to the door behind me.

"Get out!" There's a teasing tone to her voice still, like she's amused, but also not brooking any bullshit from me.

"I mean, I just think we need to talk about your attraction to me if we're going to be roommates. You know, boundaries and all that." I hold my hands open like we need to have a frank discussion about it, and I can't help but laugh as she launches a pillow squarely at my face.

"I am NOT attracted to you. Good god!" She huffs.

"Then what was the comment about liking the view earlier?"

"I was being a smart-ass when I thought you were some hookup of Jocelyn's so I could run you out of the place."

"And the way you were looking at me?" I inch a little closer to her.

"The way I was looking at you? What are you... Your ego... Can you hear yourself?" She sounds indignant but there's the slightest hint of pink to her cheeks, and her eyes flick over my chest like she's remembering what she saw before.

"I mean it's okay. I just think we should talk about it," I tease.

"There's nothing to talk about." She crosses her arms.

"Come on now, be honest. We're old friends. You can tell me." I pause to give her a chance to confess, but she continues to stare at me like I have five heads.

She glowers at me. And then I realize the perfect way to get a confession out of her as I lunge forward and wrap my hands around her ankle.

"Or I could just tickle you until you cave."

She *hates* being tickled, and it was my favorite way to torture her when we were younger. One, because it always put her into fits of rolling laughter no matter what mood she was in, and two, it gave me an excuse to touch her without admitting how much I wanted to.

"Benjamin Thomas Fucking Lawton, you will NOT." Her eyes are threatening murder.

"Oh, I think I will." I flick my thumb over her instep, and she winces.

"I will tell your mother!!" she shrieks, as I run the pads of my fingers under her toes, testing her threats and her will.

It was just like old times. Popcorn, scary movies, sleeping bags and me running around after her with water balloons, dead bugs and threats of tickling. Her threatening to tell my mother was like muscle memory, and now I had to follow through.

"I don't see how that's going to help you right now," I mock her threats.

And then she smiles, a true, genuine smile I haven't seen yet tonight and jumps out of my grasp, leaping for the door.

Her only problem is I'm one of the best wide receivers in the Pac12. My hand wraps around her middle, pulling her back from the door and into my grasp where I have prime access to tickle her ribs.

She gasps and giggles, squirming against me as she only manages to pin herself tighter against my body. She makes an attempt to press off me, this time in the direction of her bed. While she nearly frees herself, it's ultimately a rookie mistake on her part as I now have access to her ankles again.

I pull just in time to drag us down into a pile of limbs and laughter. And before I can stop it, I've made an even worse mistake. Because Violet is now straddling me, a knee pinned on either side of my hips, and her hands bracing her against my chest. Her hair's a tangled mess as she leans over me, framing her beautiful face.

I'm laughing so hard it hurts, but as she wheezes, giggling and gasping for air in intervals her body grazes against mine in a way that makes me hurt for an entirely different reason. A slight shift on her part and she is going to find out exactly how hard she's made me. How attracted I am to her. How just her laugh sets me on fire.

And in the moment, I'm no longer Ben Lawton, football god, and playboy, surrounded by girls who want me. Instead, I'm back to the kid who's wanted a girl he can't have for ages. Maybe even worse now, since it's been the better part of a decade and that familiar ache is still there when I look at her. The silence between us, as her laughter slows, is growing as awkward as I am in this moment.

"You really think you're going to win this?" I tease, using all the bravado I have left.

Her eyes open wider and shift up to mine. She looks me over, and the look on her face softens. And I wish desperately I could read minds. I couldn't tell what it meant. Nostalgia? Pity? Something else?

"Fine. I give!" She yields but doesn't move.

"So, you admit you want me?" I roll my lip between my teeth at the thought this could all be much easier than I imagined.

She sighs, looking me over again as if trying to make a final assessment.

"I admit you're ripped as hell, and if I didn't know you, that might be... worth noticing. But there is a big difference between noticing that and wanting you, Lawton. I'm sure even Nora has noticed. I just hadn't seen you in a while. You were a gangly little kid last time I saw you; you know?"

Ouch. My pride absorbs that blow, but I'm not sure how much more it can take. My ego wants to strip down and show her just how *not* gangly I am now. Have her look at me again, press her against me so she can notice every hard edge I've created by pushing my body to the physical limit every day on the field.

But I know better. That's not how you win over someone like Violet.

I release her and sit up on my elbows, trying to regain some power in this dynamic. She sits back on her heels in the process, releasing her palms from my chest. She does it slowly though, almost like she's not quite ready to let go. If this were any other girl, this would be my chance to say something clever. To kiss her palms and tell her she can touch me for however long she wants.

I'm distracted by her though, seeing her this close. The way her lip worries for a second between her teeth before she catches me staring at her.

"As long as we're being honest," I say, knowing I'm being so dishonest I wouldn't be surprised if I caught fire.

"Honest." She repeats the word as though she doesn't quite know what to do with it, but after a beat she snaps out of it.

"Besides, football players aren't really my thing, yeah? I'm more into the nerds. You met Cam." She removes herself from me entirely, leaning her back against the wall and putting distance between us.

I immediately miss the feel of her against me.

"I hear he's an asshole." I sit up and turn away from her slightly. There are likely still obvious signs of my physical reaction to her, and I definitely don't want her to know it now. Not when I've been dismissed so thoroughly.

"Sort of."

She shrugs, and I can tell she wants to talk about this about as much as I want to talk about being suspended from the team.

"You deserve better, you know." I glance back at her.

Nora had filled in some of the details for me, although I didn't know everything. But apparently after proposing to her and starting to plan their wedding, he decided he was going to take a job overseas for a year and also decided they should take a break to see other people.

"He put his career and himself first. It was smart. It's what I need to do." Her shoulder rises half-heartedly at that asshole's casual way of breaking her heart.

"What we all need to do I guess," I relent.

"Probably why Nora suggested you come here, yeah? All of us focused on getting shit straight?" She says softly, trying to be sensitive to the bounds I'd set up earlier in the conversation.

"Yeah." I pause, and then realize it's time to exit. Clearly neither of us are interested in bearing our souls tonight with so much weighing so heavily. I don't have the right words for either of us, and in front of her I have even less. I stand up and head for the door.

"You're definitely welcome here for as long as you need. Just let me know how I can help." She offers a small smile.

"Thanks Vi." I return the smile before I exit the room, softly closing the door behind me.

FIVE

Violet

"So are we going to talk about the noises I heard coming out of your room last night or are you still mad at me?" Joss smiles at me as we both grab coffees on our way into campus.

"Still mad, and there were no *noises*." I use air quotes to emphasize the noises part of that sentence.

"It definitely sounded like things were getting physical in there." Her tone is half amusement, half accusation.

"Not like that! It was just tickling..." I trail off when I realize that doesn't sound much better.

"Tickling?" she asks, pausing to cover her mouth as a laugh threatens to burst out along with the sip of latte she's just taken.

"Again, not like that," I protest, realizing tickling probably sounds even more bizarre than what she thought was happening.

"Oh, I definitely think it was exactly like that."

"It was definitely not."

"I've seen the way that boy looks at you. I'm telling you. It was definitely like that," she argues.

"What are you talking about? He does not look at me like anything other than his big sister's friend. Don't be weird!"

"You are so fucking blind, Violet. Honestly, I love you, I do. But Cam really screwed you up."

"Excuse me?" I look at her incredulously.

"He did. You barely date. You can't flirt. Now you can't even realize when someone's flirting with you." She shakes her head in disappointment and takes another sip of her latte before continuing. "I don't know your history with him, but that boy definitely doesn't see you as anything remotely related. Definitely not as a sister. I'd bet money the tickling was just his backasswards way of getting his hands on you. He wants to—"

"Stop!" I shout, not wanting to hear another word.

"What? You're telling me you wouldn't enjoy it?" She's the incredulous one now.

"Definitely not!" I protest but something in my stomach flutters the slightest bit at the thought. I wouldn't, would I? I can't stop to consider that right now, so I bluster on. "He's my best friend's little brother. I'm pretty sure she'd axe me for even thinking about it. Besides, we ran around as kids together."

"Forget the past for a minute. Imagine he's not someone you know. Just a regular guy off the street who ends up rooming with us. You're telling me you look at that body, those dimples, that absolutely gorgeous panty-dropping smile, and don't want to end up in his bed several nights a week?"

"No, do you?" I counter, wondering if I'm going to have to worry about listening to the two of them having sex given how much she's raving about him. I'm telling myself it's definitely not a twinge of jealousy I feel in my gut at the thought, one that needs to be stamped out immediately.

"Not when he very obviously has a thing for my friend!"

"He does not." I roll my eyes.

She glares at me over her cup, and I realize I need to be more convincing—for myself if not her.

"Ben does not have a thing for me. He's a flirt, and it's obvious he's used to women falling at his feet. I don't think he knows how to interact with a woman without flirting with her. It means nada when it comes to me though. It's just his charm and our shared past creating a sense of familiarity. That's it," I say firmly.

"Fine, then go out with me this weekend. Eddie asked me if I wanted to meet him at a show and he said Oliver asked about you."

"Oliver?" I questioned, not recognizing the name.

"The guy you talked to the other night. Well, the guy you said did more looking than talking."

"Oh, um..." I hesitate.

Oliver, if that was his name then, was all right. Attractive. Nice enough based on what I knew from our brief shouted conversations over the table. I'd just assumed I hadn't even registered on his radar beyond that evening, and I was surprised he remembered me at all.

"I don't know," I say at last.

"Well, think about it. I mean... if you're not going to go after the hot guy who obviously wants you, or the cute one from the bar asking about you, then what's your plan? Whatever happened to the dating profile we set up for you on that app?"

"My plan? Can't I just be single and work on my dissertation? I feel like that's a lot on its own. I don't really know that I have time or space for a boyfriend."

"Again, I'm not talking about a boyfriend, Violet. I'm talking about getting under someone new so you can forget about someone old. You're still moping and frankly, you probably need to get rid of the bad vibes he left behind up here and down there." She waves her hand over me, and her face screws up in disgust at the thought of Cam. "He's getting fucked, so why not you? Get some dick, girl."

"Yes, that's what I need, a good dicking," I say tartly. Annoyed she can still tell I'm moping, only a little, and that I've become the single friend charity case that now needs her friend to hook her up with new guys.

"Try it," she challenges.

"I'll look into the app tonight," I agree half-heartedly.

"Good." She smirks briefly before she bursts out into uncalled for laughter.

"Now what?" I say the irritation rife in my voice as I take another sip of my Frappuccino.

"Just thinking about how awkward it would be to swipe right on someone and have the app tell you he's five feet away from your bedroom."

"Joss!!" I cry, elbowing her side as she erupts into another peal of laughter at my annoyance.

———

THAT EVENING I'M SITTING AT THE TABLE, ATTEMPTING TO grade papers while intermittently stopping to look at social media on my phone. My phone pings with an alert and I pick it up to see it's the dating app I'd reopened this afternoon after Joss's lecture. I figured if she was suggesting I date my friend's little brother and desperately trying to set me up with guys who made no sense for me, I'd be better off trying to find someone on my own.

I open up the message from a guy I've matched with and it's a dull one liner asking what I'm doing followed by a "what are you looking for?"

"Sir, if I knew I wouldn't be on here," I mutter.

"What?"

My heart skips a beat at the voice I don't expect, and I look up to see Ben standing there. The shirt he has on stretches over his chest and arms and my eyes wander for a second before my brain clicks in to tell me I'm being weird.

"Um, nothing. Just Joss has me on this dating app and it's awful."

"Yeah, I tried one a while back. I don't recommend it."

"You tried a dating app?"

He shrugs and nods as if it's not strange.

"God help the rest of us if you need dating help." I sigh and pull out another one of my student's papers to grade.

Ben sits down next to me at the table, pulling out a tablet and a book to start studying.

"Do you mind?" He looks at me carefully.

"No, go ahead."

"I didn't *need* a dating app. I just thought it might help me find someone different."

"Different than?"

He smirks.

"The kind of women who usually find me."

"Ah. And it didn't work out for you?"

"Not really. I did help some friends though. I can look at your profile and matches if you want help."

Great, now I have him *and* Joss thinking I need assistance. Am I really this pathetic?

"I'll keep that in mind. Mostly I'm just trying to keep Joss happy."

"Joss?" His brow furrows.

"She thinks I need to date. That it's been too long. And I just want to stay focused on school."

"Ah well, I can back you up on that. You can just tell her

between your work and babysitting me, you don't have time."
He winks at me, and his dimples show as he smiles.

And my traitorous little heart skips a beat as I smile back.

"Going to be that much trouble?" I ask, raising a brow.

"However much you need me to be." His smile turns into a smirk.

And this man is shameless, which is going to be a problem if I can't remember who we are to each other.

"Clever." I shake my head. "Now, work on whatever that is so your sister doesn't kill me for letting her down."

"Yes, ma'am," he whispers, glancing up at me with amusement on his face before he opens his book.

In the future when my friends ask me to take their pain in the ass little brothers in, I'm going to have to ask for more information. Details like, did he grow up to be a shameless flirt with a panty-dropping smile and a distractingly hot body? Because in the future, if the answer is yes, I am definitely not taking the job of babysitting them. I am going to be lucky to survive this one.

SIX

Ben

I MEET JAKE AND COLTON AT THE GYM IN THE AFTERNOON the next week. They've been awesome about meeting me at the regular gym instead of the one at the athletic center, since I'm banned from it as part of my suspension. It sucks, but at least this way I don't feel quite so isolated.

"So, how's it going? The suspension and housing hunt and all that?" Colton asks.

"Still waiting to hear on housing. I don't think how long it's taking is a good sign though. The suspension sucks. How's the team doing in practice?"

"All right, but it's obvious you're missing from the lineup. Going to make some of these games harder without the depth in that position." Colt shakes his head as I help him get set up on the weights.

"Yeah. Fucking sucks." Jake nods from the next bench.

"Better me than half the team though."

"And thanks for that." Jake nods at me.

"No sense in everyone going down." I shrug as I spot Colt on his lift.

"Did you find somewhere to stay?" Jake asks.

"Yeah, a friend of my sister's had a spare room in her place."

"Sister's friend, huh? She hot? Single?"

"Yes." I answer all of the above questions with a single word.

"So when are you inviting me over?" Jake smirks.

"Never." I shake my head.

"Oh, he likes this one," Jake remarks to Colton.

"You think?" Colt asks, pausing for a minute to reassess the weights.

"Yeah, man. You haven't been here long enough to know Ben's habits, but he is notoriously unattached and unimpressed. The opposite of you."

"You guys going to give me shit for having a girlfriend all year, or when does that get old?" Colton asks gruffly.

"Just saying you're wasting precious time you could be out there experimenting with all different flavors of pussy. That's all." Jake shakes his head.

"I'm good with one." Colton lifts again and huffs out a breath when he lets the weight drop.

"That where you're headed now too?" Jake glances up at me.

"I wish."

"What?" Jake stops his motion and stares up at me. "I was fucking joking."

"This one's different, but don't get too worried. She still thinks I'm a fucking kid and she's the babysitter."

"I mean, could make that work..." Jake tilts his head as if he's considering it.

"Older than you huh?" Colton looks up at me.

"By a few years, yeah."

"You have a plan?" Jake asks.

"I don't think there is a plan with her. I wouldn't know where to start."

"Better figure it out. Not gonna get a better chance than being her roommate." Colton states the obvious.

"Yeah, true, but easier said than done."

"We'll figure it out." Jake winks at me, and I don't even want to ask what he means by that.

"When are you gonna settle down?" I ask him.

"Hopefully just before I clock out of the NFL due to old age. Get me a nice young model, do the kids and the picket fence thing, not a minute sooner. Commitment gives me the fuckin' hives."

"You don't know what you're missing," Colton says.

"Yeah, why don't you tell me all about it then?" Jake smirks.

"Fuck off." Colton bats back.

"All right. Less talk, more get this fucking work out done." I nod at the weights, and Colton does another rep.

———

As I'm leaving the gym, I get the email I've been dreading. The athletic department has no alternative housing options for me, and I'm on my own at least for the rest of the semester. I grimace at the idea of having to be dependent on Violet's ongoing charity for the rest of the year. But I'd looked into short term stay places and they were all well outside my budget. All my friends had full houses, and while they could offer me a couch it wasn't a place where I could keep my stuff and half of them were party houses where exactly zero studying ever got done. None of which I could afford.

Getting off suspension required my good behavior and good grades.

I stop at the little bakery around the corner from the apartment, hoping something sweet will help give me a buffer when I have to ask Violet for more time than I was expecting. They're just getting ready to close and the girl behind the counter grumpily tells me so until she looks up and sees me. Then she smiles.

"I'm sorry for coming in at the last second, but I have to try and beg for a place to stay tonight, and I'm hoping bakery goods can help me sell it." I grin at her, hoping the charm will keep her from being too pissed at me. I know at my high school job I always hated when customers rolled in at the last second.

"That sounds like a pretty unbelievable story, but I'll allow it. We don't have much left though."

"I'll take whatever you've got." I pull out my wallet and she starts gathering up pastries and cookies from the boxes she was about to put away.

"A dozen of a mix good?"

"Perfect."

I glance down at my phone as Jake texts me about a party this weekend. Part of me wants to go, but the other part of me knows I need to stay away. I trust myself not to do anything stupid, but I don't trust other people not to do stupid things in my proximity, and the fine line I'm walking means I can't afford that kind of fun.

She puts the box and some napkins into a brown paper bag for me and proceeds to ring me up. I swipe my card and then offer her another little smile.

"Have a good night and good luck!" She smiles brightly at me.

"Thanks!"

When I get into the apartment, it smells and looks like smoke.

Joss is standing in the kitchen waving a tray around, and Violet is opening the windows and the sliding glass door to the balcony. She turns around when she hears me, and I give her a questioning look.

"Joss tried to cook again." Violet looks doubtfully at her friend.

"I am not stupid enough to try to cook, Violet. I merely put a pizza in the oven. I just happened to forget about it."

"Whatever you want to call it, dearest." Violet gives her a sarcastic little smile.

"I'm going to order Thai. Just tell me what you want." Joss tosses the pizza in the trash and looks to both of us as she pulls out her phone.

"The usual," Violet says.

"Pad Thai. Just let me know what I owe you. Thanks." I nod and drop my bags by the door before I walk in to set the paper sack on the dining room table.

"What's this?" Violet peers into the bag, grinning.

"Stopped at the place you guys like."

"Did they have the muffins?" Joss whispers as she waits for the phone to be answered.

"I don't know. It's a mix of what they had left. They were closing."

"Please let them have the cookies with the little white chocolate bits." Violet pulls the box out of the bag and the napkins that were on top scatter.

One of them has writing on it and she picks it up, reading it as she does so, her face twisting with amusement. She hands the napkin to Joss, who smiles and looks at me, giving a low whistle before she's interrupted by someone asking to take her order. I can almost, almost, feel the heat rise in my cheeks. I'm never embarrassed, but these two have a crazy ability to make me feel like I'm an awkward teenage boy again.

"What?" I ask innocently.

Violet holds up the napkin, reading from it. "Enjoy the sweets. If you need another taste or a place to stay tonight, text me. Abby. And then there's a number."

"Uh, yeah. That happens sometimes."

"I bet it does. What exactly did you do to obtain these pastry goods?" Violet raises her eyebrow at me. "You're supposed to be staying out of trouble, remember?"

"I am." I snatch the napkin out of her hand and crumple it before tossing it in the trash.

"Poor Abby." Joss frowns at the trash.

"Also, you should know the pastries are a bribe."

"I mean that was obvious when I read the note." Violet snickers, having way too much fun at my expense.

"Ha! I'm being serious though. I got bad news from the athletic department about housing. They can't help me for the rest of the semester. I've already looked at some short stay places and they're all outside my budget. I was going to look for some rooms tonight online."

Violet looks to Joss who's off the phone now, and they exchange glances for a moment.

"You're going to make me keep the puppy, aren't you?" Joss purses her lips.

"I don't think he should rent a room somewhere. How will he study? And what if there are more Abbies out there? Or god forbid, a cougar finds him." Violet walks over to me and puts her hand under my jaw. "Look at this face, Joss. They will eat him alive."

They both burst out laughing, and I wrap my arms around Violet, tickling her ribs until she doubles over.

"I'm pretty sure I'm already in some sort of cougar den with the two of you," I tease.

"Not true! I have never gone after anyone younger. Joss maybe though?" Violet looks to her.

"God no. Even the older ones act like children." Her face turns up in disgust.

"So see, you're safe staying here. Assuming that's what you're asking?" Violet turns to me as I loosen my grip on her.

"Yeah. I feel like shit for doing it. But it's quiet here and I can study and get my workouts in. I just want to keep my head down and get off suspension," I say quietly, feeling awkward at having to beg for a place to stay.

"As long as you keep cooking for us a couple nights a week and no Abbies end up in common areas, I'm fine with it." Joss shrugs.

I look to Violet, and she smiles at me, a look passing over her face I can't quite read.

"Same." She nods.

"Thank you. I'll make it up to you, somehow. I'm gonna get changed before dinner gets here."

Joss mumbles something as I walk away and Violet slaps her on her forearm before shushing her.

"What?" I ask, pausing and trying not to smile.

"Nothing. She just said she needs a cookie," Violet answers. "To keep her mouth shut," she adds muttering under her breath.

"Okay..." I trail off, because I'm pretty sure Joss just said that I could make it up to Violet in bed. If that's something they discussed enough that Joss is teasing Violet about it, I'm very curious.

———

LATER THAT EVENING WE'RE ALL SPRAWLED OUT AROUND the TV in the living room, watching a crime show with a paranormal twist the two of them seem to love, and I have to admit I find morbidly interesting. It reminds me of the old school horror movies Mac, Liv and Wren used to like to watch on movie nights, and I feel a little pang of nostalgia at missing my old friends. I need to text the group chat to see how everyone is doing.

When the episode ends on a cliffhanger and Joss turns the TV off, Violet sits up and glares at her.

"You can't end it there!"

"I have work to do and then I need to get to bed," Joss argues.

"But they're just about to find the evidence. I need to know what happens," Violet protests.

"They are not about to find the evidence. They're pretending they are and then they're going to drag out the reveal for another 30 minutes."

"You don't know for sure!" Violet counters.

They have a stare off for a minute, and then Joss relents.

"Fine. Watch the next episode without me *but* do not spoil it, and that means watch it in your room because I don't want to hear tidbits while I'm trying to work in my room."

"Yes! You're the best. I love you!" Violet hugs Joss and then bounces around picking up all the dishes to put them in the kitchen.

I get up and help her bus them up, and we start loading the dishwasher together as Joss disappears into her room to work. She grabs some plates and turns abruptly not realizing I'm behind her, and bumps into me losing her balance in the process. I grab her by the hips to stop her from falling.

"Sorry. That was clumsy." She looks up at me for the briefest of moments before a soft blush spreads over her cheeks. She bites her lip and turns her head down to the task at hand, putting the plates in the dishwasher.

I release my hands from her sides way too slow, and my heart rate picks up because all I can think about is how much I want to kiss her, take her lush lower lip in my mouth and pin her up against the counter. But I stop myself because I try not to be in the habit of making stupid mistakes.

"It's okay. I'm clumsy all the time," I say, trying to make her feel better and keep the conversation going, so I'm not thinking about other things.

"Right. I bet that's why you're a D1 athlete. The clumsiness." She shoots me a look that says she doesn't appreciate the patronizing help.

"You'd be surprised. Sometimes it's like my brain short circuits."

"Uh huh. I'll believe it when I see it." She gives me a little grin and puts the last of the dishes in the dishwasher before she starts it.

"Could I watch the next episode with you?" I ask abruptly. So fucking smooth. Like I said, it short circuits, especially around her.

"Of the show?" She looks confused.

"Yeah. If you don't mind. I want to know what happens."

"Oh, um. Sure, I guess." She wipes her hands on a towel.

"If you don't want me—"

"No. It's fine. Just my room is small and there's really nowhere to sit but the bed."

Which was exactly why it was such a great idea, or bad idea depending on if you're a glass half empty or full type of person.

"Worried you can't keep your hands off me?"

Her eyes flash up to mine and she shakes her head. "I'll find a way."

"All right. Meet you in there in five?" I ask.

She nods and then heads off for her room.

I NEED THE FIVE MINUTES TO CONVINCE MYSELF NOT TO
try to put my hands on her. If she was any of the other women I
dated I'd be moving faster, trying to charm her and get her to
admit she wanted me to kiss her. Because I'm fairly certain she
does, but I also think she hates that she does. So instead, I'm
going to try to be on my best behavior with her, even if it
kills me.

When the time is up, I knock on her door, and she calls for
me to come in. She's already propped up on her bed, flipping
through the channels to get the show set up. She looks up at me
and smiles.

"So what do you think? Poltergeist? Aliens? Someone living
in the ceiling?" she asks and pats the spot next to her on the bed
when I hesitate.

I lay down next to her, fixing the pillow, and then laying
back against it.

"I don't know." I shrug as I take in the surroundings of her
room.

It feels odd to be in her space. I'd never seen her room as
kids, as only Nora had ever been invited inside or over for
sleepovers. I'd always wondered, especially as a teenager what
posters she had on the wall, whether she was messy or neat.
The room now is neat, which makes sense because Violet
always seemed put together. But there are little hints of chaos;
makeup and hair stuff spilled over the desk. A pile of dresses
and clothes draped over a chair in the corner.

"Sorry. It's a little messy." She frowns, catching me scruti-
nizing the space. "I'm used to being alone in here now."

"This is not messy. You have not seen messy until you live
with other athletes."

"Yikes. I don't know that I want to imagine that."

"Yeah. One of the benefits of being here." I smile at her.

"You really are welcome here. Joss is just teasing you, so you know."

"I just feel bad because I know you could be getting more rent for the room."

"It's fine. I'd planned on covering it anyway, so you pitching in is better than what I expected. And you cook and bring us bakery goods. Even if they are ill gotten gains," she teases me.

"Ugh." I scrub a hand over my face, the creep of embarrassment coming in again.

"Does that happen a lot?"

I shrug one shoulder. "Sometimes."

She looks me over and gives me a warm smile, her eyes drifting over me for a minute before she turns abruptly and flips on the show. The eerie music starts up, and we don't say another word before we start watching together.

SEVEN

Violet

THE NEXT NIGHT I'M STUCK AT THE GALLERY WITH Joss working on a new installation. The exhibit opens in three days, which means I have to get a bunch of the artwork up on the walls today. And day has quickly turned into night, and I'm wondering if it might even turn into tomorrow at this rate. Joss is thankfully here helping, but I can tell that even she's getting tired. I wouldn't blame her for bailing as this is one of my projects for my independent study, and she's just a volunteer for the gallery.

As I work to set another French cleat on the back of one of the paintings, my phone buzzes in my pocket and I pull it out. It's a text from Ben.

BEN

Are you guys going to be home? Dinner's almost ready

"Shit," I curse, remembering that he'd mentioned this morning he was going to cook. I'd been optimistic as hell at that hour, thinking this installation would only take maybe the morning to complete. Then everything had gone wrong.

"What?" Joss looks up from her spot at the table across the room where she's covered in polyethylene dust as she works to create a mount for one of the textile pieces.

"He's making dinner, and there's no way I'm making it back in time. You should go and maybe you can make it before it's cold."

She looks around the room and gives me a doubtful look.

"No way I'm leaving you here with all this by yourself."

"But I feel bad."

"Just tell him to put the leftovers in the fridge and we'll eat them when we crawl back in in the middle of the night like vampires."

I laugh and turn my lower lip under. I was looking forward to the pasta he was making and desperately wishing for a shower and my bed right about now.

> No. Unfortunately, we're stuck working in one of the galleries. I don't know if we'll even be home before midnight. I'm really sorry. Put it in the fridge, and we'll eat it when we get back?

> I was really looking forward to it too!

I send a little sad face emoji and then try to ignore the bit of guilt I feel that he was trying so hard to be a good roommate and we weren't even there to appreciate it.

BEN

> Which gallery?

Scotland. Why?

I'll pack it up and bring it to you guys. You
need to eat before midnight

Um. I think you are my hero

Anything else you want?

Any cookies still left? Need the morale boost
around here

You got it. Be there as soon as everything's
ready

"Yay!" I say as I tuck my phone back in my pocket.

"What?"

"He's bringing us dinner and cookies."

"Of course he is."

"Why are you saying it like that?" I look up at her.

"Because he's not bringing us dinner. He's bringing *you* dinner." She smiles.

"Not this again." I drill the cleat into the mounting frame a little too enthusiastically.

"I noticed he was in your room last night."

"To watch the show."

She goes to switch off the hot tool for the foam and sets the knife down, giving me a dramatic look in between the motions.

"Don't be dense, Violet. If I was you, I would have gotten him in bed already."

"I told you; we're just old family friends, and he's a flirt. That's all you're seeing. He's not interested in me."

"Remind me of that when he finally makes a move you can't explain away."

49

"I will because it won't happen. And besides I wouldn't let it happen."

"Because you're so not attracted to a boy who looks like he does, and flirts with you and brings you dinner when you're stuck late at work?"

"He's like a brother."

"Again, remind me... no, you know what? Remind yourself of that when you start fantasizing about him. If you haven't already." She raises an eyebrow in accusation.

I swallow hard then. Because honestly, I had thought about him in the shower. Maybe. Once. But was that really my fault? Especially when he came out of the bathroom with his hair still wet and a tight shirt on.

"And the hussy is thinking about it right now."

"Only because you put the thought in my head!"

"Uh huh. Whatever you have to tell yourself, love."

"Can we please talk about your dating life instead?"

"Nice diversion."

"I'm serious. Did the bartender ever call? And what happened to the guy you were seeing before?" I change the subject, and we discuss the many red flags she ignored from the last guy she dated because he was cute and took her on a graffiti walk for their first date.

Before we know it, Ben is texting, and I run to the side door to let him in.

"What's all this?" He has several bags in his hands, more than I would have expected for a couple of plastic containers of pasta.

"I ate the last cookie when I was cooking. So I stopped at the grocery to get some fresh ones and I also grabbed some fresh bread to go with the pasta, and some drinks."

"You didn't have to do all that." I shake my head.

"Judging by how exhausted you look; I think you might need it."

He wasn't wrong. I felt like I was going to fall over any second, and I needed to rally because this had to be done whether I had the energy or not.

"Thank you. Seriously. I owe you."

"No problem, but I'll remember that." He grins at me.

"This way." I nod for him to follow me. "There's a small lunchroom back here."

Joss was already in the room, bent over at the table with her head down like she might nap, an energy drink in her hand.

"Dinner!" I say happily, hoping it'll cheer her.

"These exhibit schedules are relentless, and I really wish they'd give us more people if they're going to keep doing this," she grumbles to the table.

"Agreed. But not much we can do but barrel through now."

"Can I help?" Ben asks as he unpacks the food.

"No, you've got homework and studying to do." I shake my head. "It's bad enough you came here to give us food. You don't need the distraction."

"Okay." He rolls his eyes at me. "Joss, is there something I can do?"

"Lots of things, but I don't want to get in trouble with Violet." I sigh. "We'll discuss it when Joss and I are less hangry."

———

AFTER DINNER—WHICH IS ACTUALLY REALLY GOOD EVEN though it's in a lukewarm state—and a couple of cookies, I feel like I can focus again. I stretch my limbs to try and get ready to mount the artwork. Joss has gone to get some more supplies, and Ben and I clean up the lunchroom.

"Let me help? I've got the homework done. I spent the time between classes in the library today, so I was just going to do some extra studying."

"You helped enough by bringing us food. Seriously. Thank you again. I could kiss you for it." I forget that I'm talking to Ben and not Joss, and I nearly choke on the last bite of cookie when I realize it. I grimace and close my eyes, waiting for a smart-ass remark on his part, but his back is to me, and he doesn't say anything for a minute.

"I'm already here, and I've got the time. Sounds like Joss thought I could be helpful."

"I guess there's a few things you could help with. For like an hour—but then you go home, okay? It's my fault for waiting too long on this and I already feel awful that Joss is stuck here with me."

"The faster we get it done, the sooner she gets to go home, right?"

"Don't make good points that contradict my feelings." I poke him gently in the ribs as we walk back out to the gallery space, and he laughs.

"How good are you with a drill?" I ask as we get back to the mess that will eventually be an exhibit.

"Not the best. But I can learn."

"No time for that tonight. But you can hold the cleats and make sure they're level and I'll drill them. We have to finish this whole wall and then that one, and then install the artwork on the cleats."

I show him the install process on one that's already done, and we do a practice one before we really get into a rhythm. And he and Joss are right, it goes much faster when you've got help. Not that I want to let them know they were right.

We're on the last one, but we're struggling to get the cleat in place because the canvas is larger than the others.

"Here, can you hold it by yourself? Is it too heavy?" I ask, and he makes a face at me like I'm stupid. Because right, he's an athlete and probably benches a bajillion pounds every day. "Sorry dumb question. I'm just going to slide under here and see if I can guide it on a little bit."

I slide between him, the artwork he's holding and the wall, reaching my hand as far as I can when I see that it's not quite clicking into place. I turn to look at him, and realize the position we're in. Me pressed up against the wall, him only inches from me. I can feel his breath on my neck and mine catches in my throat.

"Thoughts you want to share?" He smirks at me.

Fuck.

"Yeah, put it a little to your left." Which is just fantastic because that doesn't sound dirty at all.

"Got it." He moves the piece to the left, but his smirk widens.

"Stop smirking," I mutter.

"Stop looking at me like that and I will."

I look up at him, and it's a mistake because the look that passes over his face has my heart rate rising.

"Do you need help?" Joss calls out to us.

"Yes, please!" I yell, my voice coming out with a slight squeak.

He shakes his head, his eyes taunting me. "Coward's way out, huh?"

I open my mouth to say something I'll probably regret when Joss appears.

Saved by the bestie.

"What do you need?" she asks.

"I need it up and over to the left a little, but it's having trouble getting slotted, and I can't quite reach with my fingertips." I explain to her, and her mouth crumples into a little smile before she pulls her lips inward, and there is a distinctive choked laugh from Ben's direction.

"I hate you both right now. Just for the record."

"You do not. You're just tired and need to get laid." Joss calls back.

Which is exactly the kind of thing she would say if we were alone, but we're very much not alone and I feel the heat of her comment creep up my neck at the same time I feel his eyes on me. But I refuse to make eye contact with him. And if that makes me a coward, so be it.

A second later and the cleat locks into place and I can slide out from my precarious spot between the wall and the temptation that would certainly land me in one of the inner circles of hell.

"Thanks." I smile tightly at Joss.

She has the decency to look a little remorseful, and hurries back to her spot at the desk. I take a breath and pick up some of the tools, continuing to ignore him because I cannot look at him right now.

"I think we can call it a night. That puts me ahead of schedule. I should be able to finish the rest in the morning," I call out to Joss.

"All right. I'll come in after my photography class to finish this mount and get it in the case. Then we just need to put the labels and stuff up, right?"

"Yep. And I'll get them printed tomorrow morning. But for now, let's just get home."

She nods and we manage to pack everything up and head home.

———

I TAKE A QUICK SHOWER ONCE WE GET BACK, AND I RAID the fridge for a flavored water and some raspberries before I head to bed. My body groans as I stand straight again from my crouched position, and I know I overdid it today in my hurry to get the exhibit up. Some days I wasn't sure if the art *was* worth the pain.

I pop a raspberry in my mouth and close my eyes, rolling my shoulders and my neck, trying to get the muscles to relax. I was probably going to need to find where I'd stashed the ibuprofen in the drawers if I wanted to sleep tonight.

"I can fix that for you," Ben says as he opens the door to the fridge, and I jump, pressing my hand and the bottle of water to my heart.

"By giving me a heart attack and having worse things to focus on?" I glare at him, but he just laughs.

"Ha. No, by massaging your muscles. Happens to me some-times when I do too many catching drills." He takes a drink from one of the bottles he keeps stashed in the fridge.

I give him a doubtful look.

"Or you could just suffer." He shrugs his shoulders.

"Okay. Fine. I'll try it. Mostly because I don't know where the ibuprofen is."

"I have some if you need it but turn around." He sets his bottle on the counter and motions for me to turn my back to him.

I do it reluctantly because as much as I would like some relief from the pain, I'm equally nervous to let him touch me. The way my body reacted to him earlier made my brain imitate a Pollock painting, and I needed to not make stupid decisions.

I hear him rub his hands together behind me, warming them after he'd touched the cold bottle and then he places them on my shoulder, slowly and gently massaging the tender muscles there. The second he starts I know it's a mistake because warmth blooms on my skin everywhere his fingers touch and beyond, but I don't stop him.

He starts at my neck and works down my shoulder and then back up again. First on the right side, and then moving to the left. It's hard to express how ridiculously good it feels in my current state, and I stuff another couple of raspberries in mouth to keep from moaning.

Then his hands trace down my spine in small circles on either side, to the center of my back and out between my shoulder blades before he returns to my neck again; the pain melting away under his ministrations. This time I can't help myself and a little groan of relief pops out of my mouth before I can stop it. I put my fingers to my lips to cover it.

"Sorry, that just feels so good." The words come out like a breathy whisper, and I feel his fingers slow as he runs them up and down my neck.

"Yeah? Feel better?" he asks in a rough whisper. One that's so sexy, if it was any other guy, I'd have a very different response than silence. But it's him, so I can't, taking a sip of my water instead.

"Yeah," I say at last, swallowing the extra thoughts with my water.

His right hand drifts forward, sliding up the column of my throat until his fingers reach my jaw and he turns my head gently to the side, stroking beneath my jawbone with his thumb. I can hear his breathing change and my own heart is skipping beats in my chest.

He takes a breath, like he's about to say something when the door to Joss's room opens and the hallway fills with light. I jerk forward, grabbing my bottle back off the counter and tightening my grip on the container of raspberries before I drop them.

"Thanks, all better. Goodnight." I move so quickly, I can

barely get the words out before I dodge around him, headed for my bedroom.

I hear him call after me, but I ignore it, closing and locking the door behind me. Face planting into the bed as soon as I set my food and water down. I start mentally lecturing myself about who he is and how much younger he is than me, and how there are a million other guys out there and I don't need to be thinking about him.

Except when I close my eyes, he's all I see, and I can still feel his fingers sliding over my skin. It makes me imagine them elsewhere. I am so screwed if I don't get a hold on this.

EIGHT

Violet

A COUPLE OF NIGHTS LATER I LAY BACK ON MY BED, putting my earbuds in to listen to some white noise while I get some reading in. It's been a long week, and as much as I love Joss and Ben being around, I'm happy to have a few hours of quiet to myself.

My eyes catch on the book I'd purchased for my media class research. I'm still annoyed Joss got me to agree to take this class. It'd been at a weak point right after Cam had announced he wanted to take a break and try an open relationship for a while when he realized he was going to be out of the country for up to a year. I'd wanted to do something different, bold, strange. I'd wanted to take the opportunity to break the glass box around me. Because if he was going to do something different, so was I.

Except instead of going out to a bar and fucking a stranger I'd signed up for a semester long course on Sex, Media, and Art, and then signed up for a project on the female gaze in popular culture. Not exactly wild and crazy.

Meanwhile Joss was photographing naked male models for the project. One of us clearly was braver than the other, and that meant I was stuck deep in theoretical analysis that involved reading everything from Foucault to contemporary romance novels.

I glanced at the book on the shelf. I could do without Foucault and his discipline and punishment musings, but the last part wasn't terrible. I'd only gotten through a few, but the latest one was something the shelf at the indie bookstore had recommended as "dark romance".

I'd gotten through the first couple chapters, following a mafia boss and his arranged bride whose engagement was going exactly as well as you'd expect. He was a dick to her and fucking with multiple other women, and she absolutely wanted to murder him to get out of the whole situation.

Hard relate, sister. Same page here.

I open the book again, skimming the pages to figure out where I'd left off. I shouldn't be working tonight. I should take the night off, watch TV or call one of my cohorts and see who was going out for drinks. But I was tired, already in my PJ's, two glasses of wine deep, and murderous mafiosos were calling my name.

I was lost in a scene where the two of them were yelling at each other, and his temper snapped. He'd put her down on her knees in front of him and started unzipping his pants, telling her she was going to make it up to him like a good little girl.

And reading his filthy thoughts on the page sends a tingling awareness through my body, a tightness that blooms until I can feel myself starting to get wet. I glance at the door. It's shut and it's still early, and Ben and Joss should be out for hours. I bite my lip and roll it between my teeth. It had been a long while since I'd had anything close to an orgasm, and as I close my eyes the thoughts of a dark eyed dark haired mafia boss invade my senses. I can almost imagine his hands on me as I slide my hand under my shorts, letting my fingers explore, my breath hitching as I hit a particularly sensitive spot.

I open my eyes again, focusing back on the words. Trying to find the passage that had sparked my interest. Rereading his demand for her to get on his knees. I give myself a tentative little stroke, and my body responds in kind. My nerve endings, desperate and neglected since Cameron had left months ago, send little zips and sparks of awareness through me. I hate that Cameron comes unbidden into my mind. So I close my eyes again for half a second, trying to reimagine the mafia boss's warm brown eyes before I continue reading. Recentering myself and giving another small stroke to my clit has me moaning softly in anticipation of more.

When I open my eyes again to read, I see a flicker of movement out of the corner of my eye. My door is open, and a figure is there leaning against the door frame. His eyes are locked on the spot where my hand moves under my shorts, and for a moment I imagine it's the mafia boss. He looks so much like the man I'd just seen in my imagination anyway, except the suit has been replaced by a T-shirt and sweatpants.

Then I blink and reality hits. I'm not imagining the person there. He's very real. Very corporeal. And it's Ben. Watching me.

"Fuck!" I curse, and I slam the book down over my face in an effort to cover my cheeks that are blooming bright red with embarrassment. I rip the ear buds out of my ears, cursing myself for having them in and therefore missing the sound of him coming home.

He's still silent, and I can only imagine what he's thinking. Another moment of silence passes.

"I knocked."

That's it. The words that break the silence. All he has to say in this moment.

"I thought you were out with your friends." My voice is muffled by the pages still shielding my face. I may never remove the book. Just walk around with this like a paper bag on my head for the rest of eternity.

Except then I remember the cover, and the title of the book. A photo of tattooed knuckles and something about his bride to break, or his to have. I forget exactly now in this moment. I'll need to figure it out for my citations when I write the paper. If I manage not to die of embarrassment before then. All this boy brings me is one embarrassing moment after another lately. I never knew I was this much of a mess until he came to live here.

"I left early. Everyone was wasted, and I wanted to get back."

To his credit, his voice is even, unfazed. Like nothing out of the ordinary is happening.

I feel the bed dip under his weight next to me, and I cringe. I want him to leave, close the door, not speak to me for the rest of the night, and then for us to pretend like this never happened. Maybe we'd never speak again. That would be fine.

"What are you reading?" he asks quietly, and I can tell from my peripheral vision, the bit still visible beyond the pages, that he's on his side next to me, watching me.

It's the perfect opening for me to explain away this little incident, to convince him his eyes betrayed him, and his stand-in older sister was just doing a little light research on a Friday night. Absolutely nothing else.

"A book for my Sex and Media class. I'm doing a project on the female gaze, so I'm reading some of these. For research," I add, but my voice sounds throaty and uneven. I'm failing to even do the bare minimum to cover my ass here by sounding even remotely normal.

"Can I see?" he asks, still even toned.

"Sure," I agree. Because sure, why the hell not make this more awkward than it already is.

He lifts the book off my face and turns it in his hands, twisting his body so he's laying on his stomach. I'm thankful for the small mercy that he's no longer looking directly at me. At least him reading it will give me that benefit.

Then I hear his breathing change, his body shifts slightly, and I can guess which part his eyes are skimming over. Although I don't have to guess long, because he starts to read it out loud.

"She looks up at me, a hint of hesitation across her face before I see the desire consume her eyes. 'That's right, sweetheart. You're going to take all of my cock down your throat tonight, drink every last—'" Ben's voice sounds like sex when he's reading the ingredients off a box, when he's actually reading about sex? It's unbearable. Especially in my current state.

"Ben—" I manage to choke out his name, because my throat feels like scorched earth and my skin is flushed so red, I can feel the heat radiating off of me.

"I'm going to read it to you, so you can finish." He says it so calmly, so matter of factly it's hard to believe we've both lived through the same last five minutes.

"Your research," he adds.

I want to protest, but I can't breathe, let alone form coherent words. I run my hands over my face instead, wishing I could just disappear.

"'Drink every last drop of me, until you remember who you belong to.' She protests, her mind still defiant where her body has given—" He starts reading again. His voice is thick, a raw tone to it making the words that much sexier coming off the page and just like the character in the book, my own body goes along with it despite my panic.

"Ben, please. This is so..." I trail off because it feels like even saying the word embarrassing will catapult this even higher on the list of most embarrassing moments for me. Which is a ridiculous thing to worry about because this is definitely top of the list, forever.

He closes his eyes, tilts his head down, but doesn't look at me. Another small mercy I'm thankful for.

"You're helping me. Studying. Keeping me out of trouble. Now I'm helping you. So finish your research, Violet."

He turns the page and starts to read again. I can't hear the words, just the sound of his voice. The rhythmic way he speaks. The throaty quality to every word. My eyes travel over his shoulders. He has on a plain white T-shirt that's tight across them. It highlights them, stretching to meet the ridges of muscle. The line of his spine down the middle, his waist tapering to where the shirt meets a pair of dark blue sweatpants. Sweatpants wrapping around a perfect ass and draping over muscular thighs.

My fingers skim over my stomach. I seriously consider arguing with him. Telling him to get out. But somehow it feels like that would make this more awkward than just finishing what I started. So, I do the unthinkable and slide my hand back under the waistband of my panties again, touching myself tentatively. It won't take much. The adrenaline of being caught and the sound of his voice while he reads is enough to have every single nerve ending in my body turned all the way up.

I focus on his words as I brush my middle finger over my throbbing clit.

"I spread her thighs, bend her over and I can see her. All of her. Already warm and wet and ready for me..."

I give myself a few more rough strokes and that's all it takes. *Holy. Fuck.*

It's blinding as I come listening to him. Blackness enveloping me. The sound of his voice sending me off into a void I melt into. I try to stifle my reaction, keep myself quiet and still, but I can't, and a little moan tumbles out of my throat in the process. I take a breath, hoping the oxygen will help me surface again. I pinch my eyes tighter because as good as that was, I'm dreading the transition back to reality.

I hear the sound of the book shut, feel his body move on the mattress and I let my lids slide open, just enough to make him out. His head is down, forehead pressed to the closed book. It explains why his voice is slightly muffled when he speaks again.

"I'm gonna get a quick shower. Then let's watch an episode of one of those crime shows you like, okay?"

"Okay." I agree, because I don't know what else to say.

He lays the book on my desk and leaves without another word. And when he returns twenty minutes later, he climbs into bed next to me like he had before, and we watch the show in silence until we fall asleep.

NINE

Ben

AFTER THE GYM AND A SHOWER, I'M JOGGING ACROSS THE street from campus to the little independent bookstore. I'm not even sure what I'm looking for, but I'm willing to give it a shot. My eyes slide over the various section titles and land on one labeled "romance", and I head in that direction. It's just after dinner and the bookstore is quiet, the only sound a coffee machine percolating in the distance as I make my way to the back.

All I've been able to think about all day was seeing her last night. When I'd knocked and she hadn't answered, I was worried because her car was in the lot. So I'd opened the door and my heart had stopped in my fucking chest at the sight of her. I had almost wondered if I'd been knocked unconscious by the weights at the gym and was imagining it all like a dream. That was until she'd seen me and blushed so fast and heavy, she'd used the book to try and cover it up. Then it was obvious, because the fantasy version of Violet always asks me to help her and rarely ever blushes.

When I get to the section I'm looking for, I'm over-whelmed. There's a sea of covers, names and subsections and I realize just how out of my element I am.

"Can I help you?" My fairy godmother appears in the form of a blonde curvy woman with glasses and blunt bangs, about my age, dressed in a dandelion yellow sweater.

"Yeah, I'm..." I trail off. What am I doing? Trying to fucking seduce my sister's best friend by reading to her, because it's the only in I've got with her now, and I need a repeat of last night like I need oxygen. I don't think that's what this sweet little woman who's looking up at me so thoughtfully wants to hear though.

"I've got a project on the female gaze in media. I need to read some books, I guess to do some research."

Good one, Lawton. Super smooth.

"Okay," her nose wrinkles like she's thinking. "Are you looking for sweet? Steamy? Any particular genre or niche?"

I stare at her blankly and she gives me a little laugh that makes me smile.

"Okay—romance comes in a lot of genres, depending on what you like. Cowboy. Alien. Mafia. And then it runs from sweet, which is like no sex or closed door, to steamy which is open door sex. Even that's kind of a range though."

"I bet," I say staring at the shelves. "I guess open door. But maybe something less mafia?"

"Oh, started with the dark romance, did you?" She smirks at me, and I like this girl. I feel like she'd bust my balls without breaking a sweat.

"Something like that." I grin.

"I have an idea, this way." She motions for me to follow her and takes me down the aisle.

She pulls a book off the shelf and hands it to me. A bare-chested football player stares up at me from the cover. I realize I'm in my university football gear and she's observant.

"This one's still open door. Plenty of sex and female gaze for you to analyze, but a little less taboo than the mafia stuff usually is. It's about a football player and his tutor, opposites attract. He falls for her but she's not sure about him, then one thing leads to another—"

"Perfect," I cut her off, not meaning to be rude but I'm anxious to get back to Violet.

"Great." She smiles up at me. "Anything else?"

"No, that's it."

"Okay, let's get you checked out."

She takes the book back from me and I follow her to the front of the store.

I'd left Violet alone this morning, given her space and only minimal interaction. I knew I'd gotten wildly lucky with her last night, somehow played the cards exactly in the right order that she didn't throw me out when I'd picked up the book to start reading. And I'd taken the fact she'd let me back in bed to watch a show after as a good sign that I might be able to get a repeat if I could get a similar run of luck.

I slide my debit card in the machine and watch as the clerk places bookmarks in between a few of the pages, and jots notes on two of them. Then she slides the book to me.

"In case you want to cut to the good parts." She smiles.

"Read it before I'm guessing?"

"I prefer hockey players, but football players will do in a pinch." She winks at me.

I can't help but laugh though.

"Thank you. Appreciate it!"

"Come back anytime!"

WHEN I GET BACK TO THE APARTMENT JOSS AND VIOLET are spread out across the dining room table, an array of Chinese food and papers scattered across the surface.

"Hey sexy! I ordered us some take out if you want some." Joss smiles at me.

Violet glances up and gives me a barely there smile, before her eyes dart back to her paper.

Well, fuck.

"Grading tonight?"

"Yep. Fucking freshmen. They all think they're a lot smarter than they are and it shows." Joss shakes her head.

"Be nice, they're trying, and we were freshmen once too." Violet chides her.

"Please, I was born badass." Jocelyn flicks her hair over her shoulder and they both giggle at the gesture.

"Not everyone is as perfect as you Joss. Have mercy." Violet shakes her head, her little red pen tracing over the words in front of her.

"Care if I join then? I've got some studying I need to do for Geography before I can sleep."

"Of course." Jocelyn kicks out one of the spare chairs toward me, and I sit down.

Her eyes drift between me and Violet, and they narrow for a second, but she thankfully chooses not to say anything. Instead offering me some rice and Mongolian beef. I take it and pull out the chapter notes I need to go through before my quiz tomorrow. The three of us eat and work in relative silence for several hours until Jocelyn stretches her arms and declares herself exhausted.

"I'm going to bed, you two have fun." She looks at both of us again and then disappears to her side of the apartment.

"I should go too." Violet stands abruptly and starts gathering her papers together.

I close the map I've been trying to take a mental picture of for the last ten minutes and watch her put her things together.

"Do you want to watch something?" I ask hedging my bets.

She doesn't look up at me, just continuing to tuck the papers back in the folder and the folder in her messenger bag.

"Um, I don't think I can stay awake long enough to watch a whole episode."

"What about reading a chapter or two?"

Her hands still on the closure of the bag, and she clears her throat.

"Um, about that—" she starts, and I can tell I'm about to get an explanation and a lot of excuses, so I pull the book out that I bought and slide it across the table in front of her.

"I thought you could read to me."

Everything I say to her feels like I'm gambling. Normally with women, I know. I can read them, and I know if they want me or not. I can usually reasonably guess the right thing to say or do. Growing up as the only guy in a house of them taught me a lot of that. And it was a skill even my friends came to me for when their relationships were on the rocks. But with Violet I am always flying blind.

She picks up the book, her lips quivering a little when she sees the football player on the cover and a full-on smile breaking out as she turns it over and reads the synopsis.

"Lucas desperately needs Haley's help passing their statistics class and trying to charm her into helping him quickly becomes the least of his worries when he realizes she's the one girl he can't live without. Haley can't stand Lucas, but she also can't stand to go without their late-night sexts and hookups either." Violet reads it out loud, and by the end there is an all-out grin on her face.

"I stopped at the bookstore. The mafia stuff seemed a little heavy to start with, more like something you build up to."

"I see." Her lips press together as she suppresses a laugh. "And the bookmarks with handwritten notes?"

"I had some help picking it out."

"I bet you did." She smiles at them and starts pulling them out and scanning them.

"Is her number on the back of one of them?" she teases.

"She was really nice, explained a bunch to me," I say, a little defensively.

She pulls one up and reads it out loud. "Second best sex scene in a library."

"She did say she liked hockey players better, so maybe the other one involves them."

"Or she wants you to come back to find out what the first one is in person." Violet's eyes dance with mirth at being able to tease me over this.

"She was kind of cute." I shrug.

Her eyes narrow and focus on me in a way that if it were any other woman, I'd swear was jealousy. So I plow ahead, hoping that's what it was.

"So do you have time for a chapter?"

She turns the book over in her hands, and I watch her wheels follow the round. I can almost hear the clicking of the lottery ball as my luck goes from good to bad to good again, hitting each rung on the way.

"Let me get changed and then you can come in if you want."

I nod, "See you in a few."

I GATHER MY CRAP OFF THE TABLE AND STUFF IT INTO MY bag, taking that and my workout bag to my room. I take a deep breath. I can hear her moving around in her room. Opening and closing drawers and moving from one side to the other. Then the movement quiets and I hear the TV turn on against the wall. I give it another minute before I rap my knuckles against the door, trying not to seem as eager as I am.

"Come in," she calls.

I open the door, and the room is dark except for the dull glow of the TV from the wall. She's laying on the bed in an old sweatshirt with our university logo on it, and a pair of short shorts that let me see her long gorgeous legs. But her hand is wrapped around the TV controller, and she doesn't look at me.

"Changed my mind, I'm awake enough now if you want to watch something."

I bet she's awake enough now. Now that her mind is over analyzing this and running fire drills on how to exit.

I grab the book, lay it in her lap and then lie back next to her, enough that our bodies line up, tucking my arm under my head. I can feel her tense at the brush of contact, but I close my eyes, hoping for another round of luck.

"Was a long day and the offensive coach is punishing me for my suspension by making me run double the number of drills. I'd rather listen to you read, but it's up to you." I nod to the book.

She hesitates but presses the mute button and lets the TV controller drop, picking up the book and flipping through the pages.

"You want to start at the beginning, or you want to pick one of your friend's passages to start with?"

"The library sounds intriguing." I shrug.

She flips to the bookmark, and I see her smile again at the writing there.

"I'm surprised there's not a phone number on this. She playing the long game you think?"

"She didn't seem like the type to go for football players."

"Who doesn't go for football players?"

I stop myself from making the obvious accusation.

"You gonna read or you gonna talk about my future girlfriend?"

She clears her throat, and pulls the page up closer to her face, using the light from the TV to read.

"Lucas was arrogant, beautiful and entirely too fuckable for his own good. What was worse was that he knew it. Which was why my panties were off, my bare ass sitting on a library table I'm sure someone was going to unknowingly study at tomorrow, and his mouth was inches from mine asking me to admit the obvious truth. That I hated and wanted him in equal measure."

My mind immediately wanders to images of Violet sitting on a library table in front of me, bare underneath a short skirt, and I only need to imagine it for a second before all my blood starts to pool south. I roll my lip between my teeth as I listen to the sound of her breathing, the way she enunciates the words, and watch the way her lips form the letters.

"'Just admit you want my mouth on you Haley. Admit you think about it all the time. I bet you go home after we study, lay down in your bed and let your hands explore your body wishing they were mine.'"

Her breath catches and she stops reading, and I want to beg her to keep going. I'm so hard now, imagining us in this scenario, remembering what she looked like last night. I'm a hairsbreadth away from grinding my palm over my cock for some semblance of relief.

There's a deep inhale of breath and she closes her eyes and dips her head down.

"What are we doing?" Her voice is so quiet.

"You're reading to me."

"And last night?"

"I read to you."

There's a little click of her tongue and I can tell she's not amused with my smart-ass answers.

"I think—" she starts but I cut her off.

"Do you remember that summer you and Nora were already in college, but you came home? You stayed with us for like two or three weeks because you guys were moving to a new house?"

"Yeah."

"I was like 16 or so I think. You were probably 20 or 21."

"Ok..." she trails off like she's not sure where I'm headed with this.

And frankly, I'm not sure I should be headed this way, but I feel like I need to give her the same vulnerability she gave me last night.

"You guys were in the pool like every day, all day, when you weren't driving around town. And you were just perpetually in a bathing suit. The top was this bikini with a galaxy pattern on it, and it was almost too small for you because it always seemed like if you moved just the right way, I was finally going to get my wish."

"It was not too small," she protests.

"It definitely was, and you knew it." I grin at her.

"Was not."

"Trust me, I spent a lot of time looking at it. I know what I'm talking about."

"Whatever." She crosses her arms, letting the book fall off to one side of her knees. "Is there a point to the criticism of my fashion choices?"

"I wasn't criticizing. Just mentioning. It's pertinent to the story."

"Get on with it then."

"I tried so fucking hard to get you to notice me that summer. That's when I really got into football, and I thought I was bulking out. Eating protein bars and drinking shakes and hitting the gym with the other guys."

"You were getting so tall though. You were already taller than me by then. I remember your mom going on about how tall you were. Hard to bulk out that way."

"Not that it mattered. You never noticed me. Not once. Meanwhile, I had to stare at that bikini top day in and day out, hoping I'd happen to be around when the elastic finally gave out."

She punches me in the arm.

"Listen, these are the things 16-year-old guys' dreams are made of."

"Exactly. You were 16, and I was 21. If I had noticed you, it would have made me a complete perv."

"You'll be shocked to know my 16-year-old self did not care about ethical boundaries." I wink at her.

"Oh my god." She shakes her head.

"Anyway, Cameron and Tony started coming around and then I knew it was really over for me. You looked at him like he was a god. And I was so pissed, because he was shorter than me and nerdy. I couldn't fucking believe it. The girls at school noticed me every time, but not you."

"That was that summer, wasn't it? Wow. I can't believe it was that long ago."

"Yeah. Then you guys were taking night swims. Thinking you were clever, and no one could see you because of the trees and the privacy fence. But my room had the perfect view. I'd sit up there listening to my favorite punk bands, playing video games, and then occasionally look down and see you guys making out."

"So the story is that you were a Peeping Tom?"

I ignore her little dig and continue.

"Then one night I just happened to open the blinds at the right time. I saw him finally grab the ties of your suit and pull them, and that bikini top fell off. Not like a little bit, but the whole damn thing. I thought you were gonna freak out, but instead you just leaned back on the side of the pool and let him stare at you. Let me stare at you. Not that you knew. I was pissed when he touched you because I had spent weeks just trying to get you to look at me, and he just shows up and gets everything I wanted. So I decided to just pretend it was me and fuck, I came so hard watching you. The faces you made. I lived off those mental images for years. I couldn't tell you how many times I..." I trail off because she's staring at me, her mouth open, her eyebrow raised. I reach over and use the back of my knuckles to nudge her mouth closed and raise my eyebrow at her in return.

"So what you're saying is, when you make it big in the NFL and I'm at a bar, I can point you out to my friends and be like 'See him, yeah. I was his teen fantasy'?" She smirks, and I can tell she wants to joke about this, but I can't.

"What I'm saying is, yesterday it felt like I was 16 again." I swallow hard, the nerves stringing my muscles tight. I've confessed a hell of a lot in the last five minutes. Things I'd never planned to tell her.

Her face softens and her eyes search my face for a minute, her fingers absently flipping the corner of the book still half-balanced in her lap.

"Seems unfair you're always getting to watch me," she whispers at last.

"Which is why you should keep reading."

TEN

Violet

I SWEAR MY HEART STOPS FOR A SECOND WHEN I REALIZE what he's saying. I stare at the book in my lap for a moment before I turn it over. All the doors open and shut in front of me at once, other options besides the one I know I'm going to take. Other options I should take because he's my best friend's baby brother. Because he's out of my league, and he's my roommate who's separated from me by one thin wall. And let's be honest, I'm already in one mess with a man I can't make sense of.

But I don't take the smart road.

I start to read instead.

"'I do,' I answer him. 'Although in my fantasies I sit on your face, so you shut up and fuck me with your tongue.' I can see the effect my words have on him, because he reaches for me immediately, dragging me across the table to the edge. He drops to his knees and pulls my skirt up, and I can feel his hot breath against my sex...'"

I keep my eyes glued to the pages in front of me but in my peripheral vision I watch Ben's hands slide under the waist-band of his sweatpants. He raises his hips up and drags his boxer briefs down, and I can see the outline of his cock pop free under the material of the sweatpants. My tongue darts out to wet my lips as I watch his hand move up and down. He's careful to keep everything PG-13, but it feels X-rated. Maybe even more elicit because of it. My skin feels hot, and I can barely stand it.

"Keep going Violet. Your voice is fucking sexy," Ben rasps beside me, dragging my attention back to the book.

I realize I'd stopped reading and I feel a blush tinge my cheeks as I scan the page again, trying to find where I'd stopped.

"I can feel his hot breath against my sex. His hands spread me further, his eyes eating me up just before he leans forward to consume me. There's no other way to describe it. The way his mouth and tongue move over my flesh..."

I keep reading the words, doing my best not to lose my spot on the page again but I can hear Ben's breathing getting harder, and his hand works up and down. Slow and then fast, short strokes followed by a few long pulls.

Then I cheat. I do the thing that I shouldn't, because he gave me the courtesy of not doing it yesterday. But I can't help myself. I look at his face. And holy fuck is he beautiful like this. His plump lower lip pulled up between his teeth, his brow furrowed, and his eyes closed in concentration as he chases his orgasm.

I want to lean over and kiss him. At least that. In reality I want to do so much more, because I want to be the reason he looks this way. I want it to be my hands and my mouth on his body.

The muscles of his forearm flex as he works himself over

and his shirt rides up, a little patch of flesh is visible in between two valleys that form a vee. My mind tries to patch together all the glimpses of his body I've had so far to form a picture of him naked.

I'm headed for a dangerous place, so I focus back on the task at hand. On reading from this book he picked out.

I keep reading, trying to keep a steady pace as the bed starts to shift under me. His pace quickens and his arm and shoulder make the bed dip and rise in sync with him. Several moments pass by, and I have trouble concentrating on forming the words because I'd rather listen to the sounds he's making. His breathing's unsteady, and finally shudders as he rolls his hips in one last thrust up and into his hand.

I close the book and feel like I should make myself scarce, except we're in my room and I have nowhere to run off to.

He blows out a long breath, and then in one fluid motion pulls his boxer briefs back up and smooths his shirt down. He scrubs his hand over his face and sits up on the edge of the bed, not looking at me, and I stay still. I have a million things I want to say, and none at all.

"Let me get cleaned up, and then I can come back. If you want?"

"Yes," I answer him immediately.

He does the same as the night before. Disappearing for a bit, and then coming back to lay down next to me, passing out to the low buzz of the TV in the background.

"ALL RIGHT. I'M TIRED OF WAITING FOR YOU TO BRING IT up. So spill it," Joss says to me as we sit outside our favorite cafe just off campus.

"Spill what?"

"Is his body as perfect underneath all the gym clothes as I think it is?"

I know immediately who she's talking about, and a shirtless image comes unbidden into my mind. I've barely been able to stop thinking about him.

"I wouldn't know."

"You realize that I don't just stay locked in my room from 9 to 9 every night, right? I come out, I get a glass of water, I grab a book I forgot, and I know you're both locked away in your room. I've even seen him coming out early in the morning."

"We watch TV sometimes together." I shrug.

"Uh huh. Do these TV shows involve porn because you're blushing, and I don't think you'd be blushing if the two of you were in there just watching old Law and Order reruns."

I take a sip of my coffee, and glance out the window.

"You hussy. Are you watching porn with him? How is that happening, and you haven't seen him naked? I need this explained."

"We're not watching porn... so much as... I don't know, Joss. I can't tell you anything really because I don't know."

"You're killing me."

"Sorry. If it helps, I'm killing myself a little too."

"Why? And do not tell me it's because of Cameron. That fucker is out there fucking who knows what, who knows where. He gave you the green light to do the same. Not that he gets to decide, but if you cared."

"Ben isn't some random stranger I met on a research trip."

"No, he's a live-in pool boy with the body and dimples to match who very obviously wishes you would take advantage of him."

"He does not."

"Friend. Bestie. Beloved. I have seen how he looks at you. He doesn't look at you like a roommate or a stand-in sister. He looks at you like a lovesick boy, who would happily rail you to your heart's content if you would just give him any sign at all you wanted it."

"Boy is right. He's 22. He's an undergrad. The same age as some of our students in class. He should be fucking sorority girls and coeds who haven't decided what they want to major in yet. Practice for when he gets all the models and cheerleaders in the NFL. Not scorned spinsters who are two years deep in an Art History PhD they can't see the end of."

"So he's told you he's interested in you."

"Not in so many words."

"Do you want me to die? Because I might if you keep making my brain work this hard with guessing games before I've had my morning allotment of caffeine."

"He told me about a time when he was in high school when he accidentally saw me topless."

"And?"

"Apparently it was memorable for him."

"Oh my god. I bet it was. That would explain so much. You're his poster girl. The queen of his teenage spank bank, and now he's all grown up and he wants the fantasy in the flesh. I get it. Good for him. Good for *you*."

I scrunch my nose up and look at her like she's lost her mind.

"Do not tell me you're going to deny that boy, Vi. He deserves it. He cooks us dinner. Gets us baked goods. Helps us install stuff in the gallery. He gets the things off the top shelf."

"You're really selling it."

"I shouldn't have to sell it. Have you looked at him? Do we need to get you glasses?"

"It's not that simple."

"Because you're soft on him?"

"He's more than a casual hookup. With all that history, his

sister trusting me to help him..." I think about Nora and Mama Beth and what they would think of the whole situation. And I can't imagine approval being the way they'd go.

"Well, fuck. That complicates it, I guess. Still. I don't know. Might be worth a little emotional damage. You haven't seen him naked, but what about in a towel? Or those gray sweatpants that leave nothing to the imagination? Gotten a peak at the outline of it?"

I wince a little as I take another sip of my coffee and it's enough for her to note.

"Oh, we have, and it's good, isn't it? Well, if I were you, I'd jump over the cliff and into the water. That boy is a rare breed —absolutely gorgeous without all the toxic arrogance and prove-it swagger that normally comes with it. They don't even exist in the art and music world to my knowledge. Extirpated from waves of social media clout probably. So don't waste your endangered species, yeah?"

"Joss, I love you but what the fuck are you even talking about?" I look at her amused.

"Get over your feelings and let that boy have what he wants. If not for yourself, then for me and all the other women who wish they could."

I burst out laughing and shake my head.

"I love you Joss, but you are something else."

"You do love me, and I love you more!" She gives me a little scrunch of her nose, and we finish our coffees and head off to class.

ELEVEN

Ben

I'M READY TO CRASH AFTER THE WORKOUT AND DRILLS I'VE just run, when I sit down on the bench and my phone dings with a text message. I flip it open to see an image message from Violet and I open it. And it's like a beacon in the fucking locker room because immediately JB and Sam are over my shoulders and Colton is leaning in. Jake lets out a low whistle from behind me.

"Holy shit, bro!" one of them yells.

"Dude who is she? I haven't seen her at any of the parties."

"Damn." Colton just shakes his head.

"Hey, fuck off!" I yell, tucking the phone to my chest. "Can't I get some privacy here?"

"In the locker room? No."

"Oh fuck, must be a girlfriend."

"Ben doesn't have a girlfriend, do you, bro?"

"Can you two hens knock it off?"

"How about we all fucking respect his privacy before I start knocking heads around?" Colton shouts over the chatter

"Fuck man, sorry!" Sam shrinks.

"Sorry man!" JB nods and walks off.

I lift the phone again, shielding it under the hoodie I'm wearing and open the photo again. The air in my lungs catches fire because holy fuck. The picture is Violet in the galaxy bikini top, one that looks even smaller than I remember. Her hair is down, a pretend look of confusion on her face and her finger pressed to her lips. It's captioned "Was it this one?"

Yeah. That would be the one

VIOLET
It is a little small. Now

A little? A stiff breeze is going to snap it

Guess we'll see

Cruel of you since you know I'm not home
until the morning

Colton and I are going to talk to a trainer, and we're driving down tonight and back tomorrow. And I know I have an addiction to her when one night without her feels like it's going to be painful.

She sends me a little devil emoji.

VIOLET
Sweet dreams. See you tomorrow

Sweet dreams

When I get home in the morning I just want to crash and burn on the bed. I'm thankfully class-free today because my professor canceled, and I don't have to be at the gym to meet Colton and Jake until later this afternoon, so I can at least try to get a decent round of sleep in before I have to get back to the grind.

As I throw my bags on the floor, I notice a book sitting on the bed. It's the same book as before about the tutor and the football player but there's a new bookmark inside, and I flip it open. She's highlighted a passage inside and I skim through it. They're in his room studying together. She's making him go over flashcards and then without saying anything she starts to strip. On the back of the bookmark Violet has scrawled:

History flashcards tonight?

I grin and pull out my phone.

> Absolutely need to study for history tonight

VIOLET

9:30?

> Yup. My room

K. See you then

True to her word she knocks on the door at 9:30, and I tell her to come in. There's something slightly unreadable on her face, if I had to guess I'd say it was nerves.

Me too, babe. Me fucking too.

I've been looking forward to it all fucking day long, and I ran extra miles at the gym to try and wear off some of the excess energy buzzing through my body. Then I'd spent the last half hour desperately hoping she was going to be wearing that bikini top underneath her shirt.

"Got the cards?" she asks, a tumbler of something to drink in one hand.

"Yup." I'm sitting back against the pillows on my bed, my legs stretched out trying to go through some of the dates while I waited for her. Mostly they'd all just blurred together. I did occasionally get some studying done in her presence, but she was too damn distracting most of the time.

"Lemme have 'em." She reaches forward to take them and gets just close enough the vanilla pumpkin scent she's been wearing lately hits me and sends a flood of desire through me.

She sets her drink down and then curls up in the chair in the corner of the room. She's overdressed for what she normally wears around the apartment with a long-oversized top and cardigan, which she pulls tighter around her. I wonder if she might let me strip her out of them.

"You ready?" She glances up at me and gives me a little smile that makes my heart beat harder.

"As I'll ever be." I answer her smile with one of my own.

Her eyes flash up to mine, a playfulness there that I fucking love, and then she starts reading off flash cards, quizzing me on the post-Revolutionary era and the War of 1812. I get most of them and the ones I stumble on she makes me repeat several times to try to help me remember, but I'm struggling, mostly because I keep wondering if she's changed her mind or chickened out.

But then she stands up and eases out of her cardigan as she continues to read off the cards, and my eyes flicker over her form as I keep answering her questions. She's perfect in every possible way I could want, and I remind myself I need to savor every second I get with her because I have no idea how long this will last.

"Ben?"

"Hmm?" My eyes snap up to her face.

Her hand is on the hem of her shirt, getting ready to lift it, but she's .holding the card and looking at me expectantly instead of moving.

"Why did tensions rise in 1807?"

Because the British Navy was desperately hoping the Americans had a galaxy bikini top on under their shirt.

"Royal Navy was moving to restrict trade," I mumble.

"Between?"

"America and France."

"Good," she murmurs, the sound going straight to my dick.

She sets the cards down for a second to remove her shirt. When she turns to pick them up, I can see the galaxy print that's been burned into my brain. Just the motion of her leaning down makes it so that her breasts threaten to spill over the top. If it was any other woman I was hooking up with, I'd be up and off this bed lightning fast. Kissing her neck and chest, sliding the straps down her arms so I could slide my fingers under the cup and pull her out. But with her I can't. With her everything is a delicate dance of give and take, and me desperately hoping I don't do or say the wrong thing that makes this whole house of cards fall down.

She turns around and leans back against the dresser, giving me a perfect view of her while she continues to quiz me.

"President during the war?"

"Madison."

"What year does the war end?"

"1814."

With each correct answer she takes a step closer to me, and question after question I get them right, like my life depends on it.

"What treaty ends the war?"

"Treaty of Ghent."

She sits down on the edge of the bed, flipping through the

cards, and then presses them to her lips as she peeks over them at me.

"Okay. Final question. What's the era after the War of 1812 known as?"

"Era of Good Feelings."

"Perfect." She leans back against the headboard alongside me and places the flash cards back in my lap. "You get an A."

"What does that earn me?" The words are out before I can censor them, and I bite my tongue because I see the flicker of surprise cross her face.

She turns slightly, angling her back toward me. I set the flashcards aside.

"A reward for your younger self." She smiles at me over her shoulder. "Pull it."

I reach up to grab it, my knuckles grazing her spine in the process. I want to reach out and kiss her there, follow the trail all the way up her spine but I stop myself. My fingers wrap around the end of one of the ties. The top is loosely tied, on purpose I would guess, and one small tug is going to have it falling down.

I roll my tongue against the inside of my cheek as my dick stirs to life in my pants. The anticipation is killing me, and I pull, watching as the material goes slack but catches slightly around her neck. A little flick and it finishes unknotting and tumbles off, sliding down the front of her chest.

She pulls the second lower tie, and the top is off, falling down in between us. She leans back against the headboard and my mouth goes dry as my eyes travel over her breasts. They're full with two perfect pink nipples that are already beading up under my watch.

"Fuck," I curse under my breath, wishing I had better words but all the usual charming things I'd have at my disposal disappear, like always with her.

I want so badly to reach out and touch her, but I don't trust myself, and instead my hand goes to my aching dick. I run my palm over my length, trying to quench the need. Her eyes track my movements, and she pulls her lower lip up between her teeth.

"I want to know how you watched me," she whispers.

The words make my heart take on a fast pace, one I usually only feel when I take off down field for a long ball, desperately hoping for a touchdown.

"Know, or see?" My tone sounds desperate to my own ears, but I don't care.

"See," she answers without hesitating.

I go to slide my hand under the sweatpants, only too happy to do what she's asking.

"I want to really see you," she whispers again, so softly I almost don't know if I heard her.

My eyes go to hers, searching for confirmation.

"If you're comfortable, I mean," she adds.

I nod, and then slide off the bed. Standing to pull my shirt off, and then I slide my hands under both my pants and the boxer briefs I have on under them and take them off too. I hesitate before I turn around because I'm fucking nervous. Nervous that I'm still not going to be enough for her. Because I'm not perfect. I'm not the most muscular. I don't have the biggest dick. Some of the scars football has left me with, like the one where one of my ribs popped through my chest freshman year are more gnarly than sexy. And if she looks at me like I'm lacking, it's going to hurt in a way no other woman doing the same could.

"You don't have to. I can go back to my room," she says the words so softly, so tenderly that it might break me.

"I'm good," I say with more confidence in my tone than I feel and turn around to climb on the bed next to her.

I try not to look at her but when I hear the little hitch in her breathing I glance up as her hand goes to her throat, her thumb stroking the little valley at the center where it meets the top of her chest. I stop and look up at her, searching her face.

"Sorry. I just... you're very fucking attractive," she apologizes and her eyes dart to the side.

"Don't apologize. It feels good to hear you think something's improved in five years. Everything about you has."

And fuck, I cannot stop staring at her. A shy little grin breaks out across her face, and my fingers itch to touch her.

"You sure it's okay?" she asks, a vein of worry still in her tone.

"Definitely." I nod.

"Okay."

Her hands fall away from her throat, giving me a full view of her again and she straightens her spine, leaning back against my headboard. She rolls her shoulders like she's trying to get comfortable, and the movement makes her breasts bounce ever so slightly drawing my eyes back to them. Making me wish I could take one of her nipples in my mouth, roll my tongue over the tip.

I'm so hard, so fucking ready to burst I stroke myself to take the edge off, and her eyes are drawn to it like a magnet. Her tongue slides over her lower lip, and I swear I can feel it up the side of my dick. Feel her breath on me.

She looks so fucking perfect, and I wish I could go back and tell my sixteen-year-old self that this would be worth the wait. To have her here in front of me, watching me while I watch her. I slide my hand up and down, giving myself more and less friction until I hit the right pace. It's torture, but I want to draw this out for as long as possible.

She shifts again, rolling her hips this time and she clenches her thighs together, her eyes glued to where my hand pumps my cock. A bead of precum is already forming at the tip. Her tongue darts out again, and I want to beg her to use it on me. And I need something, anything to distract me from that thought.

"Touch yourself for me," I say before I can think better of it. "Over the leggings," I add because if she loses anymore clothing, I will be a fucking goner.

She doesn't hesitate, her hand immediately sliding between her thighs like she was just waiting for me to tell her to do it. Her hand is in the shadows and against the black leggings I can't see much but it's enough that it gives me the distraction I need. Especially when I hear her breathing pick up pace.

My muscles are so fucking sore from practice and lifting weights that my forearm aches as I move faster, but I mentally beg them to hold on for just a little while longer. Just long enough to let me have the rest of this fucking memory. One that's just her and me.

A little gasp escapes her lips, and she shifts her thighs further apart. I bite my tongue, a million things I want to confess, but I refuse to ruin the moment with her. I just want the soundtrack of skin against skin, her gasps, and our stuttered breathing to remember this by.

I can feel myself swell, only needing a few more strokes before I come, and I realize I don't have a towel or tissue close by, so I lean over to grab one off the nightstand. She watches me and something flickers in her eyes.

"You could, if you want..." She doesn't say the words but her free hand travels down her chest through the valley between her breasts.

I might choke on my own tongue trying to respond.

"Are you sure?" I rasp out the question.

"I want you to."

Fuck me.

I move toward her, and she slides down halfway on top of my pillows, her breasts sway with the motion, giving me the perfect angle to take her in. I ease up on my knees next to her, bracing my free hand against the headboard over her.

I stroke myself a few more times. I'm so desperate for fucking relief but I feel like I'm playing with fire by doing what she's asking. I look down at her, and she must see the worry in my face.

"Please, Ben," she whispers the words and it's all I need to hear.

I lean over her. It only takes me a half second, and I'm coming hard against my own hand, watching as the stream lands on her breasts and flows down. I'm breathing so hard my chest feels like it's on fire, and I watch her take two fingers and slide through the band of pearlescent liquid, rubbing it up and over one of her nipples. Then her eyes close, and I hear her gasp for breath and realize that her hand is still working between her thighs. I lay my forehead against my arm, sweat beading on my temples as I watch her eyes shutter closed and her body give one last little shake beneath me.

This image of her is going to ruin me. It is going to be on repeat in my head for eternity. I collapse in a heap next to her, too dumbfounded and exhausted to say anything. When I glance over at her after a few minutes, she just gives me a little smile. She stands then, grabbing her shirt off the chair, throwing it over her head, and pulling it down.

"Night, Ben," she whispers.

"Night, Violet."

And then she disappears out the door, leaving me feeling like a pining awkward sixteen-year-old boy all over again.

TWELVE

Violet

I'm sitting at my desk in my little office, peering out through the doorway and across the hall where I can see out the window. There are clouds forming in the distance and I worry about the rain hitting before my office hours are over. It's Friday night, and I'm desperate to get out of here and get back home. Joss has her annual Halloween party tomorrow night and I have several things I promised to help get ready for her.

And I might also, maybe, be hoping to see a certain football player. We've been so busy the last few days there hasn't even been the opportunity to chat more than in passing on our way in or out of the house.

Which is why when I hear his name come up outside my door, instead of minding my own business, I start eavesdropping. I can tell from the context of the conversation it's a group of undergrads discussing the weekend's parties and what costumes they plan to wear.

"Do you think Lawton will be at the football team party even though he's suspended?"

"Who knows. He's been laying low from what I've heard, so he can get off suspension."

"Why do you want to know where he's going to be?"

"As if that's not obvious. She's hoping she can be his pick for the night."

"Yeah, you can forget that unless you want to start dyeing your hair blonde."

"What? Why?"

"He doesn't like brunettes. Supposedly he's never hooked up with one."

"Blonde is too much work. Can you imagine all the appointments to keep the roots up?"

"Then apparently Lawton is too much work for you."

"Maybe it's worth it. But not before I know he's actually going to be there."

"The Delta girls will know. One of them has been hooking up with someone on the offense. We'll find out from her."

He definitely will not be there, and he won't pick anyone if I can help it.

And the tone in which I think that makes me a little embarrassed for myself. If I'm getting jealous of undergrads just talking about him? I have a problem. I do, however, have questions about this whole blonde-only rumor given that the last time I looked in the mirror I was very obviously a dark brown brunette.

———

WHEN I GET IN THE HOUSE, JOSS GREETS ME enthusiastically in the dining room.

"Ben stopped at the greens place and got us the salads for dinner."

"He did not! Oh my god, it sounds amazing."

"It's in the fridge for you."

"Don't tell me he got the smoothie things too."

"Yup. Pomegranate for me and mango for you."

I turn into the kitchen and see him mixing protein powder into his."

"Moving that boy in here was the best thing we ever did Joss. I told you."

"You were right. I was wrong. No socks all over the living room or anything. In fact, I think he cleans when I'm not looking."

Ben's face contorts as he tries to hold back laughter.

"Truly a fine specimen whatever species he is."

I reach into the fridge and grab the smoothie, stabbing it with a straw and taking a sip. It tastes like heaven after the long day I've had.

"I think I'm going to kidnap him Vi. Take him to one of those states where you can marry minors. Lock it down for the long term, you know." Joss leans over the counter, ogling Ben dramatically as she eats another bite of her salad.

"Oh yeah? Well lucky for you, I think he might be barely legal. No need to evade the cops at the state border. Mama Beth might have something to say though if she finds out."

"Is that the mother?"

"Mmmhmm." I nod, jumping up on the counter and pulling a fork out. "And she is a force to be reckoned with. She's the reason he turned out so well. A little credit to Nora too I suppose."

"I'm good with mothers. They love me."

I raise my eyebrow at Joss, knowing full well that with her

tattoos and piercings she is not always the girlfriend moms envision for their sons.

"I clean up well!" she protests.

"Well, make sure you get a blonde wig while you're at it."

"Blonde? That's not my color, and you know it. We tried it that once and it was a disaster."

"Maybe find some blonde sorority girls you can pay off to help you lure him into the car then?"

"That's a possibility. Why blonde?"

"That's the rumor on the street. Ben here only goes for blondes."

"Curious and curiouser. And you have this on good authority?"

"The peace of my office hours was disturbed by a gaggle of undergrads discussing the weekend's parties and what football and hockey players would be attending which ones. They seemed to have a pretty extensive knowledge of movements and proclivities."

"Sounds like sound ethnographic researchers in the making if you ask me."

"I thought so."

The two of us grin at each other and Ben finishes his smoothie and sets the empty cup down on the counter.

"The two of you are a menace." He shakes his head, smiling as he grabs his salad out of the fridge to eat with us.

"We know. That's the beauty of it, Benjamin. Learn to appreciate it." Joss lets out a dramatic sigh.

"Oh, I do." His eyes lift a little to meet mine, his lips curling up on one side to make one of his dimples pop.

My heart lays a little punch to my rib cage in response to it, and I was going to have to evaluate that development later.

"You going to come out with me tonight?" Joss asks as we finish up dinner.

"I don't know. Let me take a shower and see how I feel? It's been a long day, and I just want to like drink half a bottle of rosé and melt into a long sleep. But maybe I'll rally?"

"Fair enough. You want to come out with me tonight, Benjamin? I can take you to a fun little place with whips and chains. You can try getting tied up or tied down. Or are you going to be boring and go make your blonde sorority girls happy?" Joss asks him but slips me a look, letting me know she's prying so I don't have to.

"I might just stay in tonight." He shrugs, washing his silverware out in the sink.

"And break everyone's heart? How cruel." Joss gives him a mock little pout before taking off toward her room.

"Let me know the plan, Vi! The whips and chains offer stands for you too. I know the perfect guy who might be able to wake you up with some light paddling," she calls before she shuts her door.

I laugh to myself and start gathering up my stuff to head to my room, but Ben clears his throat interrupting my progress. He leans on the counter in front of the sink, the tension of his shirt highlights his back muscles in a way that's entirely distracting, and my mind wanders back to the other night.

"I left something on your bed. You can ignore it... if you want," he says the words quietly, and there's a strained quality to them that makes me nervous.

"Everything okay?" I ask.

"Yeah. It's good." He nods, but he still doesn't look at me.

I feel uneasy as I go to my room, worried I'm going to find the worst. Not that I even know what that would be.

I close the door behind me, turning to see a pile of books on the bed, nestled on top of a folded shirt. I pick them up, and a note falls off the top of the pile onto the bed. I pick it up to read it.

Hit the bookstore again. For research. Your choice. Top one sounds good though, and Signs is on streaming. Tonight?

The books are all new, a half dozen bookmarks in them, and I can imagine that they're the work of his helpful bookstore fairy again. I set them aside and pull the shirt out, realizing it's a jersey. One of his I assume, and obvious when I see his name on the back. I frown, trying to discern the context.

I reach for the book that had been on the top and turn to the spot where there's a lone bookmark. I start skimming and it's an insanely hot scene about a woman and her hockey player roommate. She's stolen his jersey because she has a secret crush, and he finds her wearing it watching a movie and slips her out of her panties before saying a word.

I slam the book closed and press it to my chest, staring down at the jersey and the note he wrote, putting the pieces together, because *Signs* was one of our favorite movies to watch in the Lawton family room on late summer nights. My skin heats at the idea of him touching me, because for all the times we casually touch during the day, we never have in the context of... this. Whatever *this*, is.

What are we doing? I want to ask him, but I don't want to have the conversation. I don't want to expose the fun we're having to the cold light of analysis. Except then he'd seemed off after dinner. Told me I could ignore it. I wondered if he was having second thoughts about the suggestion. But the ball is in my court, and I have to decide; talk to him. Don't talk to him. Put the jersey on. Don't. I pinch my eyes shut and rub my temples. Whatever I do, I have to take a shower first, so I opt to kick the decision down the road and worry about what to do after.

When I get out of the shower, Joss is waiting for me. She's already dressed up in tight pleather leggings and a corset top with macabre jewelry dangling down over the front in a bizarre mix of club wear meets Memento Mori fashion.

"You look hot," I say.

"On the hunt for a new guy. The last one finally bailed on me when I wouldn't commit on his time schedule. Want to come hunt with me?"

"I don't know. I'm still thinking. Don't hate me."

She gives me a little judgmental look. "I guess I can't blame you. If I had one that looks like that living next door that already answered when I called..."

"Stop. It's not like that."

"No? What's all this then?" Her black nails click against the covers of the books on the bed.

"Nothing."

"Well, if you're into nothing. I have some suggestions."

"You read them too?"

"Only the dark stuff. Give me a villain who likes to fuck like he might murder me after." She shrugs.

I smile and shake my head at her. "Sounds like you."

"And this?" She points to the jersey, "That nothing too?"

"Correct," I answer, throwing on a T-shirt over my underwear as I toss my robe to the side.

She gives me an incredulous look.

"What?" I ask, acting like I'm completely clueless to her point.

"I just saw what you're wearing under that. But sure, keep lying to yourself, sweetie."

I stare at her through the mirror as I comb my hair, giving a little shake of my head and nodding toward the wall. I don't want Ben overhearing our conversation and the walls are far from soundproof.

"You could come with and see if he wants to tag along?" She lowers her voice to just above a whisper.

I mull the idea over for a minute, thinking that it might be fun. But as I picture us in the club, I quickly see him becoming the center of a lot of female attention, and I'm not in love with the idea. Particularly now, since I'm obviously not blonde and it's a preference of his that's well known enough to be the subject of conversation.

"I doubt he wants to hang out with us elderly women."

"Fair, I suppose. He can get those hot young ones that are so desperate to find him at a party."

My eyes flash up to the ceiling at the thought of him with one of them tonight and my stomach flips with jealousy.

"That's what my face looks like when I'm not jealous too," she needles me.

"Someday, Joss, a man is going to make you fall so hard in love it's going to bring you down to the mortal plane with the rest of us and I'm going to relish every second of that."

"I'd just settle for one that made me want to get on my knees. In the meantime, I'm off to meet Addy."

"You two have fun. Send me updates?"

"Will do."

"Be careful. Text if you need me to pick you all up."

"You be careful too." She gives me a look in the mirror, one that's sincere and a little bit worried.

She sat through my initial melt down over Cameron and I doubt she's ready to do that again. Joss saw men as good friends, playthings, and occasionally as something slightly more. But the idea of falling in love did not occur to her, and she was unfamiliar with the pain of having your heart smashed to a million pieces by someone you were once in love with.

She gives me a little wave and heads out my door, shutting it behind her, and leaving me with the giant elephant in the room. I stare at the jersey like it's a beating telltale heart sitting on my bed. The hint of jealousy was a bad sign, a very bad sign. The fact that I want to stay in tonight instead of going out? Another bad sign. The fact that Joss of all people was telling me to be careful? The worst sign of all.

THIRTEEN

Ben

IT HAD BEEN 30 MINUTES SINCE I HEARD JOSS LEAVE alone. I know it was alone because I could hear Violet moving around in her room. And I kept waiting, hoping for a text from her. Any sign she was up for my suggestion, but it had been nothing but radio silence. I'd still been hoping up until a few minutes ago.

But now I can hear a bunch of noise in the kitchen and the sound of the TV on, and I'm pretty sure that means she took my second offer to "just ignore it" to heart. Which is a fucking blow to my ego, and after almost a week of basically pretending our last "study" session didn't happen probably means it's time to assume my luck with her has run out.

I should take it quietly. Just stay in my room the rest of the night and then pretend right along with her that nothing has ever happened between us. But instead, I'm stripping off my shirt and walking out into the kitchen to find out what she's doing, cause if she's going to ignore me, I'm going to at least try to make it painful for her.

————

"BAKING?" I ASK WHEN I GET INTO THE KITCHEN AND SEE her buried in a sea of cooking utensils, containers and ingredients.

"Shit. You scared me." She presses a hand to her chest but doesn't turn around to look at me. "Yeah, I'm getting stuff ready for the party tomorrow."

"You didn't want to go out with Joss?" I pry, because I wonder why she stayed home if she wanted to avoid me.

"Nah. She's in fine form, the kind that always lands us in trouble, and I'm not cut out for trouble tonight." she says it warmly, and I can tell she's smiling even though I can't quite see it.

"Do you want help with stuff?" I ask, as I watch her dip down into the lower cabinets looking for something, giving me a view of her ass that I need to catalog for later.

"I'm okay. Aren't you going out with your friends?"

"Nah. I'd rather stay in."

"Oh, well feel free to change the channel and watch something else if you want."

She's turned back around now but still hasn't looked up at me.

"Did you want to watch *Signs*?"

Her hands stop on the bowl, and she glances up at me, her eyes stuttering over my chest before being averted again to the task at hand.

"Sure, if you want to." She shrugs.

I grab the remote off the counter and flip to where I'd seen it available earlier. One of my best memories of her was watching this movie. We'd all been curled up on the couch watching it, Nora had been falling asleep and when a scary part came on, Violet had buried her face in my shoulder. She'd stayed like that for several minutes, while I rubbed her back and her breathing slowed. I was high on being the one she turned to when she was scared for weeks after that.

"Does it still give you nightmares?" I ask absently.

"Oh yeah. I'm definitely blaming you if I get them tonight."

"Just make sure you have a glass of water by your bed."

It had been a running inside joke between the three of us after we saw the movie the first time. When she looks up at me and smiles, I know she still remembers.

"Good point."

I start the movie, the familiar score creeping in over the air and then join her in the kitchen.

"Tell me what I can do," I offer.

She looks around and finally hands me a cake box. "You can do that if you want."

"Got it."

We work around each other comfortably for the next 30 minutes in the kitchen, until I have to reach around her for something and the incidental touch causes her body to freeze up like I've shocked her. I'd almost forgotten about her ignoring the request, lost in the movie and cooking, but her negative reaction to me brushing past her is more than I can stomach.

I drop the towel I was reaching for, but I stay like I am, caging her in slightly, my left hand still on the counter bracketing her hip. I'm half afraid she'll run when I ask her.

"How did I fuck up?" I ask quietly.

"What?" She acts confused, but it's obvious she knows what I mean.

"You can't stand me touching you. If it was too much the other night, or if my suggestion tonight was too much..."

"No. It's fine."

"Violet..."

"We're good, honestly."

She's so obviously lying that I feel insulted she thinks I'd believe it.

"Yeah?" I wrap my arm around her, splaying my fingers across her waist and I feel her stomach muscles tighten, and hear her breath stutter. "That's what being good feels like?"

"Ben..." Her voice is half warning and half confusion.

"Tell me what's wrong, so I can fix it."

"You're touching me," she whispers.

I move away from her, removing my hand even though I hate the loss.

"We don't normally," she adds, her tone softening like she's worried she's offended me.

"We do all the time?" It's my turn to be confused, because we're always touching, tickling, joking and being stupid, all day most days if we're in the same room together. I sleep in the same bed as her half the time.

"Not when we're...alone."

She's right. It's been a conscious move on my part.

"And you don't want me to?"

She's quiet, and as the silence drags on, I start to step back.

"Can I plead the fifth?" There's a playfulness to her tone and I can tell she's trying.

"You can, yeah." I laugh a little, before I decide to press my luck. "But what if I want to confess?"

"Okay."

"I think about touching you all the time. When we're alone. When we're not. Sometimes it's all I can think about."

"Why?"

I choke out a stuttered laugh at her question, I don't mean to, but I can't help it.

"Because you're you, Vi."

"I'm like a sister to you. I'm old. I'm not blonde. Is that true by the way, the blonde thing?"

"Yes."

"Why?"

I hate whoever had that conversation outside her office today, because I can't lie when I answer this.

"Because the only girl I ever had feelings for was a brunette, and I haven't met the right redhead yet."

A truth mixed with a lie is still honesty, right?

"And because you had feelings for a brunette once you can't hookup with an entirely different brunette?" Her voice is laced with a tinge of disbelief and irony.

"I tried a couple times, but it always reminded me. I felt like an asshole for thinking about someone else while I was fucking someone new."

"Have you thought about her when you've... we've..." she trails off. There is no good word for what we've been doing. She's right about that much.

"I only think about you."

She releases a breath, like she's comforted by that answer, but her body language is still tense.

"I know this was like a thing, because I'm your sister's friend. And teenage boys have their fantasies and whatever. And it was fun, honestly, but I think we have to stop now."

I try to ignore the sinking sensation I'm feeling.

"Do you want to stop?"

She doesn't answer.

"Violet... Look at me." I touch her hip to coax her around, and she finally relents.

Her eyes drift down over me, my chest, down to where I've left my joggers purposefully hanging low and then she closes her eyes, before she opens them again, looking directly at me.

"Do you want to stop?" I ask her again.

"We should," she answers holding my gaze.

"That's not what I asked." I let my hand continue to explore, letting the back of my knuckles run up under her shirt, over her stomach.

I only get halfway up her ribs when I feel satin, and the edge of boning. I close my eyes to imagine what the half corset must look like underneath the baggy shirt she has on.

"Did you put that on to go out with Joss or to wear under a jersey?"

"The fifth again," she whispers.

I try hard not to smirk, but I can't help myself and her eyebrow raises in admonishment when she sees it. I pull my hand back, remembering what she'd said about touching.

"I don't want to stop, but I don't want to fuck this up either." I tuck my hands in my pockets, because they ache to touch her, and I don't trust myself not to do it again.

"It's not your fault. It's mine." She shakes her head, staring down at the floor.

"Is there anything I can do? We can back things up, go back to how it was. Do you want to watch again?" I do my best not to let the desperation come through in my voice.

Her eyes flash up to mine for half a second at the last offer I make, and I can tell she likes the idea even if she thinks it's a bad one.

"This all stays between us, right?"

I'm confused by the question, and she sees the puzzled look on my face and continues on.

"I just mean, I don't want to be a locker room joke. Or if the university found out. I mean you're not my student, but I do teach classes. And if your family found out... I don't need Mama Beth or Nora to murder me." She rattles out the statement quickly, and I can tell it's been eating at her.

"First of all, you would never be a joke. If the guys knew I had a grad student in my bed they'd be fucking jealous and buying me a beer to get tips on how to get their own."

She laughs, and I feel the tension ease a little bit.

"But I would never talk about you in a locker room, Vi. And I'm not your student, and you don't have any power over my academic or athletic future, so I don't think you need to worry about it."

"Still not a great look. If I was a guy, and you were a female student..."

"If the power dynamics were different, maybe, but... and I'm not trying to sound like an asshole here, so please don't take it that way. I play for one of the best college football teams in the country. I'm one of their best players when my ass isn't on the bench. I don't think anyone will look at that and say you're taking advantage of me."

"No, but it's another reason Mama Beth and Nora will murder me. You *are* one of the best players. Your ass *is* on the bench, and I'm supposed to be helping you get your shit together, not fantasizing about you, watching you... Oh my god when I say it out loud, I feel like it's even worse." She presses her hand to her mouth, a horrified look on her face.

I can't help but laugh at it, even though I regret it because it just makes her face contort even more.

"Violet." I wrap my fingers around her wrist and pull her hand from her mouth. "I told you. I've been getting off thinking about you since I was a teenager. If one of us is a creep here, I promise it's me."

Her eyes light with laughter that she doesn't vocalize, but I call it a win anyway since she at least looks less horrified now.

"And I'm not in the habit of telling my mother or my sister about my sex life, so no worries there."

"I know, I just feel like... Nora knows everything. She has spidey senses, you know?"

"Yeah, but let's hope they don't extend to my dick, okay?"

We both burst out into laughter and the oven dings in the meantime. She pulls the cake out to let it cool on the stove, and puts a few more things away, the remnants of amusement still hitting her in little pangs of laughter as she works.

"We okay?" I ask after a few minutes.

She nods, giving me a small smile.

"Then I'm gonna give you space. I'll be in my room. You're welcome if you want, if not, no worries," I say, putting the ball back in her court. As much as I want her, I don't want to twist her arm and have her do anything she regrets.

FOURTEEN

Ben

AFTER 15 MINUTES GO BY AND SHE HASN'T COME INTO MY room for the second time this evening, I resign myself to the fact that I have to start giving her the distance she wants. Except I have a raging hard on and visions of what she might look like in that half corset running through my head on replay. I lay back against my headboard, staring at the shadows on the wall when I hear the door open.

The room is dark and the ambient light on my laptop is the sole source of illumination in the room. But it's enough to see she's got the jersey on and nothing else, or at least nothing I can see besides it. I pray she still has on whatever lingerie she had in store for me. The jersey would have been enough, but getting to peek underneath? *Fuck me.*

I swallow against the lump in my throat as she climbs on the bed next to me and lays down alongside me.

"Hi," she says softly.

"Hey," I answer, turning toward her and giving her a little smile.

"I didn't bring the book. I figure if... we probably need to lose the training wheels."

"They were super hot wheels though. But yeah, probably more fun if they fall off."

She rolls her eyes but rewards me with a little smile for my lame jokes.

"Should have listened in more to the undergrads today. Seen if they had any tips for seducing athletes. I skipped that part."

"The jersey thing pretty much has it covered, so I wouldn't worry."

"Yeah?" she asks, sitting up, and stretching the jersey material so she can see the entirety of the number. "Why is that anyway?"

"Why do I think it's hot to see you in my jersey?"

"Yeah."

I run my teeth over my lip trying to think of a non-dickish way to say it, and while I'm thinking she slides one leg over me, kneeling with one leg on either side of mine, hovering over my lap facing me. She holds the jersey out again and puzzles over the outlined number 87 on the front.

"Yeah, there's really no good way to say it. It's a possessive thing."

"A brand?" She eyes me skeptically.

"Sure, something like that. It's hot though, and then the way it skims the tops of your thighs like that. Shows just enough to make it hot without being X rated. You know?"

"Just wait until you're in the NFL, and you've got thousands of women wearing them." She smiles at me.

"If."

"When." She levels me with a look that says she won't listen to a counter argument.

"Now you're just trying to stroke my ego."

"Is it working?"

"Maybe." I smile at her.

There's a beat of silence and it lasts just long enough to make the tension mount between us. She worries her lip between her teeth and my eyes are drawn to it. It makes me want to do the one thing I know I shouldn't.

"I feel like I need shots for this." She breaks my daydream.

"Why?"

"I'm just... awkward. Out of practice."

"It's just me, Vi."

"You say that like you're not one of the hottest men on campus. Probably in the city."

"And you're gorgeous as fuck and get me hard every time I look at you."

She looks at me surprised, almost as if she doesn't believe me.

"Honest." I put my hand over my heart.

"Doesn't change the fact that it's intimidating."

"I intimidate you?" I laugh. "If you only fucking knew, Violet. I'm usually good with women. I can string words together, say and do the right things at the right time. With you I just fumble around hoping I don't fuck it up."

"I wish you would. It would make me feel better if you had some flaws. Might make it less awkward too."

"Was it awkward before?"

"Are you seriously asking me if it was awkward that my friend's brother walked in on me touching myself? Because yes, Ben. Like, definitely top three of my life."

"It was top three hottest of mine," I admit.

"I'm sure." She rolls her eyes.

"I'm serious. My heart fucking stopped in my chest when I walked in. I felt a little guilty at first, but then it was like winning the fucking lottery. Sitting there listening to you... I needed the shower afterwards. Even after I jacked off... it was torture sleeping next to you."

She makes a face like she's not sure, and it grates on me that she doesn't believe she has that effect on me.

I sit up and pull her down onto my lap, letting her feel how hard I am even now, just thinking about it. I use the opportunity to run my fingers over her lower back, her soft skin warm under my touch.

"Believe me now?" I ask, my voice rougher than before because the feel of her cradling my cock makes me want her so much, I can hardly stand it.

She nods and gives the slightest roll of her hips. Giving me friction I desperately want from her. Testing me she rolls them again, and she must like what she sees on my face because she starts a steady rhythm. It's just enough to tease my cock, not enough to really sate the need and she knows it.

"That how you're going to play it?" I ask her, trying to hide the need in my voice.

She nods, a grin teasing at her lips.

I sit up higher, bringing our bodies dangerously close and gripping the hem of the jersey.

"Let me see?" It's as much a question as it is a statement of need, and she nods her okay.

I pull it off, slowly, over her head and then toss it on the bed beside us. It's better than I imagined, like it always is with her. Nude with black lace overlayed on top. Perfectly holding her breasts as they sway with the rocking of her hips. She would have been hot in an old T-shirt, but her wearing this for me makes my stomach twist. Makes me ache that much more to put my hands on her, to be inside her, to fucking kiss her.

"I think I could come like this, just looking at you," she whispers.

I will give the woman credit, if there's anything she knows how to do it's make me forget how to breathe.

"Yeah? I can make it better."

With the next lift of her hips, I reach down and slide my joggers down my hips. I hadn't bothered putting on anything else tonight. The next time she makes contact with me, it's the damp lace and cotton of her panties sliding against my cock.

"Fuck," she curses.

"Better?" I groan as I grab her hips and slide my hands down her thighs.

"The best." She practically purrs the word, and her eyes shutter as she slides against me again. Her hands press against my chest, as she rocks against my cock a few more times. Then her eyes open again, slowly at first, her lids heavy and I can see the want there. The need. But as she studies my face, they flutter open again, and she slows.

"How come you haven't kissed me?" It's an honest question, more curious than frustrated.

"You ran the first time I tried."

She laughs at that answer.

"Not funny. Does something to a guy's ego, you know."

She shakes her head, smiling, but her eyes land on my lips again.

"Is that what you want? Me to kiss you?" I ask.

"Yes," she admits, whisper soft.

I run my hands up her lower back as she leans in toward me. A vein of nervousness runs through me despite how much I want her. It's not lost on me that we're both mostly naked and that I've already acted out fantasies with her that I'd never even planned on telling her about. But somehow kissing her feels like more.

I glance at her lips, my hand running up the side of her throat as I bring my own lips closer to hers in what feels like agonizingly slow motion. She inches closer to me, so close my lips ghost over hers. I look up to meet her eyes, to try to see what she's thinking but her lids are already low, her long lashes concealing them.

I lean forward, the softest brush of my mouth over hers, a first pass of her lips against mine and I already feel like it's too much. The way I can hear her breathe, the taste of her lip gloss, the way her hands go to my shoulders.

She goes to kiss me again, and I pull back, a teasing smile and her lids rise again, her eyes coming to mine.

"Now you're just being mean." She gives me a little shake of her head.

I grin and stroke the soft angle of her jaw.

"Come here," I whisper.

Then I give her what she's actually asking for, pressing my lips to hers, soft plying strokes that she answers in return before opening her mouth, her tongue teases mine and then she lets me in. Her lips are sweet, and her hands wrap around my neck, kissing me like I'm the first taste of something she actually wants. Her hips rolls again and that combined with the feel of her mouth has me dying from how much I want her. I break the kiss, and a smile spreads across her lips that I can't help but answer.

"That wasn't bad," she teases.

"Yeah. I didn't hate it." I grin. "You've got all the good ideas. What else do you want?"

"I want you inside me." Her eyes drift over me as she says it.

She's said those words a million times to me in my fantasies, but nothing's prepared me to hear her say them for real. Whatever I'd said about her being hard on my ego, I take it back. It's like this woman reads my mind and gives me everything I want. Which makes me worry that's exactly what she's doing.

"You sure?" I question, meeting her eyes.

"Yes," she says it with no hesitation, and I swear my heart skips a beat.

I lean over, pulling a condom out of the nightstand and tear the package to put it on while she slides her panties off and tosses them on top of the jersey, before she climbs into my lap again.

When I look up at her, she's watching me with an absent little half smile, and I feel a tug in my chest I try to ignore.

Her fingers run down my abs as she raises her hips, but then she hesitates and looks at me.

"Are you sure?" she asks. I see the hint of concern behind her eyes.

If I'm honest with myself, I'm not sure. I feel like this woman is about to claim me body and soul, and I'm going to be a husk when she eventually gets tired of using me like this. But while my brain hesitates the rest of me aches to be inside her, and something deep inside my chest knows I need her.

"Absolutely." I grin at her.

She slides over me one more time, testing me before she finally takes me, and I am not prepared for how good she feels. Just the feel of her around me makes me lose all focus. Her pace is agonizing at first, toying with me like she had before until I reach forward and slide the pad of my thumb over her clit, teasing her in return, and she finally gives me more.

"You feel so good," she confesses, biting down on her lower lip.

She feels like fucking sunshine on a late fall day, the ball on a touchdown route, and 50,000 people shouting my name all wrapped in one. Like she was made especially for me. Like I can't live without her.

She feels like she owns me.

But I can't say that, so instead I just watch her, trying to memorize everything about this moment. Her pace picks up and her eyes shutter completely.

"You gonna come for me, gorgeous?"

She nods, and I use my thumb to match her pace as I watch her crash over the edge, her little gasps like lightning to my cock. I slide my arms around her, flipping her gently onto her back as she rides out the aftershocks and take her faster and harder than before. Her legs wrap around me, and her fingers go to my back, the pressure of them urging me on. She cries out my name, and it's just enough to send me over after her. I come harder than I have in my life, my arms and legs weak in the wake of it, and I feel more spent than I do after a game. I bury my face in her neck, kissing her several times before I pull out of her.

She lets go slowly, like she's waking up and hadn't realized how tightly she'd been holding on. I use the opportunity to give her a moment, and fuck, maybe me too, getting rid of the condom before I climb back into bed next to her. She's sitting up, reaching for the jersey and then pulling it down over herself. And she's so silent, it scares me.

"Violet?"

"Hmm?"

"You good?"

"Yeah, just... Wow. You know?" She's quiet, but she looks back at me over her shoulder, her hair falling down over my name on the back of the jersey and her lips pull up on one side into a half smile.

"I mean definitely seeing you putting my name on you after." I smirk to hide the worry I feel.

She grins but she still reaches for the panties on the bed,

and I slide my hand over hers to stop her. She looks at my hand and then up at me, an unspoken question.

"You're not going to let me keep them? Have the full teenage dream experience?" I keep teasing her, hoping she'll relax.

She blushes though, and I feel guilty for it.

"Hey." I lean forward, bringing her chin up to get her to look at me. "What's wrong?"

"Nothing's wrong." She shakes her head. "Was just going to go back to my room."

"Or you could stay here. We could watch something?"

She gives me a skeptical look.

"I mean yeah. I might be hoping for another round later. Joss is gone, and I want to see how loud I can get you to say my name, but we can also just watch something if you want."

"Cute, but you don't strike me as a second-time type." She stands and starts to head for the door.

"Violet." I grab my pants and throw them back on.

She turns just as she hits the door.

"Where are you going?"

"I told you." She says it like I'm being unreasonable and now, now my heart is starting to race. I can feel the panic setting in.

"I'm going to need you to use more words than that. Because we just fucked and now, you're acting like you can't get away from me fast enough, and I'm starting to feel a little bruised over it."

"What? Why? I assumed this was the end game. We fuck. You get your fantasy. I get to have some *really* good sex and then it's out of our systems. Right?"

I stare at her for a minute, realizing how differently we'd been viewing this whole situation. Even though in the back of my head I'd been waiting on her to pull the plug, my stupid heart had been hoping somehow I'd have a magic dick that would convince her not to. Guess I had the answer to that.

"We agree when it comes to me getting a fantasy and really good sex, but the rest of it not so much. I like you, Violet. Whether we're fucking or watching TV. But you're definitely not out of my system." I didn't think she would ever be, but now wasn't the time for that discussion.

"I just don't want it to get awkward."

"Then come back to bed, watch something with me, or talk to me. But I want you to stay."

Her hand drops from the door handle, and I feel like I can breathe again.

"Are you sure? I really am good. You don't need to worry."

"Yeah? Well, I'm not good. I want you back in my bed. And I want you to stay there for the rest of the night. What we do is up to you, but—"

She stops me with a kiss, it's a little hesitant but she smiles when she pulls away. "Okay, bossy."

I grin and pull her down onto the bed with me, kissing her as we fall. I don't care if I live on borrowed time with her, as long as I get more of it.

FIFTEEN

Violet

"Violet!!" I hear Joss whisper screaming from across the room. I must be in a nightmare because she sounds panicked. She's telling me Cameron's here and I need to get up. But it's impossible since he's in Europe and I'm in my apartment in my bed thousands of miles away.

"Violet, I'm fucking serious, girl. Get your ass up!"

Her voice is insistent, and it feels so real it actually wakes me out of my sleep. I have to blink a few times because I don't recognize my sheets or my room.

"Fucking finally. Cameron is here. I've got him waiting outside the door because I told him I didn't know if you were here, and I wasn't letting him in if you weren't. I need you to tell me what you want me to do. But, oh. Oh shit. Yeah, you need to get out of this room and out of that..." Joss waves her hand over my form like all of me is problematic.

"Cameron?" I ask, still trying to process what she's saying.

119

"Christ, that boy did fuck your brains out. Yes. Cameron. The man you were going to marry until he was an asshole? I don't know how or why, but he's at the door right now. What do you want me to do?"

I sit up abruptly, my heart fucking racing. Remembering last night. Realizing I'm still in his room. I remembered him waking me, telling me he was going for a run. That he'd be back with a late breakfast.

"What time is it?"

"10 a.m."

"Fuck. Ben should be back soon."

"Oh god. I have too much of a hangover for fireworks. At least your boy is chill though, even if Cameron isn't."

"I have to change. I have to shower. Fuck." I stand up, shoving the jersey down because I've just remembered thanks to the cool gust of air that I don't have panties on.

"Get a change of clothes and get in the bathroom. Then I'll set Cameron up in the living room and keep an eye on him. Tell him you woke up late. I suggest inventing a reason that isn't getting railed by your hot new roommate."

"I don't owe him any explanation."

"No, but that won't change the fact he'll ask, and you'll want to answer."

She had a point.

"Get your ass going, before he starts wondering what the fuck is going on."

"Okay. Okay!"

I run for my room, stripping out of the jersey and throwing my robe on before I root through my drawers for fresh underwear and an outfit that says, *Oh hey, ex-fiancé who shouldn't fucking be here, how are you?*

I start to turn and see the jersey on the floor. I panic, wondering where to put it. Back in Ben's room is probably the best place, except I already hear her letting Cameron in and there's a good chance he sees me if I try that. So I opt to kick it under the bed instead, and then make a run for the bathroom, shutting the door just in time to hear their voices overtake the living room as Joss insists he doesn't need to go talk to me in the bathroom.

I turn the shower on, cranking the water up to high heat and collapse against the bathroom door. This is a nightmare. I haven't even had a chance to process last night, and now I'm going to have to explain it to Cameron. And soon.

———

WHEN I GET OUT OF THE SHOWER CAMERON IS IN THE living room, and it gives me enough time to change and brush my wet hair. I've just stepped out into the dining room to greet him, when I hear the front door open and see Ben carrying three coffees in a tray and a bag of pastries standing in the door.

"You're up." He smiles at me, looking bright and flushed from his run. I want to kiss him, and I almost do exactly that before I remember where I am and what's happening. That's what he does to me.

"Yeah. We have some unexpected company." I turn my attention to Cameron, but I can see a look of confusion on Ben's face out of the corner of my eye.

Cameron stands and makes his way over to me, grinning as his arms wrap around me, pulling me close to him.

"I've missed you so much Violet," Cameron whispers against my temple as he squeezes.

I glance over to see Ben, and his face is a mix of emotions as he takes in the scene in front of him before it lands on something unreadable. He walks past us and sets the coffees and pastries on the kitchen counter silently, and I wish that the floor would open and swallow me to avoid the awkwardness of this entire situation.

"Did you get something amazing?" I hear Joss asking Ben, and he mumbles something in return.

I pull back from Cameron's hug, wishing he wouldn't even touch me. We still talk via text on a semi-regular basis as quasi-friends, when he sees something that reminds him of me or when I can't find something that he put away before he left. I don't know why he wouldn't have used one of those opportunities to tell me he was coming.

"So this is a surprise," I say hesitantly.

"I know. I had the opportunity to come to a conference this weekend at the last second, and I thought it would be great to see you while I was here. Surprise you and take you out to dinner, so we could catch up in person for once. I hope you don't mind if I stay here?"

"Um, it's not ideal. We have the Halloween party tonight."

"Oh, right Joss's famous Halloween party." His lips turn down with displeasure because he never cared for her obsession with Halloween or my indulgence of the same quirky love of the holiday.

And if I wasn't already irritated with his presence here this morning, that sealed it for me.

"Well, Joss won't mind if I attend, will you?" He looks up at her as she's sipping her coffee, and she just looks to me.

I make an irritated noncommittal face in return.

"You have to wear a costume. A real one. Not a T-shirt you pulled out of your bag, so I doubt it would make much sense for you to be here Cam."

"Cut me a little slack, I just want to see my girl." He makes a pouty face at her.

"Plus we have a pretty full house tonight. There really isn't

122

a spare place for you to sleep," Joss adds on, and I could hug her for trying to help.

"I mean, I just planned to sleep in our room." He glances back at me and grins.

"My room." I correct him.

"You don't mind though, do you? I can make it worth it." He gives me a little grin that I imagine is supposed to look devious, but it just grates on my nerves that he thinks after everything *this* would appeal to me. And having it all play out in front of Ben makes me cringe.

"I don't know about that, but we can try to find somewhere if you can't find a hotel..." I trail off, only because I really don't want him to explode on me right now.

I glance up at Ben, and he's staring at the donut in his hand, doing his best to look disinterested. Cameron must follow my line of sight because his attention joins mine.

"Sorry man. I didn't see you there. I'm guessing you're Joss's guy?" He walks the few steps over and holds out his hand.

Ben looks up and shakes his hand.

"He's not my guy, Cam. He's our roommate. Violet's friend, Ben."

Cam frowns as he tries to make sense of the information.

"He's Nora's little brother," I add, giving him the information that he probably needs to put the whole puzzle together.

"You're Nora's brother? Wow. The last time I saw you, you were just a kid." Cameron smiles tightly.

"Yeah, well the passage of time and all of that." Ben gives him an unimpressed look.

Cameron smiles at him cluelessly, and Ben's eyes flick to mine.

"Ben plays football for Highland State. One of the best

players they have," Joss adds proudly, leaning her head against his shoulder and looking up at him with doe eyes.

"I didn't know you followed football, Joss." Cameron raises his brow.

"Well, we do now that we have someone who knows how to play it in the house." Joss grins, and I shoot her a look behind Cameron's back.

"No shit. Well, what position do you play? I try to watch the games, but it's been harder overseas."

"Wide receiver."

Cameron stares at him for a minute as if he's trying to make sense of something.

"Nora—not Lawton? That Lawton?" Cameron's eyes go wide.

"Yes, that one," I say from behind him.

"Holy shit. You're phenomenal to watch. And you must be excited about your draft prospects."

"I'm hopeful," Ben answers quietly.

"Okay, well why don't you get your stuff put away for the time being, and we can let them eat breakfast. I need to grab some myself," I say, interrupting because I feel like it's only growing more awkward by the minute.

"Okay. I have to run soon anyway, to get to the conference lunch," Cameron agrees. "Can I get changed and use your bathroom?"

I nod, and he heads out a few moments later, leaving Ben, Joss and me standing in the kitchen.

"He's not going to find a hotel. You know that," Joss whispers, flashing a look of contempt in the direction Cameron disappeared.

"He might. I'll tell him again."

"He won't."

"Well, I don't know what to do. Put him on the street?" I

say frustration coming through in my tone because this whole morning nearly has me in tears from it.

"Why not?"

"Because he wouldn't do that to me if the situation was reversed."

Joss rolls her eyes, and I look to Ben realizing he's been utterly silent. His eyes meet mine, an unreadable look there. I wish we were alone so that I could really talk to him about this.

"I didn't know. Honestly," I say.

"I believe you," he says softly, but I can tell from the look on his face that it has little effect on his mood.

"Vi, where are you keeping the towels?" Cameron calls out from my room, and I feel the flush of irritation return.

"I'll be right there."

I look to Ben again. "I am really sorry about this."

"It's fine." He shrugs.

But by the time I get done helping Cameron, Ben is gone with no explanation and no text. I can't help but feel like I've made a huge mistake.

SIXTEEN

Violet

By the time Joss and I are putting out food and the rest of the decorations for the Halloween party, I'm so nervous I'm trying to think of reasons I could hide in my room all night. I feel like I'm trapped. While Cameron is my ex, we have been on semi-good terms lately trying out what it's like to be friends post-breakup. He hasn't said or done anything to hurt me in recent history, and if Ben wasn't here, I likely wouldn't have thought twice about letting him crash here for a night or two for a conference. But with Ben here, and Cameron acting overly familiar? I hate it, and there's been no opportunity to take either of them aside privately to explain the situation. And it all feels like a recipe for disaster.

"You all right there?" Joss asks, breaking my concentration.

"What?" I say, blinking as I put another little bit of spider webbing around the cauldron on the table.

"Your face is doing some weird gymnastics right now. Just

want to make sure you're not overanalyzing so hard that you've broken something vital."

"Just wishing I'd been able to talk to one or both of them alone before tonight when we have an apartment full of people."

"I mean, you could make this wildly simple. Tell Cameron I don't want him here and tell him to get a hotel."

"It feels rude," I protest. "And like I said, if the tables were turned, he wouldn't do it to me."

"No, because he wants you back. So of course, he wouldn't."

"He didn't say that."

"He showed up from out of the country to surprise you. He's saying it without words."

"Well, I gave him no reason to expect that I'd be open to that."

"You're encouraging it by letting him stay here."

"I just don't want to be a jerk."

"Well, you're going to be one—either to him or to Ben." She levels me with a look that says I know the right answer.

"I'd explain everything to Ben if he was here."

"He's with some of the guys on the team."

"What? How do you know?" I stop what I'm doing to look at her.

"He asked if they could come with him tonight."

"When?"

"When he texted earlier."

"He texted you?"

"Don't put me in the middle." She eyes me warily.

I sigh, because she's right. They're friends and roommates too. I don't need to make it awkward for them.

"Have you tried texting him?"

"Not yet."

"Maybe do that then, yeah?"

"I didn't want to seem clingy."

She blinks at me pointedly.

"Okay, okay."

I go to my room to grab my phone just as I hear the front door open, and the sounds of male voices tumbling in the door. I can tell from the volume and the laughter that they've already been drinking, and when I round the corner, I see that it's not just Ben, Colton and Jake, but a couple of women that are with them as well. I tuck my phone back in my pocket, the opportunity lost, and head into the kitchen.

They're deep in a discussion about one of their friends, so I pretend to be very interested in putting candy pumpkins on top of all the graveyard cupcakes in the kitchen. I keep looking up trying to get a surreptitious glance at Ben. Whatever his mood had been earlier, he seems to be in a good one now, laughing whole-heartedly at the story Jake is telling.

"Can you make the punch, Vi? I've got to get the bread in the oven and then get the other desserts out."

"Can do." I nod.

"Is there anything I can do, Joss?" Ben turns to her, without even glancing my way, and I feel a pang of something in my chest that I try to ignore.

"You want to finish the cupcakes Vi is working on, so she can do the punch?" Joss's eyes flash up to me for half a second.

"Sure." He smiles at her.

"Anything we can do?" One of the women smiles at Joss.

"Yeah, can we help?" Jake asks.

"Nah, we've got it. Unless you all want to search for some horror movies to put on?" Joss nods toward the living room.

"Oh. I've got ideas for that." Colton takes off and the rest of them follow, leaving the kitchen a touch quieter than it was before.

"Here." I push the tray toward Ben on the counter and hand him the bag of pumpkins.

"Thanks," he says without looking up at me.

"Are we okay?" I ask softly, and he finally brings his eyes up to mine. He smiles, and it almost looks real. The only giveaway being that it doesn't reach his eyes.

"Yeah, of course. Why wouldn't we be?"

"Okay. I'm just sorry about everything."

"We're all adults. No need to be sorry." He shrugs and starts putting the pumpkins on the cupcakes.

Apparently, that was going to be the extent of the discussion. And I wasn't about to press for more or discuss last night with this many people in ear shot. So instead, I start pulling out the things to make the punch, excusing myself when I have to get down on the floor beneath Ben to reach for a punch bowl in the back of the bottom cabinet. It feels bizarre to be working in here like strangers when just last night he'd pressed me for more. How quickly a day can change things.

―――――

AN HOUR LATER AND AT LEAST ANOTHER DOZEN OR SO people have shown up, mostly Joss's friends but a couple of people from our grad program as well. Everyone mingles pretty well despite the varied interests and ages in the room, mostly bonding over the '80s horror movies on the screen and the potency of the punch I'd made. I might have over poured a bit when I was lost in my thoughts about Ben.

By the time Cameron shows up, I'm thoroughly drunk and clinging to Joss like a lifeline as I endure Ben ignoring me like I don't exist. At first, I thought he was just giving me space, but now it feels downright personal the number of times he refuses to look at me even when I speak.

Unfortunately for Cameron, I'm not treating him much better, and I can tell he's getting increasingly frustrated with me. When I excuse myself to go to my room for a minute, he trails me, and I turn to stop him before he follows me in. The last thing on earth I want is to be alone with him or have Ben see him follow me into my room.

"Did you need something?" I look back at him.

"I just wanted to talk some." He gives me a lopsided grin.

"I'm not really in the mood to talk Cam. I just want to have fun with my friends tonight."

"I mean, I'm a friend, and we could have fun if you'd just let me." Clearly, he has also had the punch if he thinks that's a possibility.

He leans forward, his hands going to my waist, and he tries to kiss me before I dodge out of the way.

"Cam," I warn.

"I know. I know we shouldn't after everything, but I can't stop thinking about you. It's why I came here, to see you."

I barely have time to think about how Joss was right, and how I should have listened to her, because we have an audience.

"Just need to get by you, man," Ben says to Cameron who is obliviously blocking the entire hallway.

My heart stops, and I look up at him, hoping he knows this is a one-sided conversation. His eyes meet mine for the briefest of moments, a flicker of irritation disappears almost immediately before he heads into the bathroom. My heart jumps to my throat, and I just want to run after him, but I've never been on this side of things with him. So I have no idea how he'll react if I do.

"Cam. We should talk sometime when we're you know, not drinking and not at a party. Okay? We can discuss things, but tonight is not a good night."

Hurt flickers over his features as he stares at me but he eventually nods and heads back to the party. I slide into my room and close the door behind me, grabbing my phone out of my pocket firing off a text.

> That was all Cameron. I am not encouraging it. I'm sorry he's here. I should have listened to Joss

BEN

It's fine. My friend Chels is spending the night btw. Hope that's okay

My heart bottoms out as I stare at the message. Tears pricking my eyes and I'm just thankful that I'm alone in my room when I read it. But I can't say anything other than okay. I told Cameron he can stay. Ben doesn't belong to me. And I have to try to act like an adult about all of this.

> Okay

I hit send and then I go back to the party, wrapping my arm around Joss's and giving her a look that lets her know I need her.

"More punch then?" she asks, a half frown on her face.

"More punch," I agree.

"I got you." She smiles and I'm just thankful that in these moments I have her.

SEVENTEEN

Violet

I WAKE UP ON THE COUCH, A CRICK IN MY NECK AND MY
body feeling like it's been through a blender. I blink a few times
at the sun pouring in and then remember that Cameron has
another round of conferences this morning.

I stumble up and try to straighten my clothes as I walk
toward my closed bedroom door. I'd managed to stay away from
Cameron for most of the evening and had fallen asleep on the
couch with Joss. I was dreading having to talk to him this
morning and hoping we could revisit the idea of a hotel for
tonight.

My eyes can't help but travel to Ben's room as I approach
mine, and I see that his door is still shut too. I let myself wonder
for a split second if he still has her in there with him before I
decide I can only handle one problem at a time.

When I open the door, I see that Cameron's already up and

getting dressed. His back is to me, his shirt and pants already on and his collar flipped up as he works on his tie.

"Morning," I say softly, heading for my dresser where I can get a fresh set of clothes.

"The sheets smell like him." His voice is sharp, heavy with accusation.

I come up short, looking back over my shoulder to see that the bed has been made and the jersey I'd tried to shove under it is now laying on top. It's turned over with "Lawton" clearly visible over the 87. I wince and close my eyes, feeling guilty for half a second before I remember that he has zero grounds to be angry with me.

"You didn't exactly give me time to change them when you showed up unannounced."

"Didn't realize you were fucking someone. Were you going to tell me?"

I stare at his back because he refuses to turn around.

"When I had a chance."

He slides his tie into place, tightening it.

"Before I left or after?"

"When we had a moment alone."

"Didn't seem to want to be alone with me last night. That why you slept out there? Worried he'd be jealous?"

Now he turns around, his jaw hard and set, his eyes burning with a mixture of anger and hurt. I don't answer immediately, trying to choose my words carefully because everyone in the house is likely still asleep at this hour, and I don't want them to wake up to us arguing.

"He didn't have the same compunctions, for the record. The two of them were up all night."

It feels like a kick in the stomach to hear it and Cameron knows because his lip curls the slightest bit in satisfaction.

"I wasn't ready for bed and then Joss and I stayed up super late."

"On the night your fiancé is in town from overseas you have to stay up with Joss?"

"Ex-fiancé. And, again, you didn't give me fair warning to change plans."

"Right. It's my fault for wanting to surprise you. For thinking we could have some time together. My bad for not giving you a chance to hide away your fuckboy's shit and tell your roommate you're not a child who celebrates Halloween anymore."

"Cam, if you want to be pissed at me, feel free. But don't drag them into this."

"Why not? He's in to you. How many times have you fucked him anyway?"

"It's new."

"I hope you're using a fucking condom. He's probably fucked his way through half the campus."

"Like you're fucking your way through half of Europe?" I snap because I hate the way he talks about Ben, the way he sees him.

"It's been three women. I've told you about every single one of them, and I'd answer any question you want to ask. They were just hookups. I didn't move them in and fuck them in our bed."

"Wow, Cameron. I didn't move Ben in to have sex with him. Nora asked me for my help because I'm here and she's not. He needed a place to stay and some help while he went through a rough patch."

"And you helped him all right. With *everything*."

"Get fucked, Cameron. Seriously. Was it or was it not *you* that told me you needed to put the brakes on things? *You* that wanted to take a break, have an open relationship, and explore other people? Was it or was it not *you* that was out fucking random women and bragging to me about it?"

"I wasn't bragging. I was keeping things honest with you."

"You can give me updates without telling me how perfect their breasts were."

"Because you didn't seem to fucking care. At all."

"I'm sorry, did you want to have an open and honest adult relationship where we saw other people, or did you want me to be a jealous scorned ex-girlfriend?"

"I wanted you to fucking care. To act like it mattered to you at all."

"I asked you not to do this, and you told me you needed it. So I adapted. I decided to take the idea seriously."

"Too fucking seriously. You were supposed to go out and have a couple one-night stands with a guy you met at a bar. Not move the first one in and start playing fucking house with him in our bed."

"First, you have no idea how many one-night stands I have or haven't had. Second, it's not our bed anymore. It's mine. You moved out."

"Yeah, and what? He thinks he can just move in here and take over where I left off?"

There's a hard knock at the door and then it pops open, Ben is standing there brow furrowed. His eyes traveling between the two of us, and then focusing on me.

"There a problem?" he asks, his tone clipped but his eyes are soft as he looks at me.

My stomach churns at what he might have heard.

"We're fine. Go back to fucking your coed, kid." Cameron sneers at him.

I see a shift in Ben, his body tightening up and his jaw setting like he's ready for a fight, but his eyes stay locked on me.

"It's fine. He's leaving anyway to get to his conference. Right?"

"Right. I made dinner reservations for tonight, after you get out of your gallery opening program."

I don't answer him, because the last thing I want to do right now is have dinner with him but saying it is only going to fuel the fire.

A blonde head of hair appears just behind Ben, and I realize Cameron wasn't lying when he said she was here all night.

"I'm sorry if we woke you guys up. I'm gonna go get some pastries and coffee down the street. I'll bring you some," I apologize, feeling insanely awkward.

"It's fine. Just wanted to make sure you were okay." Ben's eyes follow Cameron's back as he puts his things back into his bag, and then they snag on his jersey sitting on the bed. He looks down, closing his eyes.

"I'll see you tonight." Cameron turns toward me, planting a kiss on my cheek. "Love you."

The last bit more for Ben's benefit than my own, and he disappears down the hall.

"Violet?" Ben asks quietly.

"I'm fine. Any special requests for breakfast?" My eyes travel past him involuntarily, trying so hard not to imagine the two of them in his room last night. I plaster a fake smile on my face.

"No. Are you sure?"

"I'm fine." I shake my head, smiling at him because I will not cry before I get him out of the doorway. "Go get some more sleep."

My hand is on the door and I'm pushing it shut despite the look he's giving me.

"So wanna talk about it, or are you just gonna sullenly pour wine all evening?" Joss bumps her hip into mine as she fills a plastic cup with merlot. It's opening night at the campus gallery, and we'd volunteered to serve drinks and food behind the bar for a few hours so the other staff that worked on the exhibit could mingle for a bit.

"Option C. Fall into a black pit, never to be seen again?"

"It can't be that bad."

"The first words Cameron said to me this morning were, and I quote, 'The sheets smell like him'. And I'm pretty sure Ben heard the whole thing."

The little old lady whose white wine glass I'm currently filling looks up at me, her eyes practically sparkling with interest. I'm glad I can liven someone's night. I hand it to her, and she gives me a little half toast as she walks away.

"He didn't say that." Joss looks surprised, which is a feat.

"He did, and then proceeded to slut shame me," I say, once we're alone again because offering a bit of titillating intrigue is one thing but I don't need these trust funders to know all my tabloid gossip.

"Where the fuck does he get off doing that? Isn't he fucking his way through Europe?"

"That's what I said."

"I knew he would do this. All bravado when he's running around sticking his dick in French women, and then freaking the fuck out when you finally get properly railed by someone who knows what he's doing."

"He is nothing if not a hypocrite," I grump.

"That's almost his entire personality," Joss echoes my irritation.

"I think it might be the end of things with Ben. That girl

was there this morning when we woke up. And then hearing all that drama with Cameron. He's young and has plenty of options, why would he want to deal with my shit?"

"Because he's obsessed with you?"

"Doubt it. Cameron was accusing me of moving my fuckboy in and playing house with him. And honestly, it's more like, he moved in and found an easy toy to play with. Now that toy is broken and complicated and..."

"I get the metaphor, Vi. Zero possibility though." She flashes a smile to a middle-aged man whose glass she fills once he chooses the cabernet from the shelf. He eyes her tattoos and black hair carefully, and then his eyes travel down straight to her cleavage. In his defense, the dress she has on has a plunging neckline that draws your eye there, but the way he lingers on it makes me clear my throat.

"Here you go, sir." She hands him the glass and he flicks his eyes to me for a second before they land back on her.

"Beautiful dress," he says.

"Thanks, it's vintage." She smiles her fake little stunner smile at him, and he turns around.

"More like beautiful boobs. That one might be willing to fly you down to an island for a weekend."

"Ugh. No thanks. I dated a guy that age once, and they need way too much reassurance."

We both have a little laugh at the man's expense, which he can more than afford given the Gucci suit and Valentino shoes.

"Anyway, zero chance he sees you as a plaything, Vi. That boy is playing his cards so carefully, trying so damn hard to seduce you."

"It was fun while it lasted." I shrug.

"Why does it have to be over?"

"For starters, did you miss the part where he had a girl over the whole night?"

"So? For all he knew, you and Cameron were going to be breaking the bed in the next room. It was probably a defensive fuck."

"A defense fuck? Seriously? Where do you come up with this stuff?"

One of the assistant curators walks by and clicks her tongue at us, shaking her head.

"Sorry Ms. A. We'll keep it PG!" Joss chirps.

She laughs and shakes her head again, headed for a group of donors.

"I'm saying would you want to listen to the guy you're in love with hookup with his ex-fiancé in the room next to you? And if you didn't have a choice, wouldn't you prefer to be fu-have your own companion?" Joss lowers her voice as another attendee comes up for wine.

"Red or white?" she asks.

"What reds do you have?"

We pause our conversation while the asshole makes her list every bottle we have open and provide two samples before he'll make his choice.

"You're at a college gallery fundraiser, not Napa asshole!" Joss whisper yells and gives him a discreet finger as he walks away.

"I do not miss working in a restaurant," I add to the sentiment.

"Where were we?" Joss asks.

"Defensive fu- companions," I say as a woman taps the Riesling, and I top off her glass.

"Right. So give him a pass."

"Except I can't stop wondering about it. About them. If he did..."

I feel the twist in my chest again. The one that makes it feel like I can't quite catch my breath and I know I'm in trouble.

"Finally going to admit we're catching feelings, are we?" Joss raises her eyebrow at me.

My phone vibrates and I see a text from Cameron giving me the time and address of our dinner reservation.

"I don't know. Maybe. And on top of all of this I have to have dinner with Cameron. Apparently, so I can listen to round two of why I deserve a scarlet letter."

"Why are we still talking to him, exactly?"

"We were together five years? Engaged?"

"And then he wanted to fuck strange pussy."

One of the more senior curators just happens to pass by at that moment, and I swear she literally clutches her pearls.

"Sorry Dr. Carter!" Joss calls out and then turns to me whispering, "I swear we can have graphic depictions of vulvas all over the wall as long as they have an exhibit label but say the word pussy and the sky is falling. Zero sense with this lot."

"Agreed."

We help a few more guests, and then she looks at me expectantly.

"What?"

"You still haven't given me a good reason for continuing to entertain Cameron's bullshit."

"Old habits die hard." I shrug.

"I will buy you as many nicotine patches as your heart desires if you cut that one out."

"You're such a good friend."

"I know!"

Another wave of guests come to the bar, sensing the party is winding down and the free wine wells are about to run dry, and we barely get another word in for the rest of the night.

EIGHTEEN

Ben

I NEED TO GET SOME DINNER. I'M STARVING AFTER
another round at the gym and dying to get something out of the
kitchen, but I hesitate to go out to the living room. Cameron
came home a little bit ago after his conference was over to wait
for Violet to take her out to dinner. Joss had texted to warn me
about it, but now I'm stuck hiding in my room like a bitch
hoping he's going to leave, so I don't have to deal with any
awkward confrontations.

I hadn't heard everything that was said this morning, but
enough to know Violet hadn't slept in the room with him and
that he was very aware that I had been sleeping in her room
with her. As happy as I would be to rub that in the cocky fucker's face, I'm just now back in coach's good graces and a week
away from coming off the bench. The last thing I need is any
trouble that lands me on his wrong side again.

But I'm hungry, and Cameron's a professional, a doctor

who is nearly a decade my senior. I should be able to get my dinner reheated out of my kitchen without bullshit. I talk myself into doing it, but when I get to the fridge and see him drinking something on the rocks in the dining room, I know I've made the wrong decision. His eyes lock onto me the second he hears me, and I can tell from the way he stares I have a target on my back.

"Bet ya thought it was hilarious listening to me talk you and your draft chances up yesterday not knowing you were fucking my fiancée behind my back," he mutters loud enough for me to hear.

"I didn't think it was anything." I keep my tone even as I pull out the boxes from the fridge.

"If you think she and I aren't anything, you're in for a fucking world of hurt. She still texts me regularly. Still tells me she loves me. She tell you that?"

"She's told me that your engagement's off and you're sampling everything on the foreign menu," I say tightly, shoveling the food out onto a plate.

"That's rich coming from someone who's probably put his dick in every other coed on campus. You better not give her a fucking STI or hurt her in any fucking way."

The implication that I would ever put Violet in danger hits a nerve, and I slam the silverware to the counter surface.

"If you think for a second, I would do anything to hurt her, you don't know fucking anything about me or her."

"I know her a hell of a lot better than you do. You think cause she's bored sitting at home waiting for me and decides to fuck you a few times that means something? It doesn't." He stands, shoving the glass he'd been drinking out of to the side.

"I was there for her long before she even knew you existed."

"Yeah. I see that now. I never did like the way you looked at her. Never very brotherly. I guess you were always waiting in the wings, huh. But she never noticed because her eyes were always on me."

"Were. Past tense. Ask her whose name she says when she comes lately."

He laughs, hard, but his fingers are white knuckling the counter and I know he's dying to throw a punch. I doubt he's stupid enough to, I have inches, pounds and muscle on him, but who knows.

"Like I said. She's bored. Jealous of the fact I got my dick sucked elsewhere a few times. In the grand scheme of things it'll be a blip in our lives. I know you don't actually think she's going to pick fucking you over marrying me. You're a fucking boy who plays a game for a living. I'm a man who's out there saving lives. Who can give her the life she wants, the life she needs. Traveling, researching, making a difference, surrounded by people who have real influence and don't just shove each other around on a field once a week. Don't fuck that up for her." He swallows the last of his drink and grabs his keys. "And on that note, I have to go take her to dinner. Enjoy your leftovers."

The door slams behind him and the microwave beeps signaling my food is done. Except I feel like I've just gone five rounds in a boxing ring and lost my appetite in the process. The guy is an epic fucking douchebag, and I have no idea what she sees in him. But he's right. They have history. In another time-line they'd probably be sitting at this counter planning their wedding tonight.

I hear the door open again and tense, hoping he isn't back to go another round. I hear the click of heels on the floor, and Joss appears, making a show of looking around the room dramatically.

"Nothing broken then? That's a good sign. I'm too tired to clean tonight."

I give her a small smile.

"I assume from the look on your face that he threw an epic tantrum over the fact you played with his toys while he was gone."

I tilt my head in a half nod.

"He wanted to let me know where I stand."

"Do you want to talk about it?"

I shake my head. I know Joss means well, but I also know anything I say to her will be a game of telephone with Violet, and I need to get my head straight before I say anything.

"Well, if it helps, I'm Team Ben."

"Thanks Joss." I give her a small smile and dig into my food.

After dinner I head over to Colt's place. We play a few rounds of video games and have a few beers, and he lets me crash there. I say I'm too fucking tired even though it's not that late, because in reality, I don't want to be home when Violet and Cameron get there. I don't want to hear him proving his point in the room next door. And I want the last name I hear her call out to be mine.

NINETEEN

Violet

THE SECOND I SIT DOWN TO DINNER WITH CAMERON, I
know that agreeing to come here with him was a mistake. He's
angry and bitter, and there's nothing that's going to be said or
happen here that will be positive. But I'm already here, and
politeness dictates that I at least have to hear him out.

"You look gorgeous tonight." Cameron gives me a warm
smile as we sit down at the table.

"Thanks."

The waiter hands us our menus, and I thank him and open
it. This place is far too fancy for my liking, and all I can think
about is the price of everything and how I don't want Cameron
to pay for it. I don't want him to purchase a single thing this
evening because I don't want any misunderstandings. To me
this isn't a date, this is closure so that he can move on, and we
can go our separate ways. But I suspect for him this is some
strange attempt to try to reclaim lost territory.

"Do you want wine?"

"You get whatever you like. I'm probably just going to get water."

"If I get a bottle, will you drink it?"

"Probably not."

He sets the menu down, and I can tell I've already hit a nerve with him.

"I'm sorry for this morning. I should have kept my cool. It should have been a private discussion between us."

"I wish it had been." I say softly, refusing to look at him and instead skimming the menu for something cheap, but even the salads here were closing in on 30 dollars.

I sigh, because this is Cameron. He only thinks about himself, and the fact that he has a full-time job and income. Never mind that I'm still on a grad school budget just trying to get by. The diner near campus is usually the biggest treat I allow myself on any given week, if Joss and I don't spring for something from the bakery.

And the bakery reminds me of Ben, and I bite the inside of my cheek wondering what he's doing right now. I haven't heard from him all day and given that he had a guest last night I could guess where he would be spending another evening. Which makes my chest ache with jealousy and remorse. I should have told Cameron to fuck off the second he walked in the door yesterday, but instead I'd tried to keep things civil, whatever that meant. And now, I am going to pay for it.

"Can we put the knives away for tonight though? I've missed you a lot, and I just want to spend an evening like old times."

"I can try, but it really can't be like old times Cameron. Too much has changed."

I see his jaw click, annoyed that I'm not complying with his desire to just slide back into old bad habits. Admittedly they die hard. I don't want to cause a scene or argue with him in public. I want things to stay calm and him to leave tomorrow without another incident. But I also don't want to pretend anymore.

The waiter walks up before he can say anything and asks for our orders, and despite my protests he gets an expensive bottle of wine and appetizers before we're alone again. I set my menu aside, deciding on the salad after all.

"You already know what you want?"

"Yes, I'm just going to get the chicken caesar."

"You don't want to do the tasting menu?"

"I'm still on a grad school budget, Cam."

"I'm obviously paying tonight. I asked you out."

"I'd rather pay for myself but thank you for offering." I stare at the candle burning at the table, hoping this dinner goes faster than I imagine it will.

"Is this because of him?" He sets his menu down abruptly.

"Who? The waiter?" I play stupid.

"Ben."

"That I'm ordering a chicken caesar? No."

"That you're being so cold to me."

"I'm not being cold Cameron. I'm having dinner with my ex-fiancé at what appears to be a very romantic restaurant. It's not exactly a warm and friendly event, more awkward and uncomfortable. But I'm here because you asked me to be, so we could discuss things and hopefully move on from it."

"Is that what you want now? To move on?"

"We kind of already have moved on, haven't we? I mean you quite literally moved to a different continent."

"I told him this was what this was about." Cameron gives a sly little grin.

"What? Told who?"

"Ben. We had a little chat before I came here tonight."

"Why? You need to leave him alone, Cam."

"Leave him alone? He's the one sliding into my bed. Fucking my fiancée."

"I'm not your fiancée anymore. I haven't been for months. And you've been fucking other people, so I don't understand why you care who I'm fucking or why you'd be harassing them."

"I wasn't harassing him. I was just explaining the situation to him. He's young, and he doesn't understand, Vi."

"I doubt that, but please enlighten me. What doesn't he understand?"

"That he's a revenge fuck for you. And kudos. Getting an athlete and a younger guy. Making me jealous. Mission accomplished, Violet. You have my attention now, so stop playing with the kid and let's work things out. I fucked up. I know that. I want to make amends. I want to fix us."

I laugh, and then I laugh some more. It continues to just bubble up until I'm catching the attention of tables around us, and I have to do my best to stifle it while he glares at me, jaw clenched tight from across the table.

"Ben had absolutely nothing to do with you. Not even a little bit. And the fact that you'd think I'd spend my time scheming like that and use my best friend's little brother to try to get your attention is insulting, frankly."

I go silent again as the waiter brings the wine and our glasses, opening it and pouring it for us and another server arrives with the appetizer he ordered. One that looks amazingly delicious and makes me sad I won't be trying it.

Cameron takes a sip of the wine and stares off into the distance as we sit at the table.

"Why fuck him then?" he finally asks, in such a quiet lethal voice it almost doesn't sound like Cameron.

"For the same reason most people fuck, Cam. Because I wanted to. You should understand. Isn't that what you've been doing these past few months? Fucking who you want, when you want? Was it to try to torture me or because you felt like it?"

"Both. You were so indifferent. I thought it was because you wanted to get engaged and you were mad it took so long, but even after I gave you that, you just seemed bored."

"I wasn't bored. I was busy and tired. I have an insane schedule and have for a while. You remember what grad school was like? Trying to balance school and work and the myriad of projects that pop up while you barely get any sleep."

"And yet, when I leave you suddenly have time to fuck athletes."

"You are seriously fixated on this. Did you think I was just going to sit at home and hope you were going to come back and pick me again? You even told me to go see other people, do the same thing as you."

"I meant fuck that one professor who's always eyeing you or fuck some random guy you meet at a bar when you're drunk. Not go after a D1 athlete that's probably fucked half the school."

"Are you jealous of him?"

Cameron gives a wry little laugh as if I'm being ridiculous.

"Please, Violet. I can't imagine he's very good in bed. What effort does he really have to put in to all those drunken hookups with women who just want to fuck him for the bragging rights."

"Is that what you think? That I fucked him for the bragging rights?" I feel like I'm going to be sick from the anger that's boiling inside.

"Why else? You're not the kind that trips over herself for abs."

"But you think I trip over myself for that?"

"I think you knew it would get attention."

"No one even knows about us."

"You knew I would find out."

"I've already told you this isn't about you."

"Then why?"

"I told you. Because I wanted to. And if you really need to know, he's fucking phenomenal. Like fifteen out of ten, would ride the ride any time I have the chance."

His eyes flick to mine, hurt and anger simmering beneath the surface.

"That's beneath you, Violet."

"You wanted to know, so I'm telling you the truth. I'm sorry if you don't want to hear it."

The waiter returns again to take our order, but he looks hesitant to even say anything and I'm sure it's because we've been very clearly arguing. It's embarrassing to be at a restaurant like this and be visibly sparring with each other, and I think it's time for me to leave.

"Nothing for me, thank you." I shake my head.

"She'll take the ravioli and a Caesar salad. I'll have the braised lamb." Cameron bulls ahead by ordering for me, and it's the last straw.

The second the waiter walks away I start gathering up my purse to leave.

"What are you doing?"

"Leaving."

"Violet, please."

"Cameron..." I sigh. "There is nothing to discuss. You broke things off with me. You wanted to see other people. We did, we just came to different conclusions about what it meant for us. For me, it's over. I have zero interest in getting back together with you. I'd hoped maybe we could be friends or at least have some sort of meaningful closure after all the years we were together, but you're making that impossible because you're fixated on insulting Ben, and me really. And beyond the fact that he doesn't deserve any of it, he's a good friend of mine—and I love him and his family like they're my own. I'm not going to sit here and listen to it. Period. I'm sorry if you were expecting something else tonight, and I truly hope you find what you're looking for out there. I'll have your bag by the front door. You can get it when you're ready and stay at a hotel. Goodbye, Cameron."

I stand and walk away. It's harder than I thought it would be. Not because I want him back or because I think there's anything worth salvaging between us, but because it's years of my life I can't have back. Years I spent loving someone who didn't deserve it, and I've realized that far too late.

I hear him call after me, but I just keep walking, all the way until I hit the pavement of the sidewalk. And I keep walking, getting lost in the crowds until I finally tuck into one of the bars, so I can get on my phone and get a car.

Then I open my texts, and I see one from Joss warning me that Cam had laid into Ben and that Ben had left and hasn't returned. I feel the twist in my chest because it means my guess was probably accurate. He was probably back with the girl from last night, or out partying with someone new.

I can only hope he doesn't get into trouble while he's out. I don't want to fail him on every front. But really, he's been good about staying on the path, and I can't imagine this close to his first game back he would screw it up. Still, I feel like I owe him an apology on Cameron's behalf.

I'm sorry for Cameron. He's an ass. I don't know exactly what he said to you, but he's mad at me and taking it out on you. I told him not to come back to the apartment, so he won't be there whenever you get back. I'm sorry I let him stay at all. Be safe

I hit send before I can say anything else. Because I'm tempted to beg him to come back tonight. To not hookup with whoever he's with. And I can't do that to him.

TWENTY

Ben

THE NEXT DAY AFTER PRACTICE I'M EXHAUSTED AND sitting in my car, trying to decide whether I'm going to head home or drive around until I find an activity that will help me avoid Violet a little longer. I still don't have the right words. Before I know it, I'm dialing Waylon's number, it rings a few times and then a familiar voice answers.

"Hello?" a sweet feminine voice chirps.

"Hey Mackenzie," I greet Waylon's girlfriend.

"Bennnn. How are you?" Her voice lights up when she realizes it's me.

I hear a muffled male voice in the background grumping.

"Fine. Yes. I'll tell him. Will you stop? I can talk to him for a second before you!" I hear her tussling with him in the background for a second before her voice is clear again. "You still there?"

"Yup," I say.

"Waylon said I should tell you that I still do not and will never have a hall pass to sleep with you."

I laugh hard, and I didn't realize how much I needed it until I feel my muscles relax.

"Well you tell him—" I start and then hear a click on the phone.

"Tell me what? You're on speaker now. I don't need you whispering in her ear Benny Boy."

"Hey Waylon."

I hear them both laughing on the other end of the line, and I smile, happy the two of them found each other and worked through things last year.

"Hey buddy. What's up?" Waylon asks.

"You doing okay?" Mackenzie adds, sounding more concerned.

"Mostly yeah. I'm off suspension this week. I get to play, finally."

"Fucking awesome man. I'm coming out there for the game. Did I tell you that? They're having a little ceremony thing that I'm presenting."

"No man. That's badass. Do I get to see you?"

"I don't know. We'll be in and out because I've got a game on Monday. Maybe we can catch dinner after your game?"

"I'd be down."

"I'll find a place and make a reservation," Mackenzie offers.

"Yeah, just don't forget to tell your actual boyfriend where we're going all right?" Waylon teases her.

Mac had initially had a bit of a crush on me, before she and Waylon hooked up and forgot I existed, but he still won't let her live it down.

"Oh hush. Anyway, were you calling for something Ben?"

"I just... needed to talk to you guys."

"Sounds ominous," Mackenzie hedges.

"Sounds like it's a girl."

I grunt.

"There's finally a girl?" Mackenzie's voice lights up. "Oh my god. Do we get to meet her?"

"Settle down. If he's calling us, then somethings wrong. Right Benny?"

I grunt again.

"If this girl doesn't see Mr. Perfect Man right in front of her then I don't think we can help him," Mackenzie offers.

"Think about how long it took you to figure it out, darlin. What I'm more concerned about is that Dr. Love can't figure out how to hook a girl. I've only heard of that happening once in his whole career."

"Once is all it takes," I mutter.

"Oh shit. It's THE girl?" I can practically hear Waylon sitting up straight.

"Wait, there's a THE girl? How do I not know about this?"

"Cause it would have broken your little heart, and I needed that part of you intact."

"Aww, Waylon." I hear her kiss him through the line.

"Do you guys want to get a room, and I can call you back?"

"NO!" They both say in unison.

"Tell me what's going on. Waylon will be useless, but I might be able to help."

"I don't even know where to start..."

"Try the beginning," Mackenzie suggests.

So I start telling them the whole story, leaving out most of the salacious details.

"So just to be clear, the last time you saw each other, her quasi ex was slut shaming her for sleeping with you, and you had another girl with you who spent the night in your room?"

"Who I didn't hookup with."

"But she doesn't know that."

"Correct."

"Well first of all, this girl needs a friend to tell her to wake up. If she doesn't have one, I'm happy to volunteer. Second, do not listen to a word that asshole said to you. He's scared of losing her, and he's going to say and do anything to keep her, now that he realizes he made a huge mistake in the first place. Same shit Ezra did."

"He has some points though. She's fucking smart. She's getting her PhD and she has all these plans for how she wants to change things in the world, and I just play ball."

"Like a fucking god. I can't wait to see you out here on the field man. I hope it's playing for us. I put in a word or two when I can, but even playing against you. I won't mind seeing you on the other side of the field if it means you're out there. Just wish I could have the chance to knock you on your ass."

We all have a laugh, and I hope I do end up on the field in the same league as him. But I know, especially with my suspension that it's a rocky road to get there.

"Anyway, look Mac and I have made it work."

"But you guys graduated at the same time. I'll be getting drafted; she'll still be in her PhD program."

"Don't worry about all that. Seriously. If you guys love each other, you'll figure it out." Mackenzie gives me a pep talk.

"Love? I don't even know if she fucking likes me."

"She likes you." Mackenzie insists.

"Then what do I do?"

"Go there tonight and talk to her. Just tell her the truth. First, tell her that nothing happened between you and that girl. Then tell her that you have feelings for her."

"And if she doesn't have feelings?"

"Then that sucks, a lot. But at least you'll know."

"Am I pushing too much too soon?"

"I don't think so. You've spent weeks going at her pace, right? If she doesn't know if she has feelings for you by now..."

"It sucks but at least I'll know."

"Right."

"And let's be honest, it's not like you're hurting for backup options, bro," Waylon offers.

"Like you would have taken back up options on Mac?" I ask, a little annoyed, because the idea of anyone but Violet leaves me feeling hollow.

"Fair point. Sorry," he apologizes.

"Sorry. Not trying to be a dick. I'm just..."

"Strung out on a girl?" Mackenzie tries to conceal her amusement but fails.

"I'm glad someone's enjoying this."

"I am, but only because I think it'll turn out okay for you. And I'm excited to meet her. I'm so sure, I'm going to make the dinner reservations for four, so you can bring her."

"I think that's a little presumptuous."

"Let me have my fun."

"Seriously, let this girl have it, or we'll never hear the end of it," Waylon chimes in.

"Fine. Text me when you know."

"Will do."

"Love you man. Go get'er."

"Love you guys. Bye."

———

By the time I get back to our apartment, my whole body is stiff again from the rough practice. It was a challenge to be back on the field again after so long off it, but I'm determined to be a playmaker for the team again even if I have to beat my body into submission for it.

It's late and while I'd planned to talk to Violet, I don't think I have it in me tonight. I don't know whether I should go straight to bed or try to take another hot shower to loosen the muscles that feel like they might snap me in half. All I really want is to curl up in bed next to Violet, but I'm worried I'll wake her up in the process, and since we haven't had a proper conversation since Cameron left, I have no idea where we stand on that front. Or how she's feeling in general.

At least, I was worried until I walk in the door to the sounds of laughter coming from the living room. I can hear Joss talking and a male voice answering her, and the distinct sound of Violet's laughter along with another man. My eyes catch the clock on the stove as I limp my way out of the hallway. It's almost midnight.

When I round the corner, it's obvious no one heard me come in. Joss is sitting in one of the guy's laps in the chair, and Violet is sitting on the couch. Another guy is sitting next to her, arm draped over the back of it and his knee bouncing against hers as he talks. I feel a sharpness in my chest as I stare at the two of them. Cam had been one thing. I could understand why things went the way they did. This, however, was more than I could take tonight.

I know she mentioned she was going out with Joss tonight, and they're both dressed like that's exactly what they did. So that means they brought these guys home with them and given the hour it's hard to imagine that the guy next to Violet is here for anything other than sex.

"Ben." Joss's eyes widen at my appearance, and the room goes silent.

"Ben! Oh my god, are you okay?" Violet asks, noticing my apparent hobble.

It's not enough for my ego to be shattered by finding her with someone else, I literally couldn't even kick the guy's ass if I wanted to right now. I'd just fall over and crumple into a pile on the floor if I tried to throw a punch. Not that I have any right to do anything, because she and I have never discussed exclusivity. She's not even mine to fight over. Another strange pang in my chest, and I'm headed for the shower.

Violet scrambles up from her spot on the couch, and the guy clearly looks annoyed. I want to stop her before she gets too close, before she touches me, and I forget that I'm pissed at her.

"I'm fine. Just a rough night. I'm gonna hit the shower." Because no way can I fucking sleep when she's got a guy here she's hooking up with. I turn as sharply as I can manage to get out of here before I say or do something stupid.

"Let me at least take the bag!" She's at my back, but I ignore her.

"Fuck. Is that her boyfriend?" I hear the asshole on the couch ask.

Joss mumbles something in return I can't hear. I keep marching toward the bathroom like I can't hear Violet. I toss my bag into my room and go to turn for the bathroom door, but she's standing there in between me and the sweet salvation of hot water. A long hot stream of it that's going to cover the tears I feel might actually come from feeling too fucking much tonight. Too much pain. Too much frustration on and off the field. Too tired to fight it.

"Ben, please. There's gotta be something I can do. You look awful." She looks me over and concern is etched all over her face.

"You seem pretty busy. You should stay out there with your friends." I press past her into the bathroom, but she follows me.

"Do you want me to run a bath? Or get ice? What can I do?"

"I just need to shower and get some quiet time post practice. I'll be fine." I try to keep my voice level, but I'm having a hard time and it comes out harsher than I mean it.

She wilts in response, stepping back out through the door frame.

"Okay," she says softly, her eyes going to the floor and then she disappears from sight.

I shut the door, turn on the hot water and then lean back against the counter. I'm so fucked over this it's hard to think straight. It's karma I guess for all the women who I've probably hurt over the years unintentionally, that the one I want is happy to just be fuck buddies and wants nothing else from me. To fuck me when it's convenient, and fuck someone else when I'm not around.

Then she has the audacity to try to take care of me when I'm hurt, help me with school, take me in, and do every kind thing imaginable when all I want is an excuse to dislike her. I'm clinging hard to the idea of her fucking this guy and having fucked Cameron too. Maybe if I hear her tonight it'll set me straight and remind me why I can't have her. Why I have to give her space and be happy with the parts of her she's willing to share. It was after all, better than the nothing I'd had for years, wasn't it?

I climb into the shower once the water finally heats and lean against the tile. The warm water is like a balm to every ache in my body, including the one in my chest. The second I close my eyes her face is there though, and I'm wondering if she's already undressing for him in her room.

WHEN I GET OUT OF THE SHOWER I TOWEL OFF AND WRAP it around my waist, opening the door and praying that whatever is happening is either over or quiet. I cross the hallway and notice that the lights are all off now in the main parts of the apartment and her door is shut as I open my own.

So I'm startled when I see that the small lamp is on, and Violet is asleep on my bed. Her eyes blink as I shut the door, and she sits up abruptly when she realizes I've come into the room.

"Sorry, I was just waiting for you, and I guess I was tired," she mumbles as she smooths her hair out. She's still wearing the clothes she had on earlier, the ones she'd come home in which leads me to think she didn't fuck the guy she brought back with her.

"Did I fuck up your plans by coming home?" I ask, turning my back to her as I go to my closet to pull some clothes out.

"What? No. I just wish you'd let me do something to help."

"I get banged up sometimes. I'm used to it. Just takes a couple days and I'll be fine." I answer her as I grab a pair of underwear and pants out of the closet.

"But I don't like it. Especially at practice." Her arms wrap around my waist from behind me, and she rests her head against my back.

"Violet..." I sigh.

"You were gone late. I assumed you were out with your friends."

"So you thought you could get him in and out before I got home?"

"No. He's a friend of Joss's."

"That's not what it looked like when I walked in."

"He was flirting with me. That's all."

I grunt. That much was fucking obvious.

"Ben, my own best friend flirts with you constantly."

I grunt again. She's not wrong.

"Joss is harmless. That guy wanted you naked and under him," I grump.

"That's too bad." She shrugs.

I turn to face her, and she lets her arms drop from me.

"Why's that?" I push some of the hair that's still disheveled from her nap out of her face, tucking it behind her ear.

"Because there's a much younger guy I'm fucking, and he keeps me way too busy to think about anyone else." She smiles, an almost giddy look on her face that twists my heart.

"That good, huh?" I can't help but smile back at her.

She nods.

"Please let me do something for you." She gives me a pleading look.

I should have the talk with her. The big confessional that Mac suggested. Confront the truth whichever way it falls, but right now I feel too raw to face the truth. I do, however, need the answer to one question which is haunting me.

"You can tell me something."

"What's that?"

"When Cameron was here... did you?" I don't fully speak the question, and I regret it almost as soon as I ask because if the answer isn't the one I want, it's going to be too much to hear tonight.

"No." She shakes her head.

"He didn't try anything?" I'm skeptical given his self-assured smug exit when he'd talked to me.

"He kissed me. He touched me... He tried. But I told him no."

I nod. I want more details. I want to know exactly how long he kissed her. Where he touched her. But I keep that to myself.

"What did he say to you, anyway?" She looks up at me. "He and Joss said you had a run in."

"Nothing worth repeating."

"He's jealous of you, you know. You have everything in

front of you. And he wishes he did. So whatever he said, it's bullshit. Okay?"

I nod, but I can't help it that some of the things he said are still rattling around in my skull. Replaying like a bad B movie on late night television. Because some of what he said about her, I'm not sure was completely wrong.

"Can I ask you a question?" She looks up at me with big eyes that look sad.

"Yes."

"The girl that spent the night?"

"Nothing happened. We watched a couple shows on TV. Talked. That was it."

"You didn't come home last night."

"Didn't want to be here if you and Cam were going to be here."

"I guess I would have done the same."

"Seemed like the smart thing at the time."

She nods for a second, a pensive look on her face before a smile returns.

"Now." Her hands go to my towel. "Is there anything I can do?"

She grins up at me, and I lean down and place a soft kiss on her lips. She returns it, her mouth opening for me, and I slide my tongue over hers. Just that little bit of contact has me going hard, and I reach to pull her closer but groan as my muscles fight the movement.

"Fuck. As much as I wish, I think I would just hurt worse by the end."

"Yeah, no way I'm letting that happen then." Her fingers tuck the edge of the towel back in that she'd started to pull on, and I feel a little drop in my stomach at the letdown even though I know it's for the best.

"I'll let you get some sleep then, okay?" She starts to walk away to go back to her room, but I grab her hand.

"Stay?" I ask.

"Okay." Her eyes rake over my chest. "But you're going to have to put more clothes on if you want me to keep my hands to myself."

I kiss her again.

"I can do that."

A few minutes later I try to remember I have everything I want in this moment with her curled up against me, breathing softly as she falls asleep. But I can't help feeling like a coward for not asking for more.

TWENTY-ONE

Violet

BEN HAS A PHENOMENAL GAME WITH THREE TOUCHDOWNS, and by the end of it the whole stadium is screaming his name. It feels surreal to know the boy who everyone here worships. After the game Joss and I wander down to meet him where he gets out, and he's busy with Colton and Jake talking to fans who have waited for them afterward. Another guy I don't recognize who's massive and looks like a football player himself is standing with them chatting. A gorgeous auburn-haired woman at his side lurches forward and wraps her arms around Ben's neck, pulling him into a hug that he reciprocates whole-heartedly, and a tiny flicker of jealousy rises in my chest.

"Wow. Your boy is a bona fide star," Joss whispers.

"Yeah. I feel like we should probably leave him to his post-game celebrations with his friends, but I'd feel like a jerk if we didn't at least say goodbye before we leave. You know?"

"Agreed."

We make our way through the small crowd, and I tap Ben on the back softly. He turns around and grins wide when he sees me, wrapping his hand around my forearm and dragging me close to him.

"You actually stayed the whole time?" Amusement and sheer unadulterated happiness have this guy's face lit up like fireworks. The return to football has made him so giddy, and I love it.

"Of course. But Joss and I are gonna head out now." I nod in her direction. "I just wanted to tell you, you looked fucking amazing out there and say bye before we go."

His smile falters and disappointment flashes over his features, "You're going home?"

"Yeah. I figure you have a lot to celebrate with your friends." I mentally tell myself not to look at all the women fawning over him, but I can't help it, and holy hell am I getting dagger eyes from most of them for being this close to him. The dark auburn-haired girl who had hugged him earlier though is positively grinning at me, and I am more than a little confused.

"Are you Violet?" she asks, her eyes flitting between me and Ben.

"Yes?" I answer, more confused than ever now.

"Mackenzie." She stretches out her hand to shake mine and points over her shoulder to the Viking of a man next to her. "And this is Waylon."

I shake her hand and nod at the guy behind her when he gives me a chin jerk. Then I look to Ben for clarification and he's shaking his head at Mackenzie while she grins like a Cheshire Cat.

"You're coming to dinner with us, right?" She looks to me hopefully.

"Um, I was actually about to go to dinner with my friend

166

Joss." I look back at Joss who is intently studying the entire scene playing out like it's a Broadway musical.

"She can come too. Do you want to come with us?" Mackenzie looks to Joss.

"You know, I think I do." A mischievous smirk flies over Joss's face before it disappears again.

"I am really confused right now," I say quietly and look up at Ben again for direction, and his eyes snap to mine.

"Just ignore them. If you want to go, you can. But you can come to dinner if you want, too."

"Do you want me to go?"

"Honestly, I have my concerns at this point." His eyes flick to Mackenzie and then back to me. "But yes. I want you to come and meet them. Waylon used to play with me, and she's his girlfriend. He plays for Seattle now, but they're in town for the night."

"It's really up to you, Ben. I don't want to be in the way."

And then as if on cue, an older woman pushes in, "Can we get a picture? My boys really want a picture with you." She shoves her kids in front of him, and I step to the side.

He entertains their request, but the way the woman gleefully wraps her arms around him for the photo I wonder how much her sons wanted the photo and how much she wanted it.

"Not used to that part yet, huh?" Mackenzie grins and raises a brow.

"What?" I ask cautiously, wondering if my face was that readable.

"Oh, the way every woman thinks that because your guy is on a team they cheer for that they own part of him. And they reallllyyy like to touch anything they can get away with." Mackenzie's lips purse as she glowers at the woman currently fawning over Ben.

"Oh, um. He's not my guy. We're just friends. But yeah, it

is crazy the way they take advantage." I nod, continuing to watch as another group of women, these ones younger than the last, comes forward to get a picture with all three of the guys.

"Waylon, you too!" One of the girls calls him over.

I look to Mac to see her reaction and she rolls her eyes, "That one is a pain in the ass, but mostly harmless."

Waylon looks to Mac and gives her a cheeky little grin before he joins the guys.

"Except in the way she is going to blow his ego sky high tonight, and I'll have to do extra work to bring it down."

I hear Joss's laughter behind me, and I turn around to see she's made her way over.

"I think I like her." Joss gives Mac the once over.

"Mackenzie."

"Joss."

They shake hands and smile, and I can't help but feel like some sort of pact has been made between the women. My eyes narrow at Joss, but she just grins in return.

A few more fans filter up to them and take pictures and then Ben joins us over at the side. He gives a wave to Colton and Jake.

"You coming to The Aspen later then?" Jake asks Ben.

"Yeah, I'll head that way after dinner."

"You too Waylon, if you have time?" Jake nods to him.

"We'll see." He glances down at Mackenzie and nods his goodbye.

Ben's hand comes to my waist, and he tugs me closer to him and a little sliver of anxiety runs up my spine as we have never been like this out in public before.

"So, you think you can brave it?" He looks at me, and as much as I want to run home and hide under the covers rather than try to hang out with the cool kids, I nod.

"I think you got three touchdowns on your first night back, so you get whatever you want."

"Whatever I want? I'm going to hold you to that." He grins wide and his dimples pop, and a warm feeling settles in my stomach.

———

DINNER ACTUALLY TURNS OUT TO BE A LOT OF FUN, particularly when Waylon and Mackenzie reveal that they got engaged earlier in the day, and the celebration champagne starts flowing at dinner. By the time we're getting to The Aspen to meet up with the rest of the team we are all feeling more than a little buzzed. And apparently the rest of the team has wasted no time in getting wasted themselves because the place is packed and rocking.

Jake is on top of a booth table when we walk in, immediately summoning Ben to his side. He looks back at me, making sure I'm good, and I nod and smile. Joss hooks her arm around mine as we follow Waylon and Mackenzie in.

"I don't know how long I'm going to survive a sports bar. Dinner was fun, but between the stadium and this I'm pushing my sportsball limits, you know. Not to mention being a fifth wheel."

"Anytime you want to go Joss just let me know. And you are never a fifth wheel. You are my ride or die date." I pull her closer to me. "I can go with you, if you want?"

"You can't leave the boy on the night of his big return celebration. You helped him get here too, remember."

"I don't think I get to take credit for any of this."

"You get to take a little credit. Besides I am pretty sure you're the trophy tonight anyway."

"What?"

"You're not that clueless, are you?" Joss looks at me a little concerned.

"I have no idea what you're talking about, so maybe."

"He reserved the tickets for you to come to the game. The dinner reservation was for four, and you all just snuck me in."

"He wanted me to go to his game. We're friends. His friends assumed he'd have a date."

"Mackenzie knew who you were."

"So?"

"So he talks about you, to them."

"Kind of hard not to. He lives with us."

"They didn't know who I was."

She has a point. And it lands like a giant rock thrown into a pool of water, rippling through me as I try to make sense of it.

"I'm sure it's nothing." I brush it off.

"If you say so," Joss gives me a once over.

We pull up to the bar beside Waylon and Mac, order our drinks, and watch from a distance as the guys cheer and yell over Ben's arrival, clearly discussing and drunkenly re-enacting some of the plays. Waylon gets his beer and wanders off to join them while Mac stays with us at the bar to observe the chaos from a safe distance.

"I'm going to need a lot more alcohol if I stay." Joss shakes her head, and I laugh as one of them nearly knocks over an entire drink.

"It helps quite a bit." Mackenzie gives a grim smile. "This was never my scene either. I tolerate it for Waylon's sake."

"Is the NFL better or worse?" Joss's curiosity gets the better of her.

"Both? Like, it's a bit classier than college football. But in the way that the cost of the drugs, booze and women goes up and doesn't necessarily become less toxic?"

Joss and I both grit our teeth and raise our brows.

"I don't mean Waylon. He's as loyal as they come but it's a hard transition for a lot of the guys. The money and the fame on top of everything, you know?"

We both nod, like we know when we absolutely do not know. Ben is as close as I've come to any athlete, and the jobs Joss and I look forward to in the nonprofit world pay pittance salaries that will have us struggling to make ends meet. We might be roomies forever.

"Did I just see you walk in with the football team?" A voice comes from behind me, and we turn around to see two of the guys from our grad program.

Joss turns around and hugs Milo, giving a little squeal of glee at his presence and his eyes widen at the sudden contact before he embraces her and gives me a mouthed "Hello" over her shoulder. Topher gives me a nod and then one to Joss.

"You did. A couple of them anyway." I answer him at last.

"They had a phenomenal game," Topher comments, looking me over with a questioning look on his face.

"Some guys from our art program," I explain quickly to Mackenzie, not bothering to introduce them as I assume they'll be gone shortly.

"Gotcha. I'll let you all chat. I'm gonna say hi to a couple of the guys really quick anyway." She jerks her head toward the football players, and I give her a smile and a nod.

Topher comes around and settles into the spot where Mac had been, ordering a drink while I listen to Milo and Joss chat about our photography professor.

"I didn't know you were into football."

"I like to watch on occasion, but mostly Ben is on the team, and I was there to support him."

"You know Ben Lawton?" Topher's eyebrow's raise.

"Uh, yeah. I know him." I give a small smile.

"Well fuck. Could you introduce me? My whole family are

big fans of Highland football, and he's one of the best players we've had lately. I mean Montgomery and Westfield were fucking aces, but with Colton, they're just all out ballers. And Ben is phenomenal. Hope the Rampage takes him in the draft." Topher leans toward me as he fawns over Ben, a half drunken smile on his lips.

"Sure, I can introduce you to Ben." I shrug, feeling awkward about Ben's fame.

"Are you talking about Ben?" Joss whips around at his name

"Yeah, she was just finally letting us in on the secret that she knows our future hall of famer."

"Oh, yes. Secrets. She definitely knows Ben Lawton." Joss gives a little knowing smile that widens as I stare at her, and I'm starting to think everyone else had twice as much champagne as I did at dinner.

I shoot her a cutting glance before I cover for her comment, and I can feel myself blushing as I try to explain. "Yes. He's living with us actually. Just for the semester. He's an old family friend, my best friend's brother actually."

"Violet, my MVP. I need to buy you a shot for getting our boy back on the field." Jake appears out of nowhere at my side and grabs me, giving me a rough hug and kissing the top of my head in his exuberance.

I squeak at the sudden appearance.

"And you are blushing. What's got you blushing, sweet cheeks? This guy here? Bro, this guy's got your girl blushing hard." Jake is so insanely loud in his drunkenness that I just want to die, and that doubles when I realize Ben is just behind him.

"Is she really?" He looks at me, a smirk on his face that turns harder as he looks between me and Topher.

"She was just telling me that you guys live together, and

you're old family friends." Topher looks at Ben like he's hung the fucking moon, and now I'm facing my own embarrassment *and* the secondhand kind, because the celebrity crush reaction for someone I know is so new to me.

"Is that right?" Ben's eyes shift from Topher to me. "Is that what we are?"

I don't know if it's just me or if the oxygen is being sucked out of the room, but somehow, I can't breathe. Between Ben and Joss, they are determined to spill everything out in the open tonight.

"Huge fan, man." Topher holds out his hand and Ben shakes it, only glancing at him briefly before his eyes return to me.

"What do you want to drink Ben?" Jake looks back at Ben.

"Hey, let me cover your drinks for that win, yeah?" Topher asks, doubling down on his fanboy moment.

"And that has you blushing?" One of Ben's eyebrows goes up, his smirk turning smug.

I give him a look, one that I hope reads as a desperate *cut me some slack, this is awkward all around.* But he either doesn't see or doesn't care because then he leans in. He's quieter than before, but still loud enough that Jake might be able to hear him since he's standing on that side, and he has to whisper loud enough to be heard over the music.

"And I embarrass you? Or do the things I do to you embarrass you, Violet?"

"You don't embarrass me, at all," I say tersely, giving him a meaningful look to knock it off.

"Prove it."

"What?"

"Prove. It."

"We're in public. Half your team is here."

He nods and pulls his lower lip up between his teeth as he

smiles, and his dimples pop. He looks so gorgeous, it physically hurts. He leans over me, towering over me really given that he's standing, and I'm sitting on the bar stool. His fingers thread through my hair and tilt my face up to his.

"Ben..." I whisper as his lips ghost over my own.

His eyes drift up from my lips to meet mine, dancing with mirth, and I could just tilt my head the slightest bit and have his lips pressed against mine. I want to, so badly.

But a low wolf whistle out of Jake breaks the spell, and I remember we're sitting in the middle of a football bar, just this side of campus. Half his team is here, and the whole bar is celebrating him tonight which means all eyes are on us. And that is bad enough but worse yet, anyone could take a picture. Post it to social media. His mother, his sister, and everyone else could see.

So instead I laugh, nervously, awkwardly.

"Very funny, Ben," I say and push my hands against his chest to put distance between us.

His eyes darken and his dimples fade, as he pulls away, but he gives a little smirk.

"Just testing to make sure you haven't fallen in love with me. I know that's a problem for some women who spend too much time around me." He winks, and then looks up at Jake like he didn't just say one of the most dickish things imaginable.

TWENTY-TWO

Ben

I take the shot and the beer Jake's holding out, grinning at him like nothing is wrong when inside I feel sick from Violet's rejection. I chug them both, chasing the shot with the beer he's handed me. He laughs and slaps me on the back.

"Guess we need another." Jake holds up a finger to the bartender who smiles at me.

"On the house tonight for you since you won us the game." She starts pouring another one and flashes me a smile.

Fairly fucking certain if I just publicly begged this woman to kiss me, she would have stripped down to do it if I asked nicely enough. I glance at Violet out of the corner of my eye. Her cheeks are still bright red, and presumably I've embarrassed her in front of her friends. Which is rich, really, given that the dude was sitting there tripping over himself to talk to me and buy me a beer.

Jealousy swarms in my gut, wondering if this was just her

worried about people seeing us together or if she might actually like this guy and not want him to know she has a friend with benefits on the side. One I can guaran-fucking-tee he would be jealous of, given his behavior so far.

I hate that she has this kind of spell over me. I hate that I care so much more than her. And most of all I hate the fact that I put myself in this position by pursuing her, seducing her, knowing full well that she had major reservations the entire time.

———

I HAVE NO IDEA EXACTLY HOW MUCH TIME HAS PASSED, but at this point the heady mix of our win, the touchdowns, and being back with my boys again on the field and off it, makes me almost numb enough to forget about Violet's dismissal for a few minutes. At least enough that one of my old hookups is sitting in my lap, laughing and running her fingers through my hair as she tells me some story about something that happened at the game. I have no idea what she's saying, but I know it feels good to have someone that isn't trying to keep me a dirty secret buried in the basement, or in this case, the next room.

"Benny Boy, I love ya man, but Mac and I need to start heading out. We've got an insanely early flight in the morning."

"Morning? I think you mean in like four hours," Mac butts in.

"Potato, Potatuh." Waylon waves his hand.

"Oh good lord. We're getting you like a gallon of water or they're not gonna let you on the flight." She shakes her head, and Waylon and I both laugh.

"It was so good to see you man," I say, realizing how much I've missed having my old friend around.

"You too. I'm serious. Come play for Seattle, yeah? It would be great to have you."

"I don't think I get much choice in the matter."

"Well, I'll do what I can, still a rookie but some folks listen to me." He smiles a lazy happy smile. Because, I remember, he's had the best day of his life. His girl wants to marry him, and they're planning the rest of it together.

"And congratulations, man. You're lucky as hell. Don't fuck it up yeah? And Mac, thank you on behalf of all men for taking this one off the market."

"Thanks, Ben." Mac gives me a smile. "Just a little friendly advice though?"

"Yeah?" I say half-heartedly. I can guess what kind of advice she wants to give, and I don't know that any advice can help me now.

"I would tell you to knock it off, but since I'm on your side, keep it up." Her eyes dart between me and the girl beside me. "It's working." Her eyes flick over her shoulder to where I assume Violet is still lurking somewhere. "Assuming your goal is getting her mad and jealous, that is."

"Oh yeah?" I ask, suddenly interested in the idea of a jealous Violet. I didn't realize that version existed. I'm surprised honestly that Violet's bothered to pay any attention to me at all. I'd done my best to forget she existed tonight, a losing battle since she's around every corner of my mind, but I assumed she would do the same to me after she refused to kiss me.

"Just, you know, a fine line?" Mac scrunches her nose at me, like what I'm doing is beneath me.

And it is. It's so far from something I'd ever do normally. But I guess I'd never been here before, so desperate for a girl's attention that I'd try almost anything.

"Casanova over here will figure it out, Mac Truck. Don't you worry." A drunk Waylon tries to reassure her.

"Sometimes even the smart ones need help," she counters.

I shake my head, laughing at both of them and then stand up to give them each a hug goodbye, gently depositing Mia off my lap and back in the booth before I do it.

"Love you guys."

"Love you man." Waylon hugs me and gives me a rough slap on the back.

"Love you, Ben. Be smart." Mac hugs me a little tighter than Waylon and they both set off.

As I turn around, Mia is already standing, her arms going to my shoulders and then her hands wrap around my neck pulling me to her. Her lips are on mine before I get a chance to say anything. I pull away as soon as I can, but still smile because I don't want to hurt her feelings. She had always been sweet to me, and I was the asshole for leading her on tonight.

"What's wrong?" She frowns despite the smile I give her.

"I uh... can't do that."

"You can't?"

"No, he can't because his mouth is about to have my boot in it." Joss's voice is so loud it echoes in my skull, and her eyes are threatening murder. And now I'm keenly aware this is not a side of Joss I ever wanted to see.

"Whooooaaaaa." Jake stands and Colton stands with him.

"Don't even think about trying to stop me. You'll both end up the same way and that would be bad for the team. I don't know a lot about football but the three of you seem pretty key to its functioning." She points at them without taking her eyes off me.

"Any particular reason you're threatening my wide receiver?" Colton asks calmly, holding out his hands like he's trying to calm a spooked horse.

"He knows what he's doing."

"Drinking with his friends?"

"I don't know. Is that how you drink with your friends,

Ben?" Her tone says she is not amused.

I give her a look, begging her silently for some mercy.

"You staying at her house tonight? Because you're not bringing her home. Not if you want your balls attached in the morning."

"Joss, dearest. Please, let's go." Violet has suddenly appeared next to her, trying to coax her away.

"No, I'm working right now."

Despite the fact that I do actually fear physical harm from Joss, my gaze still goes to Violet. Trying to search her face but she's pretending I don't exist. Her hands wrapped around her friend's arm, trying to talk quietly to her.

"Seems like your friend wants to take you home. Maybe that's a good idea. No need to be this excited." Colton suggests to Joss, and I could have told him that was a big fucking mistake, but I have no way to warn him right now.

Joss's head snaps over to him. "You don't think so? Maybe you should come home with me. I can whip you into shape. That would be exciting, wouldn't it?"

The whole table erupts into whistles and oohs, and I can't help but laugh. He walked straight into that one. But then I remember myself again, my mind going back to Violet whose eyes are on me, clearly displeased.

"Is this funny to you?" she snaps at me from behind Joss's back.

"No."

"Then you could help instead of egging her on? I'm the one trying to keep her from inserting her heel into your eyeball, you know."

"I can take it."

"I'm sure you can." Violet's eyes dart over to where Mia had been standing and back to me, hurt crossing over her features before it's replaced again with disdain.

I feel the hot zing of irritation as she does it. Like she gets to be hurt over this when she had been hanging out with other guys tonight. And there'd been more just a few nights ago. Cameron before that.

"Can we talk?" I ask tersely.

Her eyes flick over me.

"I just need to get Joss out of here." She ignores the request.

The two guys they'd been with all night were sauntering up behind them, and the last thing I needed was for any of the guys to get into it with a couple of grad students.

"Joss?" I call her name softly and she looks at me.

"Yes?" Her eyes narrow, her brow creases.

"Why don't you ask if your friend can get you some water and have a glass before you leave? And I'm gonna talk to Violet, okay?"

"We're not talking," Violet says sharply.

"You are talking." Joss looks down at her, her brows raising in a threat, and she is clearly pissed at both of us tonight, but just more willing to hurt me, apparently.

Violet shuts her mouth, her jaw clenching as she stares off into the distance.

"Let's just talk for a few minutes and put this whole fire out, okay?" I ask quietly.

"I'm not doing it out here in front of everyone."

"Follow me."

This bar is a team favorite, and I know there's a back hallway that's usually pretty empty. She trails behind me, clearly annoyed at the entire scene that's played out, and she won't even look at me as we step into the quiet little alcove off the hallway.

"You *would* know this was here," she spits out, crossing her arms over her chest.

"I'm sorry, are you implying something? Because you didn't

complain about my experience before. In fact, I remember you getting pretty pissed at your ex over it."

She at least has the decency to look embarrassed for herself for half a second.

"I don't care what you do. Just don't bring her back to the apartment."

"Why not? You and me, we're just friends, remember? Why would you care? Or at least that's what you wanted him to believe."

"Topher? Are you serious right now?"

"Whatever the fanboy's name is."

"Yeah, Ben. Fanboy. *Yours.* He was hitting on you, not me. Good lord, you're dense."

"What?"

"He's gay, Ben and a huge fan of yours in general. It's all he's talked about. I assume he was hoping you were interested. I don't know. But he was definitely hitting on you. Not me. You notice he was offering to buy *you* drinks?"

"Oh."

"Yeah. *Oh.*"

"Still doesn't change the fact that you literally pushed me away tonight when I tried to kiss you."

"You know why."

"Because you're embarrassed of me?"

"I'm not embarrassed of you, Ben. I'm worried about people thinking I'm an asshole for taking advantage of a kid living in my house when he's trying to get his act together. Particularly your sister who I love *like* a sister."

"I'm not a kid, Violet. And I don't care what they think. Nora will get over it. So will mom. Fuck, if you really thought it through, mom would probably love it."

"Love the idea of me fucking her baby boy? I doubt it."

"We don't have to tell them you use me like your own

personal fucking sex toy."

There's a little gasp from her at the accusation, and I smirk.

"I do not do that." She glowers at me through the dim light.

"No? You sneak in and out of my room in the middle of the night. Only touch me when no one's around to see it, and otherwise act like you barely know I exist? Sounds like it to me."

"You started this by sneaking into my room, if you remember."

"I told you. I knocked. I can't help it you were too heated to notice."

"If it's all so distasteful to you then why do you keep doing it?"

"I never said it was distasteful. I love watching you and you can use me any time you want. I'm just saying you should be honest with yourself about it."

"If you think I'm using you, then we should stop while we're ahead."

"Why?"

"Because you feel like you're being used. I don't want that."

"There's an alternative you know, to using someone or stopping."

"What?"

"Giving me some of what I want when I ask for it."

"What do you want?"

"More of you."

"Like what?"

"Kiss me in fucking public for starters."

She closes the gap between us and grabs me by the shirt, pulling me to her and kisses me roughly. The way her lips move across mine I can feel the frustration radiating out from her. The glare from earlier softens though as she pulls away.

"Better?"

"If you'd done that out there, maybe, yeah."

"Noted. What else?"

"Wear my jersey when you come to my games, not just when you fuck me."

"That is such an antiquated—" she starts to protest but I cut her off.

"Maybe, but I want everyone to know you're mine. I want to look up and see you in it and remember what you look like in my bed with it on. I want you to wear it and remember what I feel like when I'm inside you... How many times you call my name."

"Stop making it sound hot." She furrows her brow, and I smirk.

I lean down and slide my fingers up the back of her neck, brushing my lips over hers and she melts into me, opening for me and letting my tongue slide across hers. I can feel her fingers creeping up under my shirt, exploring my skin.

She pulls back from our kiss after a long minute and looks up at me. "I'm sorry. I didn't think about it that way."

"It's okay." I shake my head and the way she's looking at me makes my heart and my ego swell. I'm tempted to confess everything to her. To ask for what I really want, but then she blinks like she's coming out of a trance.

"I should um, go check on Joss. Make sure she hasn't stiletto-ed Colton or Jake and get her home safe."

"Okay." I nod, still too deep in my feelings to say anything more.

"Have fun, but don't get too wild, okay?" She gives me a half smile.

I nod, biting my tongue to keep myself from blurting out more.

"See you tomorrow." She dots a kiss on my cheek and then hurries off toward the crowd again.

And it takes all I have not to chase after her.

TWENTY-THREE

Violet

THE SECOND I GET IN THE CAR WITH JOSS AND THE DRIVER takes off, I regret not asking Ben to come home with me. I know it was the right decision because he needs time with his friends and in a few weeks, I am going to have to let him go period. But the idea of him there with her, the bartender, and the dozen other women who would love to get him to go home with him tonight has me twisted in knots. And the growing jealousy I have over him makes me nervous, like maybe there's more to our friends with benefits situation than I want to admit to him or myself.

"Yes, it was stupid to leave him there like that," Joss mutters as she lays her head against my shoulder, closing her eyes.

"Thank you. That's definitely what I needed to hear right now."

"I tried to help."

"I'm not sure bodily harm would have helped."

"Depending on the guy and how it's applied..." She wraps her arm around mine and repositions me to be a better pillow.

I shake my head, laughing a little. At least it was a little levity when I need it. A flash of him kissing the woman he was with comes unwanted into my mind and I frown, staring out the window as the streets pass by.

"Text him that you're gonna sleep in his bed. Naked," she mumbles.

"What?" I raise my brow at her, not that she can see it since she's half asleep.

"It's what I would do," she says, her voice fading as sleep starts to take her.

I stare down at my phone in my hand and glance back at a sleepy Joss. She was generally right when it came to Ben. And I was generally too timid when it came to men in general, and Ben in particular. He'd said he wanted more.

So I unlock my phone and bring up the text box, typing slowly with one hand since Joss was using my left arm as a pillow.

> Since you're gone tonight, care if I sleep in your bed?

I click send and then hold my breath, my leg nervously bouncing against the floorboards of the car. I look down at Joss, worried I might be waking her up with my anxiousness, but she's still dead to the world.

> BEN
> Why?

Why? Because I'm obsessed with you, and I don't want you sleeping with anyone else. I can't say that though, right? Ugh. What would Joss say in this situation? I wish she was still awake to tell me, but she's sleeping too peacefully for me to want to wake her.

> Why not?

It's a terrible answer, and I'm terrible at this whole flirting thing. I'm out of practice from being with Cam too long.

BEN
Is there something wrong with yours?

> Your sheets feel better against my bare skin?
> And the light's a little better for the reading I
> want to do before bed

I hit send before I can rethink it, and then scrunch my eyes closed while I wait what feels like an interminably long time for a response.

BEN
Christ Violet

> Is that a no?

The car pulls up in front of our apartment and I pay the driver and gently shake Joss awake. She wipes a little drool off the side of her mouth and sits up.

"We're home."

"Yay! Bed," she mumbles, and I help her out of the car and hook my arm around hers to help support her as we walk.

I get her inside and tucked into bed before I have a chance to look at my phone again.

BEN
No

I mean, yes you can

But very unfair since I'm not there

I smile, and suddenly I have an even better idea. One I'm hoping will erase the little fight we had tonight.

I hurry to my room, stripping out of the clothes I wore and throwing on an oversized T-shirt. I grab the mafia book I'd been reading the first night he walked in on me and make my way into his room, flicking on the desk lamp so it's light enough that I can see.

I strip down completely and climb into his bed, arranging the sheets around me strategically and then press the open book over my lower face, hiding everything but my eyes and snap a picture.

Thanks. You're the best

I send the photo and then toss the phone to the side like it's molten lava before I fall back against his pillows. I am playing with so much fire here, and I know the way my heart is fluttering waiting for his response that I'm already in too deep with him to get out unscathed.

The phone buzzes again and I stare at it for a minute before I open the screen to read.

BEN

Holy fuck. A warning next time?

Jake definitely just saw that

Did he like it? Since you're busy tonight... If he's not...

I bite my lip and hit send, a little nervous how he'll respond to me teasing him like that. But the response is immediate.

> **BEN**
> Over my dead fucking body

> I mean it feels good without you here, but it's not the same. You know?

> Now I know you're trying to kill me

> Does that mean Jake is coming then or?

A little swearing emoji pops up on the screen and I grin.

> **BEN**
> I'm coming, and you better not until I get there

> If that's what you want...

THIRTY EXCRUCIATING MINUTES LATER I HEAR HIM COME through the front door, and the rustling sounds of him losing his shoes and coat before he makes his way to the room. When he opens the door, he almost looks surprised to see me there. He walks over and sits on the side of the bed without saying a word, tugging at the sheet and I let go of it so he can pull it back.

His eyes light up when he finds me naked underneath. "I honestly thought you were fucking with me."

I slide my hand over his thigh, smirking. "And how would you like to be fucked with? You want me here or on my knees?"

"Violet." The raw tone of voice he uses when he says my name and the way his throat bobs, has me moving toward him.

I grab the edge of his shirt and look up at him for permission. He stares at me, his eyes burning with an intensity that almost makes me shrink a little. I release it and pull my hand back.

"What's wrong?" I ask softly, puzzling over what has him on edge.

"Did you touch yourself before I got here?" His hand creeps up my thigh.

"Maybe." I give him a sly little grin.

"Maybe?" he asks, his eyes holding mine.

I shrug.

"Thinking about some mafia guy railing you against a wall again?" His hand slides between my legs, cupping me before he dips a finger between, and I let out a little whimper

"Thinking about you."

"I get you this wet?"

"Always."

"Fuck me, Violet." He strokes me softly, and I close my eyes. "Did you come yet?"

"No. I wanted you."

"Me or someone?"

"You, Ben." I open my eyes to see him studying me, a serious look on his face. "What's wrong?"

"I know you were teasing, but I don't like thinking of you with anyone else."

"I don't either," I confess.

A little smirk breaks on his face.

"That the reason you're naked in my bed?"

"Maybe."

"You realize that might be counterproductive if this is the reward I get?"

"I wasn't really thinking everything through." I shrug before his thumb brushes over my clit again, and I moan at the little burst of sensation.

"Obviously." He smirks and he strokes me more deliberately.

"I did have time to think about some things though."

"Yeah?"

"I'll do what you want. The PDA. The jersey stuff. But I want something too."

"What's that? To come? Because if you think I'm not gonna torment you a little after your joke about Jake..." He grins, and I roll my eyes in response before I return the smile.

Then I take a deep breath, because I'm likely about to make this uncomfortable.

"I don't want you kissing anyone else. Or fucking them, for that matter. I want you to myself. I'm not saying we have to label it or anything, and I know that's a big ask, but— "

He cuts me off before I can say more, pressing me back against the pillows and kissing me. It's rough, claiming, like he's making a point of proving that I need him. I spread my legs and he slides between them, the rough fabric of his jeans sliding over my inner thighs and the softness of the cotton T-shirt he's wearing brushing over my nipples.

I pull back and look at him, "That's not actually an answer, you know."

"Not exactly fair to ask me when you're naked and wet in my bed, you know."

"Are you accusing me of coercion?"

"Maybe."

"Is it working?"

"Yes."

"Seeing you flirt with her tonight... kiss her..." I trail off.

"Made you jealous?"

"Yes."

"How do you think I feel when I see you with Cam and these other guys?"

"It's not the same. You know you're better than all of them. Meanwhile, you have insanely gorgeous women throwing themselves at you all the time. It's unfair."

"You're right. It's worse. Because not only are you fucking gorgeous, but you are it for me, Violet. I'm not exaggerating when I say you were and are in all my fantasies. The way you look, the sound of your voice, the little faces you make, fuck... the way you taste... and none of them can even touch the way you make me feel." He leans down and kisses me briefly before looking at me again.

I can't answer. I don't even know how to respond to that. My fingers just go to his pants, undoing his belt and the button and zipper as he raises his hips to give me access, kissing down my throat as I work him out of them. I run my hand over him, already hard and hot and then rock my hips up to meet him. The head of his cock slides over my clit and he lets out a muted grunt, his head bowing to meet my shoulder.

I rock up again, and he slides lower grazing every nerve ending I have on the way until his tip nudges my opening and we both stutter at the contact. My hands run up his back and I run my nails back down it through the fabric of his cotton T-shirt and he bucks forward, just enough that he almost presses inside me before he freezes.

"Fuck. Fuck. Fuck..." he groans, burying his face in my chest. "Don't fucking tease me like that, Violet. I am too fucking weak right now."

"Like what?" I rock my hips down and he slides over me again. I let out a small gasp, grabbing the sheets in my hand because I'm torturing myself as much as him.

"Like that." He lifts his head, his eyes blazing as he glares at me, and his arms go to my shoulders to help hold me still.

"What if I want you like this?" I whisper.

His eyes shutter, and his lids lower, he leans down and grabs my lower lip between his teeth as he hovers over me. He kisses me again, buying time like he's contemplating my question.

"We shouldn't. And fuck knows right now I won't last even with a condom on."

"Okay," I answer. I desperately want him inside me, raw and unfiltered. But I'm not about to push him for it.

He groans, frustrated, and pulls away from me to tear the rest of his clothes off and throws them to the floor before he gets back on the bed. He grabs me, flipping me over and pulling me up, my back against his chest and me on my knees in one smooth motion before I can even register it happening. He slides his palm up over my hip, around and down between my legs, his fingers massaging my clit as I spread my thighs as far as I can trying to get more friction. I bend from the low pool of pleasure and his hand wraps around the end of my hair, pulling my head back and exposing my neck. I buck back in response, and I'm so wet and slick that he slides between, his cock nestled against me again.

He groans against my neck before his teeth graze the tender flesh there, and I arch my back into him and moan as he slides a finger inside me.

"Fuck. You had to offer that and now it's all I can think about. Feeling your tight little pussy clench down on me with nothing in between. I could fuck you so good that way if you let me."

He slides another finger inside me, roughly stroking me and using his palm to give my clit friction. I roll my hips and he groans, burying his face in my back. He withdraws his fingers, his hands settle on my hips instead as he tentatively presses forward, his cock lining up and teasing me.

"Tell me to fucking stop, Violet. Please."

"I can't do that, but I'm on the pill, and got tested after the engagement was off. I haven't been with anyone else."

"Fuck. Me too. I haven't ever fucked anyone without a condom."

"Me either," I whisper. I'd never truly trusted Cam, but somehow, I know I can trust everything when it comes to Ben.

"If we do this, I'm not kidding when I say it's going to be embarrassingly short." He presses a kiss to my shoulder.

"I don't care, Ben. I need it. I need you."

Another string of curses comes from his mouth as I bend forward, leaning down onto my elbows, and he wraps his arms around my hips and pelvis, pulling me against him. His fingers return to massaging my clit as he lines himself up against me again, hesitating for another second before he pushes inside me.

"Fuck. My god." He stills immediately, and I smile at the choked sounds he makes as he tries to regain his composure.

He takes another breath, and his fingers tease my clit again, making me buck back and he chokes on another swallow of air.

"Fuck me." I plead, and the request is heard because he starts to move. Two slow tentative strokes and then he picks up his pace. His breathing is heavy as he leans over me, and I can feel him tense against me.

"Touch yourself for me." It's a rough command as he grabs my hips, and I do as I'm asked. Because he can have anything he wants.

He thrusts into me harder, and the combination of sensations has me seeing fucking stars as I say his name.

"Violet, fuck..." He breathes as he shudders through his own climax. He pulls me up against him again, his mouth against my shoulder, his lips kissing a trail down my shoulder blade.

He slides out of me, and I collapse into a heap against the sheets. He's down next to me a second later, wrapping his arm around me and pulling me close to him. I watch as his chest rises and falls, still heavy with a sheen of sweat and exhaustion.

"I'm sorry... that was..." His brow furrows as he tries to catch his breath.

"Hot as hell?" I grin.

"I was thinking sloppy and not very considerate, but in my defense your body is too fucking perfect. Like next level leave-my-body-as-I'm-coming perfect."

"Uh, well whatever version that was of you... holy fuck. He's hot. And he can fuck me raw and sloppy anytime." I grin and press a kiss to his ribs.

"Fuck." He drags a hand over his face. "We should have talked about that more before we... But like I said, I get tested regularly and that was a first for me."

"Same. I wanted it, but if you regret it, I'm sorry for—"

"No. Fuck no. I get to be one of Violet Kennedy's firsts? I don't regret that for a fucking second. I might get it engraved somewhere though."

We both laugh until it gets quiet.

"I'm gonna get a quick shower but then is it okay if I stay?" I ask quietly.

"Yes, but only if you stay naked and curled up next to me." He grins.

"Deal," I agree.

TWENTY-FOUR

Ben

When I hit the field for warmups, Colton looks out of sorts. Like he can barely concentrate, and thinly veiled anger is dancing over his features.

"Everything okay?" I ask. I feel like an ass because I'm so high on how well everything is going in my life; I can barely keep from smiling.

"Nah. I'm fucking over it."

"Over what?"

"Everything at this point. Football. School. Women."

I frown. Colton had a long-term girlfriend back at his old school who from all appearances on social media worshipped the ground he walked on. He'd gone from a bench position on his last team to starting quarterback here, so the move made sense for him, but it couldn't be easy.

"You're killing it here, so what am I missing?"

"She cheated on me."

"What?" I'm shocked to hear it given everything I know, and the fact that Colton seems devoted to her.

"My girlfriend. She doesn't even know I know yet. I don't even know how to have the conversation. I feel sick man. We've been together since high school."

"Are you sure? I mean people can say anything..."

"There's a photo, and a video. Someone took it at a party."

"Again, it could be— "

"She did it. I know in my gut. She's been off lately and I knew something wasn't right. Seeing it just confirmed it." He cuts me off.

"Fuck, I'm sorry man."

"If I hadn't come here for school, to play ball. It wouldn't have happened."

I need to tread carefully here, because the wrong thing could hurt him worse, or damage our relationship, and so far, our chemistry on the field was putting this team back in the rankings.

"Listen. It's rough as fuck, but don't jump to conclusions like that yet. Okay? Let it play out. Talk to her. Take a step back and think things through."

"I'm not leaving if that's what you're worried about. It's just now I have to play ball for the rest of my life knowing I gave her up to do it."

"You don't know that yet."

"Don't I? Even if she's sorry, it's not like I can trust her anymore. Especially not when she's there and I'm here. Besides, why the fuck am I staying celibate for her while she's out there getting laid?"

I don't have a good answer for him, so I just nod silently. I can't imagine having to choose between the girl I love and football. It would be impossible. And then my heart falters in my chest.

I love her. It's the reason I'm so goddamn happy right now. The reason fucking her last night had felt so unreal. The reason I'd felt like I'd been swallowed up and drowning in fucking joy when she'd asked if we could be exclusive. I was in love with Violet, and she'd given me hope.

I blink to see Colton giving me a strange look.

"Sorry. Just having my own realization." I shake my head.

"Hopefully it's a better one than me."

"It's either really great or really awful. Definitely one of those."

He shakes his head and gives a small laugh.

"I'm really sorry though. Let me know what I can do, okay? If you need to get a beer or something."

He nods. I love Colton and Jake and the rest of the guys. What we'd built in a few months together had been phenomenal, but days like today I missed Waylon, Liam, and East. Being the man left behind when they all went off last year felt like I still had time to spare, but now I'd kill to have them to talk to about all this shit.

———

When I get home that Monday night after practice Violet is curled up on the couch flipping through channels and looking anxious as her eyes dart up to meet mine.

"What's wrong?" I toss my bag down and come sit next to her.

"Nothing's wrong."

"You look like you're going to explode from anxiety."

"This week is Thanksgiving."

"Right."

"But you've got the big game on Saturday."

"Right. I know. It sucks. I can't go home, but if you want

197

to... are you? I don't mind if you miss the game if that's what you're worried about."

"No. That's not it. Well it's sort of it... Ugh. I'm not supposed to tell you."

"Tell me what."

"It's supposed to be a surprise, and I don't want to ruin it for you."

"A good surprise?"

"Maybe?"

"Okay. Just out with it."

"They'll be mad."

"Do you want me to tickle you first? I can tell them I tickled it out of you, and it couldn't be helped. Or I can fuck you and then we can say—"

She puts a hand over my mouth. "Don't. You'll get me all distracted and this is serious!"

"Okay, then just tell me, Vi."

"They're all coming out here for Thanksgiving a day early so we can eat together before you have to be back. Renting a cabin that we're all going to stay in."

"Who is they?"

"Your mom, Nora, her boyfriend. My parents." She winces as she mentions her parents.

They're generally speaking good people, but her mom can be overbearing and her dad's only love in life is football. Which means I will be on the hook to listen to a whole lot of football stats and predictions while I eat my turkey and gravy. A sacrifice worth making if I get Violet at my side.

"Okay. And despite the usual reasons why family is sometimes rough, why are we freaking out?"

"I'm supposed to take you up there. Meaning we will both be there."

"And?"

"They're gonna know."

"They're not going to know, Violet."

"They are. Joss says I have an aura now. Like a dickmatized aura and that it is insanely obvious to everyone that we are fucking."

"I mean on one hand, good. Maybe all the guys she brings around will stay away from you." I try to keep it light, but she just shoots me a look. "But I don't think our parents are looking for a dickmatized aura."

"I'm not worried about our parents. Oh fuck, yes, I am. Oh god, your mom is going to hate me. I've tarnished her perfect golden boy!" She's being performatively dramatic, but I can tell she's worried underneath it all.

"Violet, at the risk of sounding like an asshole, I think you're overreacting. And my mom knows I was tarnished a long time ago."

"Fine. Your mom isn't the real problem though. Nora is. If Joss knows, Nora will absolutely know. Nora knows everything before I tell her."

"So counterpoint... or idea I guess?" I lift my eyes to hers, so I can read her reaction to the suggestion I think she might not love.

"What?"

"What if we just tell them?"

"Tell them? Tell them what?"

"About us. Just be honest."

"What are we going to tell them Ben? That we're fucking exclusively?"

"I was going to say we could tell them we're together, or that we're dating. That would probably be easier for them to swallow than the whole fucking part. I mean they'll likely assume given that we're both adults, but..." I smile at her, but she doesn't look amused.

"Nora is going to hate me."

"She is not going to hate you. She's just going to need a minute to adjust to the idea."

"And if she can't adjust?"

"We'll worry about that when we get there."

I hold my hand out next to her on the couch and she threads her fingers through mine.

"I'm still scared."

"Yeah, well luckily you've got the brother and the son on your side." I wink at her, and she grins.

"Yes, lucky me." She leans over and kisses me, and I grab her and pull her into my lap.

"Did you eat yet?"

"Some crackers and some yogurt."

"That is not dinner. I'm gonna fix a salad, you want one?"

"Like with the croutons and the avocado? The fancy dressing and all that?" A little look of excitement crosses her face.

I nod.

"Yes." She grins.

"All right. Just give me a couple minutes." I kiss her one last time and then head for the kitchen after she slides back off my lap.

"You can't tell my mom that though. That you cook for me and Joss. She will die."

"I mean, I have to pay my rent somehow. Isn't that reasonable?"

"Not according to her."

"Oh, what if we tell her that's why we're fucking? I couldn't afford the rent and you told me I had to find a way." I grin.

"You wouldn't dare."

"I might." I wiggle my eyebrows at her.

"Then your mom would kill me, and she's my favorite mom, so I would like to continue to be her favorite daughter."

"You don't think that's Nora?"

"With all the times Nora snuck out of the house, and the time she found the cigarettes hidden in her closet?"

"I think the guy hidden in the closet was the bigger deal breaker for which one was her favorite daughter."

"Oh, yeah, true. I almost forgot about that one. She was grounded through prom for that."

"She was lucky it wasn't forever since my mom also found condom wrappers under the bed."

"See, you're just making me more nervous."

"It'll be fine, Violet. I promise." Hoping they aren't going to be famous last words.

TWENTY-FIVE

Violet

I meet Ben on campus after his last class. His car is already packed with our bags for the overnight stay, and we just need to get going on the road so we can get out to the cabin before it's too dark. His eyes dance with amusement as he walks across the quad toward me, and I give him a puzzled look.

"What?" I ask, standing as he finally reaches me.

He slides his hand over mine, lacing our fingers, and he leans down to kiss me, softly and tentatively at first and then sliding his tongue along my lower lip until I open for him, and he dips inside my mouth. I forget for half a minute where we are and start to lean into him, until he breaks the kiss and grins down at me.

"Was just thinking how I was going to do that and then make you hold my hand all the way across campus." He turns me and our hands so that his palm is against mine and tightens his grip.

"I see," I say it like I'm annoyed, but in reality, I can't help the little smile that comes to my lips.

We pile into the car and make the drive up to the cabin, pausing in the driveway as we stare up at it and the surrounding valley. Less of a cabin and more of a lodge, it's intimidating in its size and the way the valley unfurls around it. It looks like something out of a picture book. It's gorgeous, and the air is crisp with a fresh layer of snow on the ground.

When we get to the door, my mom answers and envelopes both of us in a giant hug. Her signature jasmine perfume wafting around me.

"Hi mom," I say smiling at her as she yells for my dad and for Ben's mom to come see us.

"Hi sweetheart!" She smiles brightly. "Oh you changed your hair again. I like the color. And Ben. My god, every time I see you, I feel like you've grown a few more inches."

I give him a surreptitious little grin because I'm just waiting for her to scruff his head like he's five, but he grins in response. Just playing along like a dutiful boyfriend. My heart stutters at the thought of him being my boyfriend, at what that might actually mean for us, for me. I stare at him for a long second before I hear a whir of happiness and excitement barreling toward me.

"Oh my god. Violet! Look at you! I've missed you so much!" Mama Beth wraps me in a tight hug.

"Look at you! You look amazing." I smile back at her.

"Yeah. I've been trying a new lifestyle out and doing some dating. I've decided 49 is the new 29."

"Dating? How's that going?" I smile. Nora and Ben's dad was an epic asshole and he's been out of their lives for a long time.

203

Their mom had mostly gone it alone, with a few short-lived boyfriends along the way who were lucky if they even got to see, let alone meet Nora and Ben. She was protective of their little family unit, and I didn't blame her. Despite everything Nora and Ben had turned out to be fantastic, and a lot of it was thanks to her.

"It's a jungle out there, to be honest. But I figure with Nora and Ben gone now I can live a little bit."

"As long as I don't have to hear about the living." Ben cuts her a worried look.

"I won't share details. It's a family weekend. Give me some credit!" she says loudly as he brings our luggage in, but then she pulls me aside with a sly little grin. "We definitely have to talk some details over wine."

I grin and nod at her, noticing that my dad has finally made his way downstairs.

"Well look at that, you decided to join us after all." He always gives me a hard time, but the grin goes all the way to his eyes, the fine lines around them wrinkling under his glasses as he smiles at me.

"I did. Ben and I came up together. He had class, and I had office hours today, so we had to leave after that."

"Well we've got some pizza and wings ready. Some beer in the fridge. Don't eat too much though. Your mothers have a huge feast planned. The amount of food we lugged up here could feed an army." He shakes his head and pulls me into a bear hug before he turns to Ben.

He holds his hand out and they shake. "I hear you got yourself into a bit of trouble."

"Unfortunately." Ben scrubs a hand behind his head. "But I'm working on the remedy. I'm off the bench now."

"We all have to have a little fun sometimes." My dad shrugs it off. "But I did miss seeing you on the field."

"Hopefully that won't be happening again." Ben gives him a look.

"Violet!!" Nora yells my name from the upstairs railing and then comes flying down the steps.

"Nora!!" I yell back and she jumps at me, wrapping her arms around me and we spin for a moment.

"I'm so glad you're here. We have so much to catch up on! Come with me!" She wraps her hand around mine and drags me out from the room, already talking a mile a minute about the latest developments. I glance back over my shoulder at Ben and he just smiles up at me, winking as we hit the doorway.

———

The rest of the evening is relatively quiet with us all just getting settled in and catching up. Nora telling me about her new job, introducing me to her boyfriend, Eric, who has been brave enough to join us for the holiday, and the new apartment they're renting. Before long though, I'm crashing from the long week, and I excuse myself after numerous more hugs and chatter to escape to my room. When I'm back in my room after a shower, a text pops up on my phone.

BEN

This bed is not comfortable

Mine's not terrible. And the view from the room is amazing

I bet it is

I stare at my phone for a second, trying to think of something clever to say in return. I hadn't actually gone to bed yet, but I had tried it earlier when I'd pretended I might be able to sneak a nap in before dinner. I should be in bed, but instead I'm standing near the window, staring out at the wide expanse of Colorado wilderness where the reflection of the moon off the snow keeps the valley beyond the cabin illuminated, and the trees shimmer with an iridescent light that looks otherworldly. I love it up here but so rarely get to visit with all the demands of my program.

I'm lost in my thoughts when I feel the hairs go up on the back of my neck. A second later, I feel a body pressed against me and a hand goes over my mouth. I gasp despite it and turn abruptly to face the intruder when I recognize Ben in the dim light. I punch him softly in the arm as he relaxes his grip on my side and drops his hand from my mouth.

"Sorry, just didn't want you to scream."

"You scared me. I didn't hear the door."

"Good. Hopefully no one else heard."

"Great to know anyone can sneak in my room. But you shouldn't be up here." I chastise him.

"Couldn't sleep. And then you had to mention the view." His hand slides down my hip.

"I meant this one. Isn't it beautiful?" I turn around and pull on his arm to bring him over to the window.

"Yeah. It is." His arm wraps around my middle, and his lips brush over the side of my neck. He's barely even bothered to glance out the window.

"Ben..." It's half warning and half sigh, and my voice sounds breathy even to my own ears.

He pulls me tight against his body, and his chin rests against my shoulder as he finally looks out at what I'm trying to show him.

"I'm looking. I'm looking. It's just hard to care about that view when I have this one."

His fingers slide under the hem of my oversized T-shirt,

softly brushing over my stomach, and teasing against the band of my panties.

"I want you," he whispers against the side of my temple, before he presses a kiss there.

"Someone could hear us."

"Then I guess you'd better stay quiet."

"That's easier said than done when you're touching me."

"Fuck, see you say things like that, and I can't help myself." His lips brush against the shell of my ear, and his breath against my neck has me arching into him.

His hand slides down between my thighs, and he strokes me through my panties, making me spread my legs further. I lean back against his chest and kiss his neck.

"I want to taste you, here. Feel you come on my tongue."

"Ben, fuck, you cannot say things like that..."

"Will you let me?"

"There's no way I keep quiet through that."

"So you won't let me..." He nips at my earlobe and cups me through the cotton, bringing me flush against him, and I can feel him pressing hard against me.

"I don't know," I whisper through the darkness.

Except I do know already. I will give him anything he wants, and this isn't exactly a hard ask. Other than the fact that being silent while he puts his mouth on me is going to be nearly impossible.

"Or I could just go back to my room." He lets me go abruptly to prove his point, grinning as he does it. I'm caught off balance by the loss of him and stumble forward, catching myself on the desk in front of the window.

"Don't," I say finally, giving in as he pretends to walk away.

I can see the little look of self-assurance on his face through the dull light and where with most men it would irritate me that they know they have this kind of hold over me, that they were smug about it, with Ben, it makes my stomach flutter. He closes the gap between us again, and roughly tugs my panties off, letting me step out of them before tossing them back toward the bed and then lifting me up on the desk.

He slides the chair in between my legs and sits down, spreading them wide to accommodate his shoulders as he bends down to kiss my inner thigh. I immediately inhale on the brush of his lips against the sensitive and tender skin, pulling back slightly, and I'm thankful that the desk doesn't bounce against the wall with the motion. If I can keep my mouth shut, we might not wake the whole house.

"I have a confession though." His voice is deep, thick with want as he toys with me.

"What's that?" I ask, gasping again as he drags a finger through my wetness to test me.

"This is a first for me."

"What? The desk?" I puzzle at him.

It seems strange anytime I hear he hasn't done something given the number of women I can assume he's been with. I can't imagine there's much left to explore that's new, but a bolt of jealousy sears through me at the thought of him with anyone else.

He shakes his head, nipping his way along my inner thigh and sliding a finger in and out of me as he looks me over in the moonlight. I roll my hips to match the pace of it before he pulls it away again, and I give a little pout at the loss. His eyes raise up to mine and he looks at me thoughtfully, raising a brow as he slides the tip of his finger against his lips, tasting me.

"I know you're not saying it's the first time you've ever fucked a girl with your mouth." I laugh at the absurdity.

"That's what I'm saying." His voice is soft, almost defensive in response.

"What? How is that even possible?"

He ignores my question.

"So you're going to have to walk me through it. Tell me where you want my tongue, how you want my tongue." He uses his thumb to part me and grazes my clit.

I'm trying to process that revelation, wrap my brain around how to believe it but I can barely think straight.

"You can't ask me for that. Unless you want us to get caught." I try to whisper, but I struggle as he makes another pass over me.

He smirks and looks up at me, sliding another finger inside me and curling them in a way that has my breath stuttering.

"I just haven't been able to get it out of my mind. I get off to the thought of it every day." He leans forward, sliding his thumb to the side and presses his mouth to my clit, a tentative kiss that has me biting down on my tongue to keep from moaning.

"I can't, Ben. I can't take it."

"You can. I believe in you." He slides his tongue between with one long stroke and I come up off the desk, unable to stay still with the feel of him.

The man is going to break me, no way my body can withstand him or the orgasm I can already feel building just from the few slight touches he's given me so far.

"You should just fuck me, Ben. Put me out of my misery, please."

"No. I've waited way too fucking long for this, and you taste even better than I imagined. So no fucking way. Now, tell me how you want it."

I could scream from frustration, but instead I decide to embrace it. I had imagined this before, and if he was going to insist on me running things, I was going to ask for what I wanted.

"Get naked."

"Now you're just buying time."

"No. I just want to see all of you while you do it. I want to watch your muscles flex and see how hard it makes you and then I want you ready because the second I come; I want you inside me. So strip."

"Fuck. I like you bossy." He stands and does as he's told. He grabs the back of his collar, pulling his shirt over his head and then pulling his pants off, revealing that he didn't have anything on underneath. His cock is fucking perfect, the size, the shape, just like the rest of him. I reach out and stroke him with my hand, leaning over and running my tongue over the tip because I want him to suffer too. He inhales sharply at the contact, and I grin before I sit back again.

"You're a liar too, because you said you were trying to sleep. And you planned to come in here the whole time."

He leans forward, catching my lips with his, his cock brushing against my core. "Like I'd give up an opportunity to fuck you with a chance of everyone hearing you. It was just a little white lie. Forgive me?"

"Right," I say, and then slide forward on the desk so that the tip of him nudges my entrance. "You could just fuck me. Make it up to me that way."

"This is how I'm making it up to you." He shakes his head, showing an immense amount of self-control that I don't have right now. He pulls back away from me and sits down again.

"Tell me what you want, Vi. I want you to teach me exactly how to make you come."

I take a breath because this isn't my wheelhouse, bossing a guy around, and least of all someone that looks and feels like Ben does. But I also want to be brave enough to do what he's asking of me.

"Tease me with your tongue. My clit. Just barely touch me with it," I whisper, and on command he does what I ask. It's torture to feel him, and I run my fingers through his hair, gently, closing my eyes to try to hold on to the feeling of pleasure and agony wrapped up into one.

"Put your fingers inside me again. Slowly, in and out." He follows the instructions perfectly, hitting a tormenting rhythm that I want to give him a gold star for.

"Fucking fuck, Ben. If this is beginner's luck for you then I don't want to know what you're like when you've got experience." I can feel the weight of my orgasm, the building wave of it and I know it's going to be white hot. His mouth and his tongue are fucking spectacular.

I slide a hand up my shirt to give my breasts and my nipples the attention I need to bring me closer to the edge, and as I look down, the sight of him between my thighs nearly has me coming.

He looks up at me, breaking his concentration, his eyes darkening as he sees my hands move under my shirt. He pulls away from me and I whimper, the cool air whipping across my flesh where he's left me exposed.

"Take it off," he grits out the command roughly, and I do as he says, his teeth pulling at his lip as he watches. "Fuck you're gorgeous, Vi. So fucking gorgeous. Touch them for me, yeah? Let me watch you."

I do as he asks, thankful that his fingers are still inside me, working me to the same rhythm he had before.

"Does that feel good?"

"Yes."

"Good. Tell me what you need."

"You. Your mouth back on me. I'm so close, Ben."

He kisses and nips at the skin on my inner thigh for a moment, stalling, but then returns his mouth to me, kissing me like he needs it to breathe.

"Spread me with your fingers and use your tongue on me

again. Be rough. I need you to be rough with me," I plead quietly, trying to remember that while we're tucked away upstairs, we still need to be careful.

He does as I ask, and it pushes me to the fucking precipice, just hanging there with his mouth and hands holding me in the balance. My whole body eager to do whatever he wants.

"Suck on me, then hard with your tongue and fuck me harder with your fingers. Please. Fuck. Please, Ben." I sound like someone else. Someone desperate. Someone he's broken into a million pieces.

He does it on command, and I would swear that a supernova has just ruptured inside me from the way my nerve endings melt at the feel of it. He stands abruptly, his hand going to my mouth, and I realize I'd started to cry out despite my best efforts. I rock forward on the desk as I ride out the aftershocks, and he slides inside me.

He fucks me rough, hard, sloppy, like he can't control himself and his hand slips off my mouth and slides down my throat, wrapping around the base of my neck. And I wish I could memorize every second of him.

"Christ, Violet. The way you fucking feel is insane. I can't. It's embarrassing..." he mutters, gasping for breath.

"Come inside me. I want to feel you, please," I beg him.

He thrusts into me, hard and fast, a few more times before his fingers curl into my shoulder, pinning me in place, and I feel him coming.

He hits me just right, the perfect rhythm and one of the aftershocks of my first orgasm creates another wave and this one is even more devastating than the first. Sending bright waves of satiating lightening through every single nerve in my body, flooding with me with too much and not enough at the same time. I run my hand up the back of his neck, anchoring my fingers in his hair as I brace myself against the last of his waning thrusts.

He collapses against me, his chest heaving against my shoulder, his body racked with attempts to get more oxygen into his lungs. He pulls out, and I feel the warmth of him against my inner thighs. I feel so sated I'm not sure I've ever been happier than in this moment, a dumb sort of happy that has my brain foggy and my limbs heavy.

He raises his head finally, cupping my jaw with his hand and sliding his thumb over my lower lip, back and forth like he's concentrating or debating something. I purse my lips, kissing the tip of his thumb.

"Be honest, that could not have been your first time," I say smiling at him, studying his face to make sense of what he's trying to see.

He smiles absently in return. "It was."

"I get one of Lawton's firsts? How lucky am I?" I make a little gasp and press my hand to my heart, grinning hard at the thought of it.

"I wanted it to be you." His voice is raw, like it might crack.

"What?" I say, because I can't have heard him right.

"I shouldn't tell you that. Fuck..." He looks down at the floor. "But I couldn't imagine, didn't want it with anyone else. And fuck, it was worth it."

The way his eyes travel over me, the way he looks, it's reverence. Like I'm some treasure he's managed to unearth. Like he's been given the keys to the Louvre and told to explore to his heart's content, and I'm a particularly fascinating piece of art that's touching him in a way he hasn't felt before. I rub my hand over my sternum to try and stem the swell of emotion that's coming as a response. One I'm not sure I can contain.

I try to reason with myself that we've both just come hard from the best sex of my life and neither of us is being sensible in this moment. But something deep inside whispers that it's more. That the reason my body responds to him the way it does is because he's more than I've ever had before. That I only thought I knew because I had no idea at all.

"I don't know what to say. I can't... I just..." I stumble over my words, tongue tied as I try to sort through my emotions. Trying to understand how or why he would have saved that for me. My mind is trying to make sense of it, reasoning he's young and it's just a lack of opportunity. But a wiser voice tells me he's had plenty of chances, was probably downright begged for it in the past.

He kisses me, disrupting my thoughts again, and it's so incredibly soft. Tender strokes of his lips against mine make my heart feel like it's going to leak fucking stardust and rainbows, and I can barely stand it when his hands slide up my legs. It feels like I'm barely held together as it is and any more touch from him could have me falling apart. He breaks the kiss then, but his lips hover just above mine, and he must feel the same because his fingers are biting into my flesh like he's trying to hold on for dear life before he speaks again.

"I love you, Violet. I've been in love with you."

And my heart explodes. It must, because I have to put my hand to my chest to try to hold it in and I can't breathe. There's no air. There's no desk. No room around us. There's just him in front of me. His breath against my lips as he adds to the devastation he's already caused and kisses me.

After a moment he pulls away, his eyes drifting over my face.

"You don't have to say anything right now. I know it's a lot, but I just, need you to know."

Then he kisses me the same soft careful way he had before. And it can't be real. It absolutely must be a dream. Ben Lawton cannot be in love with me. No one, least of all me, gets that lucky.

"Stay with me. We'll set an alarm or something. But I need you to stay with me tonight," I whisper, and he kisses me again before he pulls me up into his arms.

"Okay. Shower first, alarm, then bed, yeah?"

I nod and he carries me off with him.

TWENTY-SIX

Ben

IT'S THE MORNING, AND DESPITE THE LACK OF SLEEP I'M freshly showered after a quick run this morning, and I feel fucking amazing. I jog down the stairs, desperate for caffeine and starving for one of the pastries I'd seen Vi's mom put out in the kitchen last night. I hear the distinctive sounds of Nora and Violet talking downstairs and smile at the thought of her from last night, knowing I finally have all of her.

"Is there something going on between you and Ben?" Nora asks, her voice just loud enough to be heard over the sound of the percolating coffee.

I stop in my tracks, my heart slamming to a standstill in my chest. I lean against the wall of the hallway, holding my breath because I don't want them to hear me. It's not the way we'd planned to tell them, but at least she had Nora alone to tell her first.

"What?" comes Violet's half-choked reply.

"You guys are just awfully close. Touchy." Nora's voice is laced with suspicion, and I was going to hear about it later from Violet, that she was right, and I was wrong about people figuring us out.

"Touchy? I don't see how we're touchy or at least any more than we were as kids. We've always joked around."

"Ben isn't a kid anymore."

"Obviously."

"And I know he always had a thing for you growing up."

"What?"

"You weren't that oblivious, were you? He was such a little try hard. Trying to find excuses to bother us at our sleepovers, watch movies with us. Even when he was in high school. You don't remember any of that?"

"No, I just remember him being a kid."

"Oh god. It used to irritate me so much. We would fight about it, and mom would tell me to leave him alone, that crushes were normal."

"Your mom knew?"

"Anyone with eyes knew, Vi. Apparently, you *were* that oblivious."

They laugh, and I feel my heart falter with embarrassment. At least I'd told her myself first. Slightly less humiliating that way, but only barely.

"Anyway, I just thought that with you and Cameron breaking up and then him moving in with you... I didn't think about that when I suggested it. I know you're vulnerable, but he is too with everything he has going on."

"I know he is. I've been trying to help him," Violet says defensively, and I badly want to interrupt this entire scene, wrap my arms around her and tell my sister where she can shove the implications she's making about her best friend.

217

"Right. And you've kept it strictly helping? Nothing else has happened between you?" Nora presses.

"We're just friends, Nora. He's moving out at the end of the semester." An insistence to Violet's tone, makes the lie that much more painful to hear.

My heart sinks in my chest, bottoming out in my gut and rolling over there until I feel like I might actually be physically sick. I didn't realize it was possible to hurt this much this quickly.

"Okay. I'm sorry. I just got a vibe and I... don't know, I'm reading too much into it again. Just be careful, okay? He might have a crush on you again and make it weird."

"I can handle Ben, Nora." Violet gives a little laugh, and it breaks me.

"Morning!" I say walking in, forcing a cheerful tone despite the fact I feel like I've been summarily ripped open and gutted.

Both of their eyes dart to mine, worry that I've overheard them etched across their faces before Nora smiles brightly at me. And even if I hadn't heard them, I'd be suspicious at this point because Nora is not a morning person, and her smiling at all in the morning would be a bright red warning flag.

"Morning. Sleep well?" Nora asks.

"Didn't get a lot of sleep, honestly. Rough night." I smirk, glancing at Violet before I pull a pastry out of the box and put it in my mouth.

Violet sputters on a sip of her coffee, spilling a little and wiping it with a napkin.

Nora looks at her briefly but then looks back at me.

"Yeah, there is a weird smoky smell in my room that I don't love."

"You should try one of the other ones. It's not like there aren't plenty." Violet joins in the conversation, I assume to try and cover her little mishap, which just presses my buttons more.

"Did you have to switch rooms?" I ask, looking pointedly at Violet before shoving another bite of food in my mouth and licking my fingers.

"No. Mine was fine," she says quietly, watching me before taking another sip of her coffee as a pink flush blooms over her cheeks.

"Huh. Got lucky then." I flash a gritted smile at her before I grab a mug out of the cabinet.

"I guess. I think I'm gonna walk down to the river and get some fresh air with my caffeine to try to wake up before our moms start putting us to work." Violet smiles at Nora.

"You have fun with that. I don't have patience for snow this early in the morning," Nora gripes. And there is my real sister.

I shoot the shit with Nora despite her grumpiness, discussing which room she and Eric might take instead of the one she has now and talk about how we can help mom with cooking today, but the whole time I'm listening for Violet to head outside. Because if she thought she was going to get to just slink off, it isn't happening.

Nora heads back to her room a few minutes later, claiming she wants to change but I have feeling she just wants to go back to sleep. Which is perfect because I don't want her watching me. I throw a jacket and shoes on and head out the back door, following the winding stone steps down to the river. I spot her standing there staring out over it and walk my way out to her. She doesn't hear me approach over the sound of the water and my first instinct is to lecture her about how she's not safe out here if she's not paying attention.

"So how are you going to handle me? Like you did last

night? Fuck me into silence or do you just plan to try to ignore me the rest of the trip?"

She startles and gasps as some of the coffee sloshes out of her cup and onto the ground, still dripping from the edge as she turns to look at me. She has the decency to look ashamed and turns her head away from me again no sooner her eyes meet mine.

"Ben..." she starts, looking despondent.

"No. We agreed we were going to tell them we're together. I don't want to lie to my family, Violet."

"You don't understand. Your sister—"

"I heard the whole conversation."

"Then you heard what she said. She thinks I'd fucking seduce you and use you as a rebound."

"Well, we know she's wrong about half of it."

"You still think I'm using you?"

"It certainly fucking feels like it. I thought we were past this, after last night I thought we were on the same page. But the second you're confronted in the daylight you lie to your best friend. Rather lie than admit you love fucking her brother?"

"Christ, Ben. You make it sound dirty."

"I feel fucking dirty."

"Well that makes two of us. I panicked, okay? The way she framed it. I just feel like..." she trails off.

"Like what?"

"Like I fucked up. Royally."

"So I'm a mistake now?"

She doesn't answer. Just stares out into the wilderness beyond the river looking miserable, and I can feel my chest caving in, a black hole forming where my heart should be.

"Well, I have to say it is a royal fuckup considering how many times you repeated the same mistake. Over and over.

Begging me for it. I mean, just last night, how many times was it?" I ask bitterly.

"Ben!" she hisses my name, and her eyes look glassy like she might cry, and it pisses me off. Because *I* want to cry and fucking scream at the same time for her to stop jerking the fucking chain around. I almost hope she'll make up her mind already and call it quits. Put me out of my misery. I can't take anymore of having her in half measures and sneaking around.

"You need to figure out what you want, Violet. Because at this point you're lying to everyone, including yourself."

Her phone dings with a message and she looks down at it.

"Seriously?" I mutter.

"It's Nora," she says sharply before she opens the message. Her eyes skim over it and then all the color drains out of her face. "Oh my god."

"What?" I say, taking several steps toward her to close the gap between us because despite how angry I am with her, I'm honestly a little nervous she's about to pass out and fall into the river.

She doesn't answer. She just holds out the phone for me to read the text Nora sent her.

> **NORA**
>
> Your mom is looking for you because she has a surprise. Doubt you're going to like it.
> Cameron is here

"You have got to be fucking kidding me!" I bark out a harsh laugh.

Her fingers go over her lips and she fiddles with the mug in her hand. Her eyes are wild and distant, full of panic. I stare at her for a beat, trying to even make sense of how Cameron would be here. Why her mom would have him come up given they called things off months ago.

"Do they know you and Cameron broke up?" I ask sharply, the second the realization pops into my head.

"They knew we had a rough patch a few months back and that he's been overseas," she mumbles, not looking at me.

"But you never told them you called the engagement off. That things are over between the two of you." I'm half accusing her and half explaining to myself what I should have figured out before now, because I'm an idiot. "No wonder you don't want them to know about me. Because they still think you're marrying the doctor!"

"I was going to tell them this weekend, before we told them about us."

"Were you? Or did you just tell yourself that you would to ease your conscience?"

"I was going to tell them. I'm still going to tell them as soon as I can think straight."

"Don't bother. I'm done. Tell your family, don't tell them. Hell, fucking marry him or don't. I don't care anymore. I'm done being your secret. I deserve more than that. I deserve someone who wants to be seen holding my hand. Who I don't have to beg to kiss me in public. And you deserve to be with someone you're proud of. Someone you want to tell your parents about and have as your date when you go home to see your family."

"Ben, please." Her face looks pained, and her eyes are watery, and I want to give in. To give her one more chance, but I can't.

"No. No more, *Ben, please,* or *Ben, please fuck me,* or *Ben, please don't tell anyone.*" I start to walk away.

"He knows about us, remember?" she calls after me, panic still in her voice.

"What?" I stop and turn, trying to understand what that has to do with anything.

"Cameron knows about us. And when he realizes they don't know..."

I grimace, tucking my hands in my pockets as I shrug my shoulders.

"I wanted to tell the truth. So you can figure it out on your own, Violet."

TWENTY-SEVEN

Violet

As I watch Ben climb back up the stairs toward the house, my heart feels like it's been shattered into a million pieces, and I feel like complete and utter scum. Probably because I am. He has been everything for me, patient, thoughtful, always giving me space. And I have been awful to him. The idea of going into the house like this to face Cameron is about as appealing as lighting myself on fire. Celebrating the holiday with both of them at the table is even worse.

I briefly wonder if it's possible to just run away into the woods. Although I doubt I'd survive long in what I'm wearing with only half a mug of coffee. I try to retrace how I ended up here. I'm sure Joss would say something about the road to hell and good intentions.

I take a deep breath. Trying to convince myself that somehow someway I'm going to get through this. Probably with everyone hating me at the end. But, given that I'd clearly hurt Ben—a man with one of the kindest hearts I've ever met? I probably deserve what's coming to me. I probably deserve to end up with someone like Cameron. That might have been my mistake in the first place with all of this, thinking I could have things I shouldn't be allowed anywhere near.

I wait another ten minutes, until my fingers are so cold it hurts to hold the mug and my coffee is gone before I start the trudge up the stairs. Apparently, that was a few minutes too long, because my mother and Cameron emerge at the top of the steps, dressed like they were about to come looking for me.

"There she is!" my mother announces in a voice that's a little too shrill for this early in the morning. "I've got a surprise for you, Violet!"

I smile tightly up at her. My eyes flicking over to Cameron for a second. The rest of us look like we've barely woken from bed, but he's already dressed for the day, his hair styled, a shirt and tie on under his long wool winter coat. If I didn't feel so much disdain for him, I might be able to note that he looked good. Europe was doing him good. Fucking other women apparently made him need to invest in his wardrobe and appearance. Good for him.

"Violet," he says my name in a warm familiar tone that would leave you thinking we didn't spend the last minutes we'd seen each other arguing publicly in a restaurant about me fucking someone else.

"Aren't you excited?" My mother's brow furrows.

"Yes. Just tired and cold," I lie. They're coming fast and furious this morning.

"I don't know why you came out here anyway. The steps are icy." She shakes her head at me like I'm a misbehaving toddler.

"I noticed."

"It's good to see you." Cameron wraps his arms around me when I reach the top step and pulls me close to him.

It's an infuriating display he knows I have to participate in because of my mother's presence. As much as I plan to tell my mother the truth, this hour of the morning, outside, right after she thinks she has done *a good thing* is not the time I want to discuss it. It will be explosive, and after talking to Ben this morning, I don't have it in me. And at this point, *when* we discuss it might be the only aspect I have any control over.

"You're freezing though. We should get you inside." Cameron rubs his hand over my back, and I wonder if I could rip it off discreetly as he ushers me back in the house alongside my mother.

They exchange a few more pleasantries before she wanders off, and I use the time to ditch my coffee mug in the sink. I can hear my mother and Mama Beth plotting the menu and plan of attack in the dining room, and the smell of the turkey they've already put in the air fryer is enveloping the room.

"Do you want to talk in our room?" Cameron asks when I finally turn to face him.

"Our room?" I laugh, because I don't know what else to do besides cry.

"Yeah, your mom got me set up when I got here."

"Why are you here?"

"Why doesn't your mom or dad seem fazed that I am?" he hits back.

I glare at him.

"Just, come talk to me Violet, please." He gives me a pleading look and it's revolting. I think about that for all of two seconds before Ben's voice echoes in my head. Him telling me not to say "Ben, please" anymore and I wonder if this is why. I wonder if this is how much he can't stand me. I can't dwell on that thought because it hurts to imagine that he might feel about me the way I feel about Cameron.

"Fine." I reluctantly follow him into my room, and he shuts the door behind us.

"What the hell are you doing here?" I ask, the second we're alone.

"I wanted to see you. I want the chance to prove to you it's not over between us."

"It's over Cameron. It's been over for months now, and you absolutely know it's been over since Halloween."

"I know I fucked up at Halloween. I was immature about you being with someone else. I realize now how hypocritical I was. It was your choice who you slept with while we were on a break, and I should have respected it the same way you did my choices."

"No shit, asshole." I shake my head. I'm too upset right now to say anything reasonable or levelheaded. Plus I'd tried that before and this is where it got me.

"Can we please keep this civil?"

"Civil? Is it civil to show up to my family holiday weekend unannounced to try to strong arm me back into a relationship with you?"

"That's not what I'm trying to do."

"Then what are you trying to do? Enlighten me." I sit on the bed, crossing my arms and he leans back against the desk in the room.

A flashback from last night comes burning back into my mind, and my heart goes tight with the memory of Ben. The way he had looked at me, the things he said. I wanted to jump up now and run to look for him and apologize, beg him to forgive me.

"I want a chance to say what I should have said when I saw

you last. I honestly am sorry. I was blindsided. I owe you an apology for all of that fucking bravado shit I said."

"You owe Ben an apology too."

"That's probably true."

"It *is* true. He didn't do anything wrong. He just got stuck in the middle and you were awful to him."

"Yeah. I thought about that." He honestly sounds like he is sorry, and I will give him a smidgen of credit for it. Not that it does much in this context.

"So what is it you want to say? And before you say anything, you should know that I literally cannot imagine *anything* you could say that will change my mind at this point. I'm so far over us, I don't even think about it, or you. I'm not saying that to be mean, I just want you to know where things stand."

His face falters with those words. I know they come out harsh, but it would be what I would want to know before I poured my heart out to someone. Especially if they knew they were just going to reject me anyway.

"If that's the case, why does your family still think we're together?" Anger laces his tone.

"You know how my mother is. I haven't talked to her much in the last few months, and I haven't wanted to hear her go on about how old I am and how you're a doctor, and the million other objections she's going to have about our breakup."

"You think she's not going to be thrilled to hear about Ben though."

I feel like I walked right into this trap.

"Except she doesn't know about that either, does she?" His eyes sparkle with that knowledge.

"Why would I share the details of my private life with her?"

"Because his mother is her best friend? You're all here together, having a cozy holiday."

"All the more reason it's no one's business."

"Does your best friend know?"

"Cameron. I thought your point here was to convince me I made a mistake in saying things were over between us."

"I just think it's interesting they don't know we're over, and they also don't know about Ben. Feels like that might be your subconscious trying to keep the door open for us."

I laugh. "Don't be ridiculous, Cam."

"I'm not being ridiculous. I'm being honest. Maybe you should try it. Seems like you're keeping secrets from a lot of people these days and that doesn't seem healthy."

"I feel like we're retreading old ground in regard to your honesty. Do you have something new to say or not?" I really want him to focus on us rather than on Ben and me. I don't even want him to talk about Ben right now.

"I'm still in love with you, Violet. I tried—hard—to forget you. To find someone else. To feel something else, but it's always you at the end of the day. I know now I fucked up asking for space. I was just scared—the commitment, planning the wedding, the idea of forever just really got to me."

"You proposed to me," I interrupt because this really feels like he's trying to frame it like I trapped him when getting married had been far from my mind when he proposed.

"I know, but when I did it, I felt like I was just following the path. Painting by numbers. I got my MD. I finished my initial fellowship. Now it was time to get married, and I was the guy, so I needed to propose."

"Well that makes me feel like... absolute shit." I give him a bright fake smile.

"I know. I screwed up. And then I panicked because I screwed up. I thought the wrong things were the problem. Now

I realize how much I took for granted, how much I love you, and how there's no one else for me but you. I know you can't forgive me overnight, and I know you're not going to forget what I've done, but if you give me another shot... I will do everything in my power to make it up to you, Violet. I can give you the life you want. We can travel. We can do research. Raise money for the arts. Live where you want to live—east coast, west coast. I don't care as long as you're with me."

The tears break freely now, because everything hurts so much. That Cam is finally saying all the things I wished he would have said so many months ago. That him saying it now just feels hollow and empty, because the only guy I want to be with is the one I've just hurt so much I'll be lucky if he ever speaks to me again. That I've put myself in this stupid unenviable position by trying to keep up appearances and worrying about what everyone would think instead of just being honest.

"Violet don't cry, sweetheart. Please. I know I hurt you, but I can fix it." Cameron gets down on his knees in front of me, his elbows on my thighs as he reaches to pull my arms away from my face as I sob into my hands at the insanity of all of this.

"I need space right now, Cam. Please go." I manage to get out between the tears. I don't have the heart to tell him I'm crying about Ben and not him, because it would be cruel to say it, but I can't sit here and pretend with him either.

"Okay. Whatever you need." He stands, looking back at me with a pitiful glance before he leaves the room.

All I need right now is Ben, and he's all I can't have.

TWENTY-EIGHT

Ben

I STAND OUT ON THE DECK, WATCHING THE SUN SET behind the mountains and the shadows fill in the valleys of snow and evergreens. I take a sip of the whiskey Violet's dad poured for me hoping it'll warm me up and run the ice around the edge of the glass.

"So, how long have you and Violet been a thing?" Nora's voice is behind me, and I'll give her credit for being sneaky because I didn't even hear the door open.

"Don't know what you're talking about." I shake my head, and take another sip of the whiskey, a bigger one this time because I know my sister well enough to know how this is going to go.

"Let's pretend for a minute that I'm not an idiot, and that I've noticed the way you look at her, touch her, and the way you've looked like someone punched you in the gut ever since Cameron showed up."

"I don't give a fuck about Cameron," I say shaking my head.

She leans on the railing of the deck, and peers up at me through the fading light.

"So if I told you they made up and they're upstairs fucking right now, you wouldn't care about that?"

I feel like I've been shot in the chest.

"What?" I ask sharply.

"Exactly." She gives me a smug little smile.

"There's something wrong with you, you know." I stare down at my sister, trying to remember that she usually has good intentions as I take a deep breath.

She shrugs.

"And Violet doesn't want you to know. She thinks you'll be pissed at her. That she took advantage of me, which is fucking hilarious." I can't help the smug smile that comes to my face.

"I mean, I am pissed at her. At both of you. For exactly what's happening right now. Because you're fighting, and now I'm stuck in the middle, and who am I supposed to choose? My baby brother or my bestie who's been by my side since we were in diapers?"

"You don't have to choose. We're adults."

"But she hurt you."

I shrug. "It's not her fault. I thought that... I don't know. I hoped for things she couldn't give me. She was in a not-great place after Cameron, and I should have left it alone."

"You were in a not-great place after your suspension."

"She didn't take advantage of me, Nora. I pursued her. She fought me the whole way."

Her eyebrows raise.

"Not like that. She wanted to fuck me. She just objected to it for all the same ethical reasons you're going to rake her over the coals for."

"And yet she did it anyway."

"Yeah," I say grinning, thinking about the greedy way she'd looked at me, touched me, wanted me. At least I'd have those memories.

"Gross, brother. Just gross. Also see, this is the other reason it's a problem. I want to hear about her latest hookup. I want the juicy details of the guy she's dating, and if her latest hookup is my brother? Ruins all of that girl talk."

"You'll live. You've had her for twenty years. You could afford to share her for a few months."

"So it's over?"

"She doesn't want what I want." I shrug.

"And let me guess. You want to fuck her and all your jersey chasers, and she wants something more committed than that."

I laugh, because I'm sure that's what everyone would assume. I'm the jackass commitment-phobic fuckboy and she's the sensible committed grad student. But that my own sister can't even tell what a sad fucking sap I am for her is somehow funny to me.

"I could have warned her, but then I get it. That would have been an awkward conversation." Nora sighs.

"You should have warned *me*. And I shouldn't have moved into the apartment with her and Joss. Fuck," I curse, staring up at the sky.

"What?" Nora looks up at me puzzled.

The sun has dipped far behind the mountains now, and it's getting dark fast.

"I shouldn't have moved in with them. I knew the second you told me the room was free because Cameron and her called things off that it was going to be way too much of a temptation."

"Yeah, well, but I knew she would be a safe place for you to land and would help keep you on track and out of trouble. And it sounds like she did a good job of that. You and her both. I don't want to detract from your hard work, but I do think she played a role."

"She did. She was pulling for me. And hey, having her at home made me never want to go out so..." I laugh and shrug my shoulders, taking the last swig of whiskey from the glass.

"Again, gross, but I guess good for her if, you know, you weren't my brother." She gives a little shudder. "And poor Cameron. Does he know?"

"He knows. He came home last month and figured it out on his own."

"Oh my god! See! That's the kind of gossip I thrive off of, and she didn't tell me because of you!" Nora punches my arm.

"Well, you can talk to her about it now, just don't tell her I told you."

"First, I have to yell at her for corrupting my baby brother. And then comfort her because your dick ass broke her heart."

"I didn't break her heart."

"I mean, telling a woman that she's not enough and you want to also sleep with other women when she has feelings for you is uh... rough. Maybe not heart breaking, but definitely not a feel-good kind of situation."

"I know."

She stares at me for a second, and then lets out a little gasp.

"Nooooo."

"Yes."

"Who? I mean, she's over Cameron."

"I don't fucking know, Nora. She didn't say in so many words, she just doesn't want to be with me. We were gonna tell you guys this weekend and then she panicked this morning and told you there's nothing going on. Then Cameron shows up... I'm over it. If this was one of my friends, I'd tell them to move on and find someone else."

"Are you sure it just wasn't overwhelm from all of us? I

mean, I get her being nervous. If she had a brother and I was fucking him, I'd be nervous as hell about telling her or her parents."

"Mom is not anything close to her parents and the way they are."

"No, but you are mom's baby boy, and she knows that."

I roll my eyes.

"So you wouldn't give her another chance?"

"I don't see the point. She's been pretty clear how she feels. Besides, you think Cameron would be here if he didn't think he had a chance?"

"Cameron is a delusional narcissist who thought he could put Violet up on a shelf and come back and get her when he was ready. He doesn't factor what she wants into what he does. I wouldn't factor anything he does or doesn't think into what you do."

I shrug and shake my head because I don't know what else to say.

"Also, she'd be an idiot to pick him over you, and Violet is a lot of things, but she's not an idiot."

"Thanks, I think." I frown at my empty glass.

"Love you." She wraps her arms around me and gives me a tight hug, and I return it.

"Love you too."

Then she disappears into the house, and I'm left alone with my thoughts again. Ones that just keep returning to the same woman who's in the house right now with her would-be fiancé.

TWENTY-NINE

Violet

THE SECOND I SEE NORA'S FACE; I KNOW SOMEONE HAS told her. I know she knows, and the dread wells up inside my chest as she nods for me to follow her upstairs. I follow behind her, slowly trudging up the stairs because I don't think I can handle any more confrontational encounters today.

We get to her room, and she shuts the door behind us, turning around to look at me.

"If you're going to kill me, just make it quick, okay? It's been a long one." I sigh as I sit down on the edge of the bed.

"I'm not going to kill you. Just lecture you a little about lying to your childhood best friend."

"I mean, if you think about it, I spared you. Did you really want to hear that I was sleeping with your brother before you finished your first cup of coffee?"

"Not exactly, but of the two of you I think I would have preferred hearing it from you."

"I'm sorry. Honestly, Nora. I should have told you a while ago. It's my fault."

"Well, I forgive but I don't forget. Gonna be pretty hard to erase the mental images conjured up by it." She shakes her head.

"Again, sorry. But just to be clear, I did not pursue him or seduce him."

"You were the senseless victim of his wit and charm?" She looks at me like she can hardly believe it.

"I mean, that and other things. Do you really want to be asking these questions?"

"Probably not. He gave me enough insight already."

"So he told you?"

"No. It was obvious. The two of you are so obvious to anyone who knows you well enough. He just confirmed it when I twisted his arm."

"I told him you would figure it out. Now I just have to hope our parents don't know."

"They haven't said anything if they do."

"Well here's hoping Cameron doesn't blurt it out."

"Yeah, about that. How do you keep that from me?"

"Oh god, Nora. He showed up the morning—I mean, do you want to know?"

"I mean... yes? No? Shit. I'm just going to pretend it's not my brother. It's some hot professor or someone. Go on." She makes a little gesture and I continue the story of how Cameron showed up the morning after Ben and I had sex and the awkward party, and dinner.

"Wow. Yeah. See I would have loved to know all about that. I would have had lots of advice—namely that you not let Cameron into the house."

"Joss gave me that advice, don't worry."

"Because she is wise AF and you should really listen to her

more often. I wish I had a Joss."

"Hey, you have me!"

"Yes, but you're much nicer than her. Joss just tells it like it is, no sugar coating. I need that sometimes."

"Fair enough, I guess."

"I still love you. Even if you are breaking my little brother's heart." She narrows her eyes, and I shift under her gaze.

"I didn't mean to. I did fuck up though. Lying to you. He overheard it and is furious with me."

"Was that the reason for the animated chat in the snow?"

"You were spying on us?"

"I told you; you were being weird. Both of you. And when I saw him follow you outside... Like you wouldn't have done the same thing!" she answers defensively.

I sigh.

"I'm not trying to break his heart. I have feelings for him. I want to be with him, I just was so worried what you'd think. What our parents would think. And I guess I feel like maybe he's right to some extent even though I don't want it to be true."

"What?" She gives me a curious look, and I make a face, trying to warn her that the answer to her question is going to be something she doesn't want to hear. "What is this random hot professor that is totally not my brother right about?"

"That I may or may not have initially slept with the professor because he was incredibly convincing, and quite good and definitely made me forget that Cameron existed."

She cringes a little but seems to recover.

"So it was just physical at first but then?"

"I don't even know if it was ever just physical. I mean he is an easy person to like. To be friends with. It's hard not to be drawn to that, you know? It's just he is distractingly good in bed and it kind of became about that. And I didn't know what was lust or love, so..."

"Love?" she interrupts.

"I think so."

"Like love because you've known each other forever and he's like family, or love like you're in love with him?"

"Both?" I say, giving a little shrug, still nervous that she's going to be upset.

"Have you told him that?"

"Why? What did he say?"

"See, again why this situation sucks because I love you both and I feel like I owe you both silence."

"No, I get it. It's fair, Nora. And I don't mean to put you in the middle. It's just I want a chance to explain to him, to work through it."

"Just give him some time and space first. He's feeling bruised right now. But he'll get over it and be more reasonable. You didn't make the best decisions, but they're understandable ones and Ben is the kind of person who doesn't stay mad long."

"I hope not." I look at my best friend and whatever she sees written on my face, she reaches over to give me a hug.

The drive back from the cabin is brutal. I'd hoped I could use the time in the car to talk to him, to explain things and apologize but as we'd gotten in to drive home, he'd told me he had a headache and just wanted to focus on the drive. It'd taken everything I had to just keep quiet and stare at the passing scenery.

I thought that would have been the worst of it, but his lack of appearance anywhere in the apartment for several days was proving worse. I would have taken anything at this point. A wave before he left for classes, a smile when he got back from practice, but there was nothing. The only reason I knew he was at least occasionally still staying at our place was the smell of his body wash in the shower in the morning, and water droplets on the tiles. Otherwise he was gone. And I was beginning to think any chance we had was long gone with him.

———

Which was why when I heard his name outside my office, I immediately started eavesdropping. It was the same group of women as before, or at least some of them as I recognized at the least one of them for her distinctive voice.

"He's going to the frat party this coming weekend, for sure. I have it on good authority."

"Whose authority? Because the last time it was London, and she told you that he was somewhere he was never going to be."

"Colton and Jake. Jake actually invited me."

"Wow. He invites you and you're going to go after Ben anyway?"

"I mean, it's not my fault he invited me."

"Isn't it? You have been flirting with him a lot."

"Because it seemed like Ben was unavailable. With the whole suspension he was MIA. Now he's back, and now I'm blonder and have a chance."

"Well, good luck. You'll need it. Every chick on campus is going to be after him when they hear he's back."

My gut churns at the statement, because she's right. Ben is going to be inundated with women who want to make up for lost time if this group was any example. And he was going to forget that his older sister's dowdy best friend who was pushing 27 years old with no money and no prospects even existed. At least I wasn't a burden to my parents. I had that going for me still, right?

I probably should do what I originally planned to do. Get my act together, focus on school, career opportunities, and what life could look like post-graduation. That would be the best way to spend my time, instead of pining over a boy who was well out of my league to begin with and involved history that now came with a very complicated set of baggage.

But I miss him, and now that he's gone, I realize how much about him I took for granted. I'd be thrilled just to have my roommate back who teases me while we make dinner in the kitchen or watches a movie with me at night asking me how it's possible that CGI that bad could really give me nightmares. But even more so, I want the Ben I love back, and that's the one I think I'm least likely to ever see again. I'd been so lucky to have him, and so stupid to lose him—in one of the dumbest ways imaginable.

I wonder if it's possible to win him back over. If he did love me, I had to imagine there might be a way, but I was at a loss for what that was. Every explanation I had for not telling my parents, lying to Nora, or for Cameron showing up not once but twice, seemed to fall short of everything he had given me. And if I was honest with myself, he'd given me everything. Asking for very little in return. The real jerk move I'd made wasn't getting involved with him in the first place, but not appreciating him while I had him.

———

And now he was out of town on a road game, one that I was sitting on the couch watching, curled up next to Joss as she worked on editing photos of mostly naked male models.

"I miss him." I pout, curling my legs under me and leaning my head against her shoulder. I stare absently at her screen as she works on the latest photo.

"Me too," she agrees.

"How do we get him back?"

"I think that's mostly a job for you, since I'm pretty sure it's not me he's avoiding,"

"I tried apologizing via text. I've tried to wait and see him in the morning, but I never know when he's here or not."

"Did you try waiting for him in his bed naked again?"

"I should have never told you that."

"Oh you definitely should have. It was one of my proudest moments as your friend." She grins, and I manage to get a little laugh out of it.

"I'm pretty sure if I tried that, it would backfire."

"Well, you could leave a note in his room, or make him dinner one night. Turn his tricks around on him."

"Maybe," I say, my mind running with the possibilities for a minute. "The biggest issue is that I barely know when he's here and time is getting shorter. He's supposed to find a new place to live and it's already December. Has he said anything to you about moving out?"

"He's barely talked to me, and I doubt he would tell me. He knows I love his sexy ass, but he also knows where my loyalties lie."

"And how lucky I am to have them." I hug her.

"Ouch. Careful. That one tattoo is taking its time to heal." She hovers her hand over the spot.

"I'm sorry," I apologize, and then try to peek at it under her sleeve. "It's going to be gorgeous when it does heal up though."

"Yes. Oh, there's an idea. Get a tattoo. Just have them put LAWTON on your back permanently."

I laugh hard at the idea, but the more I think about it, the more I wonder if it wouldn't be the craziest thing to do on earth.

"Or his number?" I say, thinking out loud.

She stops what she's doing and looks over at me. "No... Really? You're really thinking about it?"

"I mean, it would convince him I was serious about him, right?"

"Seriously crazy, but in a way I love and would definitely do myself if I was in love with a boy like him."

"And if it goes wrong, I mean I'll still watch him play. And there's laser removal, right?" I look at Joss.

"Right... Are you serious about this?" She eyes me with wary excitement.

"Maybe. I don't know. I think I might miss him enough to try anything at this point," I confess, as I watch him line up on the scrimmage line on the TV again, reminding me he's hundreds of miles away.

Because the truth was, I couldn't stop thinking about him, wanting him, missing him. I love him in a way I have never loved anyone, and even if he rejects it, I want him to know.

THIRTY

Ben

WE WIN THE GAME, BUT I STRUGGLE TO BE AS HAPPY AS MY
teammates are about it. We're well on the way to another championship game this year, one I hope we might actually win.
One we could win if Colt, JB, Jake and I continue putting up
points and our defense continues to be an immovable force on
the field.

But unfortunately my heart is also an immovable force.
One that can't seem to forget my roommate even as I try to
avoid her. It's been torture with her still sleeping in the room
next door. I've been crashing at Colt's and Jake's place. I've
gotten up at the crack of dawn to go for a run in the freezing
cold or get to the gym extra early just to avoid having to see her.

I'm terrified of it if I'm honest, because I feel like seeing her
is going to make all my resolve come crumbling down. One
more look. One more I'm sorry, and I'm a goner. And I don't
want to fall back into old habits.

"You all right?" Colt asks as he jumps into the seat next to me on the bus.

"I'm fine." I shrug, staring out the window as I watch them finish loading the bus with luggage and signal to the stragglers to get their asses in gear from across the parking lot.

"Two touchdowns tonight, should make you more than fine."

"Just not feeling the celebration tonight."

"Me either, if I'm honest."

"Never were able to resolve things with her then?" I ask, knowing by the look on his face already that the answer won't be a good one.

"Nope. We're officially done."

"That sucks man, I'm sorry," I say, not knowing anything comforting to say. I think half the reason I was able to give easy advice to my friends before was because I didn't truly understand what it was like to be on the wrong side of a relationship with someone you really cared about. It's easy to be objective and level headed when you're not the one hurting.

"Yeah. How's things with your girl? I assume not great given that you look like this."

"Also over."

"She cheat too?"

"No. Just didn't want the same things."

"Yeah, that'll do it in pretty quick."

I nod.

"I wish there was a way I could forget she even exists to be honest. I still miss her, even though I don't ever want to see her again."

"Yeah." I nod, because fuck if it isn't relatable.

I can't say that I never want to see Violet again. I know someday when this finally stops hurting and I have perspective again, I'll want to see her. Hopefully we can even be friends again, or at least get along at family events. But for now, I just wish I could have temporary amnesia. Forget the way she looked at me, the way she felt, the way she tasted. Everything about her fucking haunts me.

One of the worst parts about it being that the curse has extended beyond brunettes now to all women. I can't even picture hooking up with someone else because when I so much as think it, Violet's there in my head. Her sweet smile as she quizzes me on history wearing a galaxy bikini top. Teasing me about my weakness for seeing her in my jersey. Cooking dinner together in the kitchen. Tickling her mercilessly until she surrenders. Spread out in front of me saying my name.

Sometimes I think she's actually broken me, because in the darkest moments in the night, when I can't sleep, and I wonder if she's still awake in her bed, I hope that I've at least ruined her the same way.

THIRTY-ONE

Violet

As I stand outside the frat house post-game a couple of days later with Joss, I suddenly just want to run back to the car and drive off.

"No," Joss says loudly.

"What?"

"You're thinking about chickening out, and the answer is no. It's too late. You got the tattoo. You stalked social media to find out where he would be tonight. You dragged me to a college party at what appears to be a frat house. You're committed. No backing out."

"This is going to be humiliating if it goes badly."

"Too fucking bad." Joss gives me a steely eyed look, and I know she's not gonna let me back down. Which is why she was here with me.

I take a deep breath. She was right. I wanted Ben back; this was the only way I could imagine proving to him that I meant it.

"All right. Let's do this."

When we get inside though, I immediately regret my appearance. So many of the women are dressed to kill in here. Even Joss is in a leather skirt and corseted top that makes her look like a knockout, and I'm standing here next to her still wearing the black jeans and jersey I wore to the game.

It had seemed like a good idea at the time, to wear the jersey with his name on it. I thought it would help make my point given his feelings on it, but now I just feel frumpy and out of place.

As we start walking in, I can already see a few eyes on us, wondering at how we belong in this particular scenario. And the truth is, we don't at all.

"I'm sorry I couldn't just do this on my own," I whisper to Joss as I see her grimace and shake her head at the entire scene.

"You can do it Violet. Go get your man." She nods to the other side of the living room. The farthest point from us that's still in the room where Ben is sitting with a group of guys I recognize from the team, flanked by women who all clearly want their attention.

I take a step to the side to get a better look at him and note there's a gorgeous blonde at his side. She's dressed in an outfit even sexier than Joss's and his left arm is wrapped around her resting on her hip. They look beautiful together. Perfect even. A match that makes sense. I want to be sick, but I can't stop staring at them. I glance back at the door again.

"Nope. You're doing this. Barbie has been there for what, all of ten minutes—maybe a few hours if we're stretching it? And he's wanted you for years. Get him."

I take a breath. She's right. However this turns out, even if he laughs me out of the place. I owe him this. He put himself out there for me over and over, and even if all this does is give him a chance to reject me, it's fair enough.

He's currently laughing and chugging something from a plastic cup, smiling at his friends as his dimples pop. I see Jake at his side reenacting some play from the game, and I can't help but smile at the two of them. I run my finger over my wrist, still a little tender from the ink there. Now or never it is.

I slide through the crowd dodging bodies and make my way to him. I cringe a little more when I notice two kids from the class that I'm currently TA-ing sitting on a couch not far from him. No matter how this went, if they paid attention it was going to make class super awkward Monday. But it had to be done.

Someone slides out of the way in front of me, heading off to get another drink and it provides me a straight line to him. I walk up, taking a deep breath to try and calm the erratic beating of my heart in my chest.

"Ben?" I say, far too softly and he doesn't hear me at first over the laughter and music.

"Ben!" I say it more forcefully this time and his attention is torn away from Jake and the others searching for the person who called his name.

"Lawton." I add his last name and I see the recognition hit his eyes when he finds me.

It's not a great welcome, confusion followed by something else I can't entirely read settles there. He jerks his chin up, like I've seen him do to the fans of his around campus. Acknowledging my presence but doing nothing to give me any credit.

"Would you sign my jersey?" I hold up the Sharpie I'd tucked in my pocket, and he just stares at me like I've lost my mind.

"Wow. Looks like you've got a really big fan." The beautiful blonde is still at his side, and she laughs, her eyes glittering with an air of superiority that nearly makes me crumple under its weight.

But I've come this far, and I'm not stopping. My presence and my appearance have gotten the attention of more people around us, but he still doesn't move to speak or take the pen from me.

"Yes, I am a huge fan," I admit and then for lack of anything better to do, I hold out the marker for Ben to take.

He stares down at my hand like it's a fucking cobra that's popped out from a basket ready to bite, and then his eyes land on my wrist. His face changes, alters as he studies it and realizes what it says.

He leans forward and takes my hand in his, twisting my wrist and turning my palm up so he can get a clear view of the tattoo.

"Holy shit, bro! She has your number fucking tattooed on her." A player from the team I don't recognize slaps him across the back, and I hear the blonde giggle again at his side.

I study him, trying to read his face or guess what he's thinking, but he just stares at my wrist, unmoving.

I shrug at the guy commenting. "It's a good number."

I'm just hoping the embarrassment I'm feeling at the attention and Ben's silence isn't reaching my cheeks.

"That's commitment to a college player's number," Jake whistles.

"I'm pretty sure he's going pro." I smile at Jake, thankful for someone familiar and for the small smile he offers in return. I doubt he's on my side in this. He seems like the kind of guy who would convince Ben he was better off playing the field than getting involved with me, but I'd take it.

"And if he doesn't keep that number?" the other guy, the one I don't know, asks, his eyes glassy with all the alcohol he's consumed.

"Someone like him? He'll keep his number. But if he changes it, that's what the other wrist is for." I give another small shrug, trying to sound casual even when I don't feel it.

"Wooow." The blonde rolls her eyes and then flicks them over me, clearly wishing I could fuck off to wherever I came from so she can resume her flirting.

Ben stands abruptly then, like her comment has woken him up and his grip around my wrist tightens. He starts to walk off, dragging me across the room, down the hall where he opens a door and pulls me into it.

"Ben?" I ask softly at first, and then louder again when he doesn't respond. "*Ben?*"

He flicks on the light and illuminates the small bathroom. It's beautiful for a frat house, still keeping some of the original fixtures and architecture.

He still hasn't said anything to me, though. His face is clouded, anger and irritation dancing over it, and I know I've fucked up by trying to make amends. I guess I knew how this was ending.

He flicks on the faucet, and I have no idea what he's doing.

"Ben? Are you going to say anything?" I ask quietly, afraid that even talking is going to make him angrier.

"Wash it off," he bites out, pointing to the water.

"What?"

"Wash off the fucking tattoo, Violet. It's not funny."

"Given that you have tattoos Ben, I'd think you'd know they don't wash off," I say sarcastically, and it's a mistake because he practically snarls at me in response.

"Stop trying to be cute, Violet. It's obviously a temporary tattoo. Now wash it off." He pumps the soap onto his hand and pulls my wrist under the water, lathering over the spot where the number is etched into my skin.

And even though I should be worried about the way he's

reacting to this, focused on the fact that he is furious with me, I'm mesmerized by the feel of his hands on me again. The way his fingers run over my pulse, and the heat of his body against mine. The smell of the citrusy soap melds with the smell of him, and I bite my lip because being alone with him for five seconds has me already wishing for more.

He scrubs harder at the tattoo, running his nail over the outline of the seven before he finally relents. His face softens slightly for a moment, a puzzled and then shocked look, before his eyes snap to mine. Anger settling over his features again a moment later.

"You got a permanent fucking tattoo? Have you lost it? You realize they're forever, right? I don't even have my number tattooed on me."

I pull my hand back from him sharply, wiping the water against my shirt and cradling my wrist against my side.

"Yes, Ben. I realize that's what permanent means. God, you sound like my mother, now."

"Your mother?"

"She said the same thing when I told her and asked what I was going to do if you... reacted just like this actually." I laugh at my own fate and the fact that my mother is going to love the fact she was right.

"Your mother knows?"

"Yes. I video chatted with her and dad the other day. I explained everything. Dad suspected. Apparently, we were 'very transparent'." I sigh.

"What did you explain?" His brow furrows.

"I apologized for not telling them about Cameron and I breaking up, and how that all ruined Thanksgiving. And I told them that I'd had feelings for you for a while. That I was pretty sure I was in love with you. And that I had royally fucked things up with the way I treated you. I doubted that you were going to forgive me, but I had to try. And no matter what I was always going to be one of your biggest fans, for everything you are and everything you've taught me these last few months." I feel my voice starting to waiver, like I might cry at any moment, and I stop talking and stare at the ground. I'm willing myself to have some sense of composure. That breaking down in tears in a frat house bathroom is an experience I could continue to skip.

He's silent though, and it's killing me. Normally he telegraphs everything, and I know what he's thinking. But his face is blank. A solid canvas of nothing and I'm starting to feel ridiculous for having tried to win him back, especially in such a public way.

"I'm sorry if it... if this whole thing embarrassed you. I just wanted you to know, to see, that I don't care who knows that I'm... you know." I sniff back a sob and laugh to try and cover it up.

"You're what?"

"In love with you. Obsessed with you? Crazy maybe?" I try to laugh it off but a few of the tears roll down.

His hand goes up to my cheek, his thumb wiping them away as he cups my jaw.

"Are you sure that's how you feel, and this isn't like guilt because of all the history between us and our family and—"

"Ben. I'm sure. I've been in love with you for a while, I just got scared." I cut him off because the doubt on his face makes me feel even worse, that he can't even believe me when I am telling him.

"And I pushed you instead of being patient."

"You were very patient. With Cameron and all the stunts he pulled. With me wanting to hide everything."

"You had your reasons. You and Cameron were together a long time. You were gonna get married. You were worried about Nora. Just because I'm hurt doesn't mean I don't understand."

I stare down at my wrist, wondering at how he was so much younger and yet so much wiser than me. Wondering at how I'd ever gambled with losing him. I take a deep breath, and raise my eyes to his again.

"Does it mean you'll forgive me?"

His eyes soften and he looks at me like he might still want me even after everything.

"Yes."

The tiniest bit of hope is blooming in my chest as I stare at him, his warm brown eyes with the flecks of gold in them still watching me carefully.

"I love you so much. I understand if I'm not what's best for you right now or what you want. But I hated the idea of you not knowing how much I felt, after everything you shared with me. So, I just needed you to know, okay?" I smile, tentatively.

THIRTY-TWO

Ben

HER PALE AQUA EYES ARE SET OFF BY THE REDNESS around them, so glassy from the tears falling down her face, and I hate that I'm the reason she's crying. I have my own guilt at having pushed her so hard and fast on being with me when she was still trying to recover from her last relationship, and I wonder as much as she does if I'm right for her.

"You're always what I want," I confess before I lean down to kiss her because I can't hold it back anymore. Not when she's here offering me what I've always wanted. When she has my number tattooed on her wrist, telling me she's in love with me. She kisses me back, but I can feel the hesitation in it, like she's still worried.

"But not what you need?" she asks when she pulls away.

"That too," I admit.

"I feel like there's a but coming..."

"Are you sure you're over Cam?"

She laughs in response, her fingers brushing away the last of her tears.

"Literally all I thought about every time he was around was how much I hated him for making things harder for us. And how insane it was that I wasted so much time with him when I could have had someone who made me feel the way you do."

I smile in response to that because it's too hard not to.

"I did warn him you really loved saying my name." I smirk, and her answering grin makes my chest hurt with want.

"You didn't."

"Might have."

"Good. He deserves to know the truth."

I kiss her again, wrapping my arms around her waist and dragging her close to me. Her arms encircle me, and she runs her palms up my back. The smell of her shampoo and the feeling of her pressed against me is more than I can take, a sensation that had become all too familiar and then was ripped away from me. I've missed it. Missed her.

"So does everyone here." I grin.

She looks up at me and rolls her lower lip between her teeth.

"How loud do you think you could be?" I whisper the question, raising my eyebrow in challenge.

"How hard do you think you can fuck me?" she counters, a devilish little grin on her face as her hands go for my pants, unzipping them so quickly her palm is on me before I can think straight.

"Fuck," I groan as she works her hand over me, and I get harder under her touch.

"How do you want me?" Her tongue slides over her lower lip as she stares at my cock.

"Screaming against this fucking wall as soon as I get these

off," I answer her as I shove her jeans down, and she uses her free hand to help me as she kicks off her shoes.

I lean over running my hands up the back of her thighs and grabbing her ass, before her eyes snap up to mine, worry suddenly crossing them.

"What?" I ask softly.

"Do you have a condom?"

And I realize the real question she's asking.

"I didn't touch anyone else, Vi. I just came on my hand every fucking night wishing it was you."

Her grin returns slowly as she studies my face. "Good. Now it is, so make it count."

I haul her up against the wall, sliding inside her and pinning her there with my cock. Her arms wrap around my neck and her legs wrap around my waist in return, a little gasp as she rolls her hips to get herself into a better position. The movement has her pussy clenching down on me and making me grit my teeth.

"Fuck, you're so fucking good."

"I need this. Need you. Please." Her lids are heavy and she's looking at me like I'm the only thing she can see.

It's all the encouragement I need to take her hard against the wall with the sound of my skin on hers and her little gasps and moans as I fuck her. Her fingers thread through my hair, massaging my scalp and pulling on the ends when I go deeper. She's so wet and warm, so hungry for it with every little noise she makes that it's taking all my focus not to come immediately.

"I'm already close, Ben. Fuck. Just a little more. A little harder," she begs, and I fuck her hard into the wall, half worried and half pleased at the idea that she might have a few bruises on her ass from the way my fingers are digging into her.

"Yes, fuck. Fuck," she curses.

The way her back arches, the way she whimpers for me as I

take her, all while knowing she etched my number into her skin; it feels like I could fall for her all over again, maybe even harder the second time around.

"Come for me and let them know you're mine."

And true to her word she fucking screams my name as she comes, her tight pussy bearing down on my cock and making me come hard inside her until I see pure fucking black as I ride out the last of it.

The door suddenly pops open and my head swivels, seeing Colt standing there wide-eyed as I glare at him.

"*Fuck!* Sorry. Sorry!" He covers his eyes with his hands and stumbles backward.

"I told you they're fine. She's just getting railed. But no, you couldn't listen to me..." I hear Joss's voice trail off as the door shuts again.

Violet's body is shaking, still pinned against the wall, and I turn my head back to her, and she's laughing so hard she's crying. I slide out of her, and release my grip on her slowly, letting her feet touch the floor and she doubles over as I go to pull my pants up.

"That's the second fucking time he's gotten to see more of you than I would ever fucking want," I curse.

"Well, you got your wish. Pretty sure everyone heard."

"And you're fine?" I ask, doubt coloring the high of having her again.

"Are you kidding?" she says, as she cleans up and puts her clothes back on. "I hope your little blonde heard and eats her heart out."

"You're kind of vicious." I grin as I watch her slide her pants back up over her thighs and notice the red marks from my hands.

"When it comes to your fangirls, yeah. They can look all

they want, but they don't get to touch anymore. You're mine now." She pokes me in the chest.

I pull her close to me again, pressing a soft kiss to her lips before I take her in again. She's too fucking beautiful for words, and I don't know if there are even the right words to explain what it means to finally have the person I've wanted, loved, wished for, for so damn long.

"You *are* mine, right?" She looks up at me, wide-eyed like there's a chance I would say no.

"Always have been, you just didn't know it yet."

Her lips twist into a grin. "I love you."

And I kiss her again, because I cannot get enough of her.

EPILOGUE

Violet

WE'RE SITTING IN ONE OF THE MEDIA ROOMS AT
Highland, gathered around Ben as the NFL draft plays out on
the big screen on the wall on the far side of the room. His mom
and Nora sit on one side of him, and I sit on the other.

He's too distracted to watch the current draft pick, his knee
bouncing up and down under the table as he spins his phone
around again in his hand. He's waiting on the big call. The
important one that tells him where he's going after college.

I am an absolute basket case of emotions. So damn proud of
him, so worried for him because of how stressed he is, and so
thrilled that he's finally getting the reward for everything he
worked so hard for. A small, deep-down part of me is also sad,
because I will miss him so much when he's gone.

We've already talked about how we'll make it work. Wherever he goes we'll video chat and text. During the season I'll fly
out to see him and his games as often as I can, and during the

off season he'll come stay with me here in Denver while I work to finish my PhD. I have another year at least, and then I can finish my dissertation off campus if I need to, or at the very least part time.

I glance down as his phone lights up, his face a war of emotions all at once as he answers it. He nods over and over again. A series of "yes sirs", and "mmhmms", and "will dos". Mama Beth starts to cry, and Nora grabs her hand, tightly lacing it with her own as they listen. I run a hand over his back briefly, before he stands, pacing back and forth.

"Okay. Yes, sir. Thank you. Yes, looking forward to it, sir."

He ends the call, and we all look up to him, waiting to hear but he's like a deer in headlights staring at the screen again. I follow his eyes and realize the team picking next. I had secretly hoped it might be the Denver Rampage, but for all the right reasons this was going to be the better pick for him.

"And? Don't keep us in suspense, Benjamin!" Mama Beth chastises him.

He blinks and looks down. "It's Seattle. I'm going to Seattle."

A moment later and the representative from Seattle is on the TV. He sits down again, as the Highland athletic media department has their camera pointed at his chair so they can show his reaction live.

"And for our next pick, Seattle selects Benjamin Lawton, wide receiver out of Highland State University..." the man announces, and tears prick his eyes as if he's finally realizing that it's really real. That he's going to the NFL.

Mama Beth and Nora jump up to hug him, pinning him tight and he looks to me, grabbing my hand and I lace my fingers with his. I mouth the words "I love you" and he grins at me and then back at the camera.

"Thank you. I can't wait." He nods to the camera, and I

can't help but imitate the grin on his face like it's contagious. His friends and everyone around us erupt into cheers and he's swarmed with hugs and people wanting to congratulate him. I step out of the way, letting everyone get a piece of him in this moment. Wanting to be able to watch him soak it all in.

Joss walks up behind me and hugs me.

"I know you're excited for him, but I also feel like you need this hug too." She gives me a knowing look, and I hug her back.

"He deserves it though. And even still, I can't believe it. Seattle? With Waylon? Like a dream for Ben." I shake my head and smile, watching as he's engulfed in another round of hugs.

I see his phone ring again in his hand and he picks it up. A video chat from Waylon who is screaming at the top of his lungs, and he and the guys on the team holler back and forth at each other through it, sheer joy and chaos.

Joss and I just laugh.

"Jocks, am I right?" And I watch as her eyes shift away from Ben to one in particular.

"Mmm. It was your idea in the first place." I side-eye her.

"And aren't you glad you listened to me?" She gives me a devious little grin.

We stand there for several minutes just taking in the chaos next to each other when Ben suddenly looks around, worried.

"I think he's looking for you." She nods.

I walk back toward him where the crowd is thinning and when he sees me his eyes go soft, and he smiles. He comes forward and grabs my hand, lacing his fingers with mine and pulls me over to the side away from the rest of the crowd.

"Congratulations! Can you believe it? Seattle. How thrilled were Waylon and Mackenzie to hear?" I grin at him.

"Marry me." It's more a statement than a question, and I can't believe that I heard him correctly.

"What?"

"Sorry, that came out wrong. Marry me? I'd get down on a knee but that's going to attract a lot of attention that I'm not sure you want. We can do it more official later. With the ring and the kneeling. But I don't want to do this without you."

"Ben, I think you are very fucking high on the fact that you just won the football lottery right now, and you need to take a breath." I smile at him nervously because as much as I want to say yes, this feels like a blindside out of the blue. We've barely been together six months, and that was counting the unofficial time.

"No. I've known this is what I want. I just wanted to know what my future looked like first, for you to know what it looked like before I asked."

We stare at each other for a minute, our eyes searching, and I can feel my heart kick up in my chest. My mind racing with the idea of being married to him, of what Beth and Nora will say. Of what my family will say. I can already see Joss over his shoulder looking at us, and I can imagine her planning my honeymoon and dragging me to the lingerie shop and I laugh.

"What? Is that a good laugh or a bad laugh?"

"Good."

"So, you will?"

"Yes, but you should... you should be sure Ben. Let today's news settle and think about it before—"

He picks me up off the ground, and I instinctively wrap my legs around his waist, and he spins me around, kissing me and smiling until we both almost fall over.

"I won't fucking change my mind, Violet. So, get used to the idea of being my wife."

"I love you," I say softly because I have no other words to express how much I feel for this man. How much I want him. How much I need him. How much I've always been his even if I didn't know it yet.

BONUS EPILOGUE

Ben

1.5 years later

Violet's barely off the plane before we're driving to look at a house that had made our short list. We had a brief window of time where the realtor could meet us to show the house, Violet was actually in Seattle, and I wasn't at practice or a game. She's sitting next to me in the car, distracted and scrolling videos and when I hear a song play for the fourth time in a row. I raise my brow and glance at her for half a second before I put my eyes back on the road.

"Do I want to ask what you're watching?"

"Fan thirst trap videos."

"Of?"

"You, silly."

"The answer to my original question was no then." I sigh. I've seen enough of them to feel wildly awkward about the fact they even exist.

"Okay but some of these are really fucking hot though. I sent one to Joss the other night. She agreed and wants to know when she can shoot the calendar. I told her when I had the money to buy every copy. Oh, and then I almost sent it to Mac but I didn't want to have Waylon glaring at me the next time we all go to dinner."

"Which is tomorrow night by the way."

"Oh yay. That place down by the marina again I hope?"

"Yes."

"Perfect," she answers absently. "I brought some stuff from Denver for them."

Another song cues up on her phone and I hear it repeat twice.

"Oh damn. This one is good. They've got one of you smiling on the sidelines all slow motion with your dimples popping and then you stretching on the field before a game. My god this is so fucking good."

"Vi..."

"Yes?"

"You realize I'm in the car with you. Like actually sitting here."

"Yes but you're not doing *this* right now, are you? And these videos. Oh my god. They make me want to fucking jump you the second I see you. I should be annoyed but honestly, I think I'm going to write some of these women a thank you note... Oh! Here's one of Waylon. I gotta forward this to Mac. Then maybe I can win some points with him."

I shake my head and smile because even if she is a little strange, she's my favorite person in the world.

"What?"

"You."

"Oh hush, you love me." She turns her phone over in her lap and she reaches over, running her fingers over my thigh.

"And you'll love the inspiration the videos give me later, I promise."

"Fuck. Don't start. I haven't seen you in weeks and we have to look at this house first."

"Do we though?"

"Yes. You said you want to move in after the wedding, right? We're running out of time. Especially if we need to hire someone to update anything or landscape."

"Okay, Boss."

I flash her a little look because that was her favorite thing to call me lately.

"It's really pretty here. Are we sure we can afford this kind of view? I mean I feel like we need founded-an-internet-startup money for these views."

"We can afford it. Another one of the guys lives in this neighborhood. And it's got water access."

"We could get a boat?" She says in an excited voice.

"Says the person who can't swim."

"Which is exactly why I need a boat, Benjamin." She laughs and her smile is infectious.

I hate the gaps in time that we're separated, when she's in Denver finishing her degree and I'm here playing, but I love having her back again. It's only another month before she'll be back here full time and a couple more months after that I get to make her mine permanently. It almost doesn't seem real.

A few minutes later and we're touring the property. She's trailing behind me as we weave in and out of the different rooms.

"What do you think?" she asks softly.

"I think I kind of like it?" I ask her hesitantly because I actually like it quite a bit, but I'm more worried about her finding a place she loves. She's starting her own consulting business once she moves here and needs the office space at home until she gets it off the ground.

"I think... I really like it." She looks around the upstairs one last time and we wander down the steps and down a hall on the main floor to find two rooms side by side.

The first one is a big room that's set up currently as a den with massive TVs on the wall, a bar area and some gaming tables.

"Looks like this could be a Ben cave." She gives me a little smile.

"I don't hate it." I tilt my head as I give it the once over. It's a little mature for my tastes but nothing me and the guys couldn't fix up on a weekend after the season's over.

The next room has two big doors and they open up to a massive office/studio space. The realtor had mentioned an artist owned the property and that made me hopeful that Violet might have some ready-to-use spaces.

"Oh my god!" Her jaw drops and she lets my hand go as she spins around, taking in the massive expanse and the cabinets, shelves and desk that are already installed. "This is insane. I can already see it. Art work that's waiting can be over here. I can set up a little conservation work area here. Have my desk here, and these built-ins would be perfect for all of my books. And then over here by the windows I could have a little meeting area when people come for meetings. It's honestly perfect."

"And the views." I nod to the massive picture windows that overlook the yard and the water down below, because I know when she sees those it's probably going to be case closed.

She walks over closer to me and stares out, her eyes going wide as she gapes at the gorgeous view.

"And our little caves would be next to each other so I could take breaks and come bother you. I think I'm in love. " Her eyes practically sparkle as she runs up and grabs my hand again, squeezing it tight as she takes another look around.

"Yeah? You think so?"

"Do *you* like it?"

"I do, but I want you to pick something that works for you Vi. You'll be here a lot more than me. I want you to be happy with it. Make sure it works for you."

We walk over to the other bank of windows and from there we can see the deck and stairs that lead down to the small boathouse and dock.

"Mama Beth and Nora will absolutely love coming over here. We could sit outside and have drinks and chat while we watch the boats and stuff go by."

"As long as they're not here *too* often."

"I mean, agreed... because I also saw the size of the tub and shower upstairs. And I have ideas about some bedroom remodeling. We also might have to have some built-ins put up there for our book collection." She gives me a devious little grin.

I smirk and shake my head before I kiss the top of her forehead.

"I can't help it I'm a wee bit obsessed with you." She tries to look a little sheepish.

"Oh, I'm not complaining." I grin at her, picturing what she'd look like in here working with coffee in her hand in the mornings.

"I love you." She stands on her tiptoes and places a soft kiss against my lips.

I pull her closer, kissing her back as she wraps her arms around me. It never gets old with her. It's the strangest feeling in the world, but every single time I kiss her, it feels like a different version of the first. And I love her more every single day.

"So we doing this?" I nod to our surroundings and then raise an eyebrow.

"Yeah, I think we're doing this." She grins at me before she grabs my hand again and we hurry down the stairs to put the offer in.

ALSO BY MAGGIE RAWDON

Pregame

Play Fake

Delay of Game

Personal Foul

ABOUT THE AUTHOR

Maggie loves books, travel and wandering through museums. She lives in the Midwest where you can find her writing on her laptop with her two pups at her side, in between binge watching epic historical and fantasy dramas and cheering for her favorite football teams on the weekends. She has a weakness for writing characters who banter instead of flirt.

Join the newsletter here for sneak peeks and bonus content:
https://geni.us/MRBNews
Join the reader's group on FB here:
https://www.facebook.com/groups/rawdonsromanticrebels

instagram.com/maggierawdonbooks
tiktok.com/@maggierawdon
facebook.com/maggierawdon

ACKNOWLEDGMENTS

To you, the reader, thank you so much for taking a chance on this book and on me! Your support means the world.

To Kat, thank you for your constant help, support, and patience.

To my beta readers, thank you for always holding my hand and giving me constant support and encouragement.

To my Street Team, thank you so much for your constant support and love for this bunch of friends.

Made in the USA
Las Vegas, NV
21 January 2025

16825563R10154